She was th  **ted...**

Kristen   worth."

Hot adrenalin streaked through Rider, leaving his limbs quivering, his mouth dry. He felt the blood drain from his face, felt his fingers and toes grow numb as his body pulled the blood into its core, trying to protect itself from the shock.

Kristen Skipworth. The name hovered in the air like a storm cloud, echoed down the corridors of his brain like footsteps in an empty chamber. His gut twisted in revulsion.

He recoiled from her outstretched hand. Kristen Skipworth, the latest best guess of the best researchers had traced the problem back to her. The entire problem.

He stared at the woman who was known in the future as the Mother of All the Deviants. Something wasn't right. Something in her amber-green eyes paralyzed him.

He flexed his fingers slowly, willing them to move, willing his body to act like the weapon it had been conditioned to be. His fingers weren't cooperating, though.

The eyes watching him clouded with worry. He tore his gaze away from her. She was a Deviant. She'd get inside his head if he let her.

A violent wave of nausea ripped through him and he welcomed it. It was a relief after the confusing emotions she evoked in him. He'd kill her all right. But killing her wasn't enough for him. First he wanted her to know why she was dying, wanted her to feel all the pain her descendants had caused down through the centuries.

Quelling his revulsion, he forced himself to grasp her hand in his, wincing at the anticipation of a blinding wave of nausea that never came. Her touch rattled his brain. Instead of increasing his sickness, multiplying his hatred, her touch soothed his beat up emotions. Her fingers were cool and light. Her skin exuded peace and caring.

He slowly raised his gaze to hers, using all his strength to dredge up enough hatred and anger to make his voice quietly menacing as he squeezed her fingers. "How do you do, Kristen Skipworth. I've been sent from the future to kill you."

To Michael, whom I love.

Other Books by Rickey Mallory

Heart of the Hero
Shadow of the Cat (Coming in 2006)

Time Rider

∗∗∗

Rickey Mallory

TIME RIDER
Published by ImaJinn Books, a division of ImaJinn

ISBN: 1-893896-54-4

10 9 8 7 6 5 4 3 2

PUBLISHER'S NOTE:
This book is a work of fiction. Names, characters, places and incidents are products of the author's imagination or are used fictitiously. Any resemblance to actual events or locales or persons, living or dead, is entirely coincidental.

Books are available at quantity discounts when used to promote products or services. For information please write to: Marketing Division, ImaJinn Books, P.O. Box 545, Canon City, CO 81212-0545, or call toll free 1-877-625-3592.

Cover design by Rickey Mallory

This book was previously published as an electronic book by Dreams Unlimited.

ImaJinn Books, a division of ImaJinn
P.O. Box 545, Canon City, CO 81212-0545
Toll Free: 1-877-625-3592
http://www.imajinnbooks.com

ONE

He was still out there, frightened, hurting, furious.

His anger and pain flowed like a red watercolor wash over Kristen's dreams. Giving up on sleep, she dragged out of bed and wrapped a wool robe around her.

There was no escaping him. She'd tried. Music, wine, even the sleeping pills left over from Skipper's death, and still his pain and fury reached her.

At first, she'd thought the insidious feelings were a return of the sympathetic aftershocks that had rocked her after Skipper died. But those echoes had long since faded. So when the fear and pain had reverberated inside her two days before, she'd been plunged back in time to the harrowing weeks after her twin brother's funeral.

Back to nights of black panic when she would jerk awake out of a sound sleep, senses alert, only to remember for the twentieth, or fiftieth, or hundredth time, that it couldn't be Skipper. Skipper was dead.

Finally the ghostly sensations had faded, like the phantom pain of an amputated limb, and Kristen had been left with an aching void where her twin brother—her other self—had been. She'd always lived with him inside her, linked to him in a way other people could never understand.

When he'd died, a part of her self had been ripped away. It had taken her a year to get over the worst of it, a year before Skipper's song had completely faded.

Sometimes now, the silence left by his death overwhelmed her. Oh, she gleaned things from others around her, but they were just feelings, a weak manifestation of the empathy she'd shared with her brother. They'd always been there, as much a part of her as the sound of the wind. She'd learned a long time ago to detach herself from them.

She'd been doing really well, too, until two days ago, when *he* had showed up in her mind.

Tonight was the worst so far. She pushed her hair away from her damp forehead, wishing she could push him away as easily. Wandering into the kitchen, she opened the refrigerator and stood for a couple of minutes letting the cool air drift around her.

Tonight his intrusion was almost total. Tonight he was stealing her identity. She squinted in the harsh refrigerator light. He was so weak, so thirsty.

She sniffed carefully at a carton of orange juice before turning it up to swig the contents like water. A dribble of juice ran down her chin, and she wiped it with the back of her hand.

What was she doing? She stared at her dripping hand, at the juice carton. She had never guzzled juice straight from the carton before—it was almost like she drank to assuage *his* thirst. She thrust it back into the refrigerator and slammed the door, wiping her mouth again.

As she started to turn away, her gaze caught twin circles of bright gold shining from the top of the refrigerator.

Her heart leaped into her throat.

"Sam, you scared me!" Damn, she was jumpy tonight. It wasn't as if her cat didn't perch on top of the refrigerator every night.

"Get down! You know you're not supposed to climb up there." She wrapped her fingers securely around the cat's supple middle and pulled him down, ignoring his growl of protest. "Now stay off this time."

He pointedly ignored her, waving his tail like a banner as he strutted toward the door. Kristen frowned at him. "I don't want you going out, Sam. Okay?"

An irritating yowl was her only answer, so she sighed and opened the door. "How did I get mixed up with a tomcat like you? Moira would say you're just another stray I picked up."

A deep sadness settled on her as she went into the living room and gazed out over the city. The city was always sad. Sometimes she thought she would rather die than have to feel the anguish of all the mournful souls.

Thankfully, Skipper had helped her learn to detach herself from their pain, or she might have been locked away or killed herself by now.

He'd taught her the careful balance between empathy and detachment that made her such a good doctor. She'd gotten pretty good at it. Pretty good.

But not good enough to block *him*.

He was still out there.

His pain was getting worse.

She put her palms on either side of her head, wishing she could squeeze him out of her brain.

He knew he was going to die.

Kristen moaned quietly, pushing her fingers through her hair.

"Get out of my head," she muttered. "I don't want you in here! I don't want to know who you are, how much you hurt!" She hated it, these new realizations she was having. "How in the hell did you get inside my head?"

He was going to die. Not from his injuries, not even from starvation, although if she concentrated, she could smell the yeasty odor of a body feeding on itself for lack of any other nourishment.

He knew he was going to die, but he wasn't frightened of dying. No, the knowledge of his dying lay within him like his soul. It nourished him. He embraced it like a lover.

That wasn't the fear that was eating at his guts. He was afraid of something entirely different... he was afraid of her—

Kristen jerked. Had she fallen asleep standing up? As she looked out over the city again, the lights seemed brighter somehow, and harsher.

"Who are you? Why are you so afraid?" She rubbed her temples. Her thoughts were getting crazier and crazier. Why would anyone be afraid of her? Especially someone she'd never met, never even seen.

The garish lights made her head hurt. Savagely she pulled the drapes closed, shutting them out, wishing she could shut out his pain as easily. Pulling her robe tighter around her, she curled up on the couch, dozing fitfully, disturbed by strange dreams of falling through a dark abyss, hurtling toward hell.

When Sam's indignant yowl woke her, she realized she'd overslept. She squinted sleepily at the clock as she jumped up to let him in. "Sam! You're late!"

His meow managed to combine righteous indignation and martyred patience.

"Well, all right. *I* slept late, but you should have yelled louder. I was up half the night."

She fed him and put on coffee, then rushed to dress. It was already after eight on Friday morning, and she was due at the Street Clinic at nine.

***

"Dr. Skipworth, just what is the problem here? You sick?"

Kristen looked up, startled, to find Moira standing, fists propped on ample hips, glaring at her.

"No, Moira. No. I'm just tired I guess. I haven't slept well the past few nights." Kristen stretched her arms and flexed her neck, toying with the idea of confiding in Moira. But no. She'd given up trying to talk to anyone about her empathy years ago. No one understood—no one but Skipper.

She'd spent all afternoon trying to catch up on her dictation, but *he* kept intruding, kept wrenching her attention away from her notes.

He was getting weaker. Today, his fury and fear were tempered by a weary resignation that frightened her more than his anger and pain had. As he grew weaker, his emotions became harder to ignore.

Somewhere between this morning and now, she had begun to care what happened to him. She wanted to run to the windows and shout *"Don't give up!"* But she didn't know who she would be shouting to.

"Kristen?"

She wrenched her attention back to Moira, brushing the nurse's hand away from her forehead. "I'm not sick. I've just got something on my mind."

"I'd say so. You know what time it is?"

"No."

"It's after five, and you didn't eat lunch. You not going to eat supper, either?"

"I ate lunch! Didn't I?"

Moira shook her head, her lips pursed. "No, young lady, you did not. What you did was wolf down a stale doughnut with your third cup of coffee. Now, you going to tell me what's going on?"

Kristen stood up, groaning at the stiffness in her back. She stretched again. "Nothing's going on. I'll leave in a few minutes, okay?" In the middle of her stretch, a searing pain stabbed her. She gasped and doubled over.

Moira reacted instantly, moving to her side. "All right, Miss Doctor Smarty Pants, out with it. You still have your appendix?"

Kristen laughed shakily, trying not to grimace. "Moira, I don't have appendicitis. My stomach's just cramping from hunger. I'm getting ready to leave. You go ahead. Bill's here, isn't he?"

Moira's black eyes snapped as she assessed her. "Okay, I'll go on. But you be careful. Do you want a ride?"

Kristen shook her head. "It's only a couple of blocks, and I could use the exercise." She rubbed her rib cage. It almost felt like cracked ribs. What was going on here?

"I'll tell you what you could use, young lady. You could use some fun. You could use a social life. You work too much. When was the last time you went out on a date?"

Kristen wrenched her thoughts away from the pain. "A what? A date?" She shrugged. "It's been... a long time."

Kristen shook her head as she stacked the papers on the desk. What would Moira think, what would anyone think, if they knew just how long it had been?

"Well, you might think me cold, but your brother's been dead for two years. You need to get out, have fun, quit moping."

Kristen couldn't concentrate on Moira's words. Another searing pain ripped through her side, and her head began to throb. A frightening thought had just occurred to her. Was her empathy growing? Getting stronger? Her heart drummed in her throat. If that were it, wouldn't she be feeling it with other people, not just *him?*

And how would she ever stand it without Skipper's help?

"Kristen?"

Kristen looked up. "I'm sorry, Moira. I guess I'm more tired than I thought."

"Go home. Call a friend. Go to a movie."

Kristen waved her hand at the nurse, still overwhelmed by the pain and fear she could feel in *him.* "I'm fine. Really. But you're right about dinner. I am hungry."

Moira shook her finger at her. "Then get out of here. And Doctor Skipworth," Moira said. "Don't pick up any strays. You got that? One of these days one of them poor souls you're always dragging in here is going to turn on you."

Kristen shook her head wearily. "No, they won't, Moira. You don't understand."

"I understand you trust people too much."

"It's not trust, exactly." She spread her hands. There was no way to explain. "Besides, this is different."

Moira propped her fists on her hips. "What's different?"

Kristen's head jerked up at Moira's question. Had she said that aloud? She was really letting it get to her tonight. "Never mind. I'm just tired. I don't know what I'm saying." She shrugged and smiled sheepishly.

Moira just shook her head and left, muttering to herself.

Kristen shut her eyes. She couldn't feel him any more. Where was he?

Oh God, had he died? She covered her eyes with her hands and pressed hard. She had wanted him out of her head, but the void was worse.

Where was he? She felt a faint echo of the pain in her side and breathed a sigh of wary relief, unsure if it was because he was still alive, or because she'd been given a respite from his insidious, oppressive sensations. He must have gone to sleep or lost consciousness.

Turning off the dictating machine, she walked out into the receiving area. "I'm going, Bill. This was one of the slowest days we've had in a while."

Dr. Bill Maxey looked up from the book where he was logging the daily count of controlled drugs. He gave her a sharp look, then smiled. "Good, maybe it'll be a quiet night, too. I could use one. Today was a rough day at the hospital."

"When are you going to quit working two jobs?"

"When Anne decides we have enough money to put the baby through college."

"So when are you getting a third job?" Kristen grinned, and Bill laughed appreciatively.

"Oh, by the way," she said, "Walt is in there." She gestured toward the exam room. "He's just about slept it off. You can kick him out if anyone comes in."

Bill grimaced. "I thought I smelled cheap wine. How long you think his liver's got?"

She shrugged. "I'd have thought it would have given up years ago. Bye."

Kristen breathed deeply of the cool air, allowing its clean bite to clear the dregs of pain and fear from her head. The city was growing dark, the haloed streetlights barely making shadows on the mist-damp streets. There were fires burning in drums along the alleyways, their flames bent by the chill breeze wafting in from the bay. Small groups in tattered clothes huddled around the drums, reaching out with claw-like hands toward the flames, begging for warmth.

She shivered and drew up her shoulders, trying to insulate herself from their desperation as much as from the cold, but both still seeped inside her jacket. She only lived a few blocks from the clinic, but on nights like this, when her senses were flayed open like a wound, she wished for a fast car and a house in the mountains—miles from another living soul, where she could hide from their pain. Or maybe she could get on Skipper's boat and take off across the seven seas.

"Lady, got 'ny change?"

Kristen looked toward the voice, squinting in the darkness. It sounded too young, too vibrant, to be another of the pathetic homeless people who crouched in doorways. A small form huddled back against the shadow of a building.

Kristen considered walking past—for about one second. There were so many people who needed help, and so few who were willing or could afford to give it. She remembered Moira's warning, took a few steps onward, then turned back with a sigh.

As she approached, the small figure crouched even lower to the ground.

"Only asked for change," the little voice grumbled, cowering as if Kristen were going to smack it.

"Who are you?" Kristen whispered. "Aren't you awfully young to be out here like this?" She tried to see underneath the hooded jacket, but the figure just huddled deeper. "Why don't you let me take you to the clinic, and you can call someone?"

The voice changed, grew older somehow, and less hesitant. "Ain't you been told not to pick up strays?"

Kristen recoiled in shock at the familiar words Moira had spoken only minutes before. "Who are you?" she asked.

The cowled head raised, and Kristen looked into eyes as black as deep space shining out of a small, pinched face. She was buffeted by a total absence of emotion, as solid as a wall, as if the tiny figure was deliberately holding itself apart from her.

"I'm nobody, and I don't need nothing," the vibrant voice said.

As Kristen stared openmouthed, the figure melted back into the shadows. For an instant, she debated going after the little waif, but a grinding pain caught her in the midsection.

She drew in a deep breath, wishing she'd accepted Moira's offer. She didn't like to walk this way at night, although it was the shortest route home. There were too many weirdos, too many vestiges of despair wafting from the dark corners of the alleys, waiting like the fog to seep into her soul.

Sometimes, she questioned her decision to become a doctor. She'd thought her empathy would make her a better physician. It had, but the constant assault was too wearing. Sometimes after a busy week at the hospital, she would sleep for twenty-four hours straight.

She'd almost quit after Skipper died, but then Bill had asked her to help out at the Street Clinic, and she'd found a measure of peace there. It was fulfilling work, gave her a paycheck, gave her something to do besides sit at home and feel guilty.

Cold mist gathered in her hair and ran in rivulets down her forehead and cheeks as she turned down the deserted street. She walked as fast as she could, hoping she could outrun the returning sensations of otherness *he* was evoking in her.

He was still out there. Weak, resigned, hurting.

A shudder not born of the misty cold racked her. There were no words for the hollow fear and desperate agony of someone else's pain. No poems celebrating empathy, no sonnets sung to it.

She considered the questions that had always plagued her. Why didn't everyone feel the misery of the sick? Why weren't others crushed under the hopelessness of streets full of homeless people? She didn't think other people had to steel themselves against the world's pain.

She didn't think she could bear it if this one died. She wiped water out of her eyes. His pain weighed heavier on her than anyone's ever had, heavier even than losing Skipper.

Suddenly, an ice cold hand wrapped around her ankle, and pain and terror shot through her. The edge of her vision went black, and she hit the pavement with a bone-jarring thud.

When she could focus, she found herself staring into shocking blue eyes glazed with fear and agony and locked on a space somewhere to the left of her head.

"You!" she whispered, her pulse pounding in her throat.

A shard of coherence flashed in the eyes for a brief moment, then they glazed again.

It was *him*. As soon as his icy hand had closed around her ankle, she had known. Known even as his concentrated pain and fear and brave dregs of anger knocked the wind from her lungs.

She wanted to jump up and run, wanted to scream for help, but she couldn't. His despair and fear held her more tightly than his grip on her ankle.

"Who are you?" she whispered, trying to move, but his relentless fingers didn't let up, although his eyes were still glazed and witless.

She reached out to peel his fingers away. Her foot was starting to tingle. When she touched his hand, he groaned, and she felt a tightness—a tightness and a searing pain along her midsection. His ribs.

Her fingers froze above his then changed course, stretching to touch his face. It was as cold as his hand, and her fingers came away stained with half-congealed blood. She moaned, her own head throbbing with pain that had to come from him.

Moira's warnings echoed in her brain, but she brushed aside worries about disease or danger. His distress was the only thing that mattered. She had to help him.

"No..." he muttered, his voice cracking like thin ice.

"Can you walk?" Kristen wrapped her fingers around his hand. "Hey, can you walk? We need to get you to a hospital."

"No!" His eyes were closed, his brow furrowed in pain.

"Well, can you try? Look, I need to get some help." She maneuvered around until she was sitting up, not easy with his grip still tight on her ankle. "I can't move you by myself, and I think you've got broken ribs. Plus a bad cut on your head."

"No! Hospital!" He spoke shortly, in little bursts, obviously trying to minimize the torment of breathing.

"I can't help you! You've got to let go!" Kristen cried desperately. She couldn't breathe, either. The grinding in her midsection had her doubled over.

She pried at his fingers again. If she could stop him from touching her, it wouldn't hurt so bad, and maybe she could concentrate. She'd never experienced anything like the way his every emotion, his every pain, transferred itself to her through his fingers. She gritted her teeth and worked on steeling herself against him.

Finally he let go. He sat up gingerly, grunting and grimacing with each movement. For a few minutes he rested his head against the wall and took shallow breaths that puffed out in silver clouds of mist. His hair, wet and plastered to his head, looked to be a dirty brown.

With his incredible eyes shut and his hand no longer transferring sensation to her like an electric charge, Kristen gathered enough wits to study him.

A dark splotch discolored the side of his head, and a knot had risen on his temple. His jaw was clenched tight, his lips compressed and grim with pain, the tendons in his neck corded with tension. He was well-muscled but thin like a runner, and she noticed the peculiar odor of starvation about him.

His hands were elegant—a surgeon's hands, or an artist's, with fine tapering fingers, currently white-knuckled against his side. His body was long, too, encased in filthy jeans and a pull-over jacket.

She looked back at his face, where pale thick lashes rested against his gaunt cheeks. Her chest hurt from compassion and the echo of his bruised ribs.

He opened his eyes.

Kristen started. For the first time his eyes were lucid, re-flecting a wary curiosity and sharp intelligence. They were the most intense blue she had ever seen in eyes, and they seemed to cut right into her soul. She blinked and wiped mist off her face. "Can you stand?" she asked.

He stared at her for a long time, then with a grimace that showed white, even teeth, he nodded. He braced his shoulders against the brick wall and inched himself upward, groaning, but pushing persistently.

She stood and tried to help him, but when she touched him he growled and jerked his head sharply, sending another rend-ing pain through her side and his, no doubt, so she left him alone. She certainly didn't want him to puncture a lung if his ribs were broken. Walking a few steps toward the street, she pretended not to notice how hard it was for him.

A ragged sigh and an easing of the ache in her side told her he had made it. She turned. He was taller than she'd realized, and he slumped against the wall with both arms wrapped as tightly as possible around his middle. His face rivaled the mist for pallor.

"Can you walk?"

A short, sharp laugh surprised her. "Sure, lady," he grated. "Have—this dance?"

She stared at him, her lips twitching. A sense of humor? Even if it was caustic and barbed. "I don't think we'll see many cabs around here, and I've got to get you to a hospital, now!"

"No!" The pain faded from his eyes, and an unreasoning anger took its place. "Leave!"

"I can't," she whispered, wanting to cry because he was so desperate, wanting to cheer because he had regained the will to be angry.

His eyes darkened to indigo and narrowed to slits. "Can't?"

She shook her head, dislodging droplets of mist from her hair, and wiped her face with both hands. "No. You hurt too badly. I can't leave you." *I can't leave you, and I can't stand to be close to you.*

"No!"

"Look, we're not getting anywhere," she sighed, spreading her hands helplessly. "The Street Clinic's about two blocks over."

His eyes blazed as fear, anger, suspicion, all flashed across his face in a matter of seconds. "No ID, no credit," he whispered, closing his eyes and leaning his head back against the wall.

Kristen knew most of the strength that had served to get him upright was failing him. He wouldn't stay conscious much longer. In fact she could feel the warning buzz inside his head that signaled he would soon pass out.

"Okay, okay. I don't know what your problem is, but I'm not standing out here in the cold all night. Come on."

He shook his head, and she wasn't sure if he was trying to clear the buzzing, or if he was still refusing to be helped.

"Look, dammit! I'm not going to hurt you," she shouted.

His head fell back against the wall, and water dripped down his cheeks like tears. He'd given up fighting. Even as triumph lifted her spirits, her breast tightened with pity, because she could feel from within him that he wasn't used to defeat.

She gritted her teeth as she lifted his arm and placed it around her shoulders, steeling herself against the sensations caused by his touch. He growled again, but he didn't protest. Kristen was fairly sure that if he could have found the strength to push her away, he would.

He leaned on her helplessly, his rock hard body heavy against her, his breath shallow, uneven. The taut muscles of his abdomen moved against her side.

He was in superb physical condition. Probably a good thing, too; otherwise he would have been dead by now. His body had obviously started digesting protein because he had no fat reserves. That accounted for the odor of starvation that clung to him. As her doctor's brain clinically analyzed his condition, her woman's body began to react to his physical presence.

The waist she had her arm around was hard, the muscles like long straps of steel. The arm clutching her shoulders was corded with tendons and muscles, their suppleness undulating against her skin as they walked. If she looked down, she could see the hard thighs under the material of his jeans.

A thrill tightened her stomach, and embarrassment flooded her face with heat. Where had that unprofessional reaction come from? She was a doctor, and he was a sick man.

But she couldn't ignore the unfamiliar ripple deep in her belly as his body moved next to hers. She'd never been affected like this by a man before. She'd never felt so aware of another human being in her life.

She concentrated on his feelings rather than hers. From every square centimeter of him, she absorbed his fear and pain. She wished she could wall herself up, away from the feelings, but strangely she craved them too, because they were an echo of everything she'd lost when Skipper died.

TWO

They stumbled into the clinic, Kristen staggering under the weight of the barely conscious man. "Bill, get Walt out of the exam room!" she snapped.

"What the hell... "

"Go! I can't hold him up much longer."

"Let me... "

She shook her head. "No! Just clear out the room." She urged the man in her arms to take just a few more steps, to make it just a little farther. He muttered something that sounded like "little general," his head lolling drunkenly on his neck.

Walt came out of the exam room squinting against the bright fluorescent lights, cursing and snorting. "Can't even get a good night's sleep anymore!" he grumbled, shrugging into a decrepit coat.

"Get out of here, you old reprobate," Bill laughed. "You've slept all day long. Just because you're too cheap to get a hotel room when your wife kicks you out for drinking. Go home!"

Bill helped Kristen get her vagrant settled on the exam table.

"Where'd you find this one? Was he attacked by aliens?" he asked, peering into the man's eye.

She made a face at him. "That only happened one time, and you know that poor guy was diagnosed as schizophrenic."

Bill chuckled as he checked the other eye. "Concussion. Nasty bump."

She nodded, her own head aching. She rubbed her temples and examined the cut on his forehead. It wasn't bad, but Kristen felt the torn skin, the bruised flesh, as if it were her own.

Bill slit the jacket with a scalpel and slid it off the man's arms. "Look at this, it's filthy. No, it's beyond filthy! We'll find him something from the stash. Whew!"

Bill dropped the offensive garment in the trash can.

"Think he's got any broken ribs?" Kristen said, but Bill interrupted her.

"Kristen, you're going to have to stop bringing in these bums. One of these days you're going to pick up somebody dangerous."

She glanced at him irritably. "Trust me. Like I've told you before, I can spot them. They won't hurt me." She probed delicately around the man's rib cage, still marveling at his physical condition. A monstrous, dark blue bruise marred his pale skin. She probed it gently, eliciting a ragged groan, although he didn't wake up.

"I can't feel any breaks. Could be he's cracked a couple. Hard to tell without x-rays," she said shortly, tamping down the well of sympathy and pity that were overwhelming her. Her emotions were rampant, out of control. What was the matter with her?

"Yeah, look at the contusions," Bill remarked. "He's black and blue all over. Did he get hit by a truck?"

Kristen shrugged. "That, or he ran into a very angry mugger," she muttered.

"Where'd you find this guy?" Bill's voice was tinged with suspicion and awe. "This is no homeless derelict. Look at that muscle tone. He's been working out, or he's in the service. Never saw this kind of physical conditioning outside of sports or the military." He grinned at her. "Going to take him home to live with your other tomcat?"

"Bill! Don't be crude. He is strange, isn't he? He's starving—you can smell it—but with his lack of fat stores, it wouldn't take but a couple of days for his body to start digesting protein. Maybe somebody dumped him there in the alley."

"Any ID on him?"

Kristen shrugged again. "He said he didn't have any."

"Yeah, right," Bill snorted. "Take a look."

The thought of searching his pockets made her face grow hot. She couldn't believe she was acting like a schoolgirl about this guy's body.

Bill must be right, she thought, her brain latching onto a logical reason why the thought of touching a man—no, a patient—would stir her so. It must be the perfection of his form that fascinated her. That was all. Determinedly, she thrust her hands into his pockets, her eyes closed, her mind deliberately blank.

The bell rang out front.

"I'd better wait on that customer," Bill said wryly. "Let me know if you find anything interesting in there!" He leered at her as he left. She made a face at him, humiliated that he'd noticed her reaction to the man.

Kristen didn't find anything in his pockets, so she turned her attention back to his injuries. It was a relief, him being unconscious, because when he was awake she could hardly think. She worked quickly, trying to finish before he woke up. She cleaned the cut on his head and quickly closed the ragged edges with sterile strips, then bathed his face where sweat and blood and dust had mingled.

His features were cleanly sculpted and strikingly beautiful except for the grim, set lips and the furrowed brow. He looked to be about thirty-five or so. It was hard to tell because of his youthful body, but his face looked old and jaded, deep lines running from his nose to the edges of his mouth, deep creases at the corners of his eyes. She didn't think those creases were from laughter.

She traced a finger down one of the lines, a finger that trembled as it smoothed the skin across his gaunt cheek.

She was amazed at her sudden boldness and at the depth of feelings he evoked in her. She would have never touched him so gently, so intimately, had he been awake. In fact, she'd never really touched a man at all, not like this. Her entire experience with men had been the few kisses and dates she'd endured in high school before she'd decided she wasn't cut out for romance. Her empath's brain had never been able to endure the duplicity of the boys who'd touched her and whispered sweet words while, inside, they churned with single-minded lust.

As her thoughts wandered, her finger traced the deep creases at the corners of his mouth. Unless she was very much mistaken, those were lines of pain. She'd even seen them in children on the cancer ward.

Her heart filled to bursting with compassion. The pain etched into his face wasn't the brief trauma of cracked ribs or bruises. It was old pain, deep pain. Pain no one should have to bear.

Blinking hard, and chagrined at her reaction, she distracted herself with familiar, professional acts. She took her penlight from her pocket and lifted his eyelid. Yes, he was concussed. She flashed the light in his eye, then away, then back, watching the response of the pupils.

You could tell a lot from eyes. Hypertension and diabetes both left their marks on the eyes, as did half a dozen other ailments. Not to mention grief, joy, anguish. Kristen touched the lines around his eyes, smoothing the tender skin. Yes. You could tell a lot.

She jerked her hand away, once again dismayed by her

unprofessional reaction. Taking a deep breath and blinking slowly, she turned her attention back to her examination. She shined the light through the pupil, leaning closer to look at the back of his eye. Something...

Suddenly alert and intrigued, she didn't have to force herself into professional reaction. Some odd sort of scar tissue shone from the depths of his eye, back toward the retinal wall. Could he have had a detached retina repaired? She looked in his other eye. It was clear. She looked back at the right eye, searching its depths. There was something else, too. Something opaque, foreign-looking. She moved the light so it shone from different angles. The object looked like a minuscule cube, and when the light hit it just right, it reflected, as if at least part of it were made of glass.

She blinked and rubbed her eyes. She was too tired to figure it out. When he woke, she would ask him.

Right now, though, she needed to get him undressed and examine him for further injuries. The filthy jeans molded his legs like the hands of a sculptor, the buttons strained across the front. She started to call Bill in to undress him, but if she did that she'd never hear the end of it.

Her face burned as she reached for the buttons. They were some kind of molded plastic, with a logo she'd never seen before. She had undone all but the last one when his hard hand grabbed her wrist.

"No!"

Astonished that she hadn't known he was awake, she jerked against his grip as anger pummeled her through his touch. His fingernails were broken and bloody, his knuckles scraped, as if he'd tried to claw his way out of some dark prison. Looking at them, she could feel the burning pain on her own knuckles. She had an astounding urge to kiss the knuckles and the broken nails, to hold him and tell him he was safe now. What was it about him that stirred these feelings?

She looked at his face. His eyes were like shards of cobalt glass cutting her. Could he tell what she'd been thinking?

His fear streaked through her, wrenching her thoughts back to her job. She twisted her wrist against his steely grip. "Is the word 'no' the extent of your vocabulary, Mr..."

"No."

She stared. Was that his caustic sense of humor surfacing again? His hand on her wrist sent flashes of pain up her arm.

She couldn't tell whose pain it was, his or hers.

"If you think you can sit up, I need to clean you up and wrap your ribs."

His expression remained unchanged.

"It'll help you breathe. Also, I need to get these filthy clothes off you."

"No."

"Look, *Mister!*" She said, straining against his grip. "I don't have time to stand here for hours and listen to your limited discourse. I've already put in a full day, and I'm ready to go home. But I found you, and I feel responsible for you, and I'll be damned if I'm going to leave a job half done. So, you've got two choices. You can get up and walk out of here, or you can let me get your ribs wrapped and give you something to eat so you can rest for a while. I don't really care which!"

Something flickered in his wary eyes, which might have been amusement, although it never reached his lips. He turned over on his side and hoisted himself up using his shoulders and hands. He grunted once. By the time he sat up, his breath was shallow and fast, and sweat beaded his brow.

"I'll—take—number one," he whispered and tried to stand. He gasped and stared at her, shock and fury on his face, then his eyes glazed, and he collapsed like an abandoned marionette back onto the table.

"So, *Mister*," Kristen whispered, pushing his hair back from his forehead. "You made your choice." She gently turned him onto his back and strapped his arms down, thankful he had passed out. She couldn't concentrate on her job when he was awake, transmitting his every emotion to her through his touch and piercing blue eyes. It was hard enough to concentrate even when he was unconscious.

She probed his muscled wrist for a good vein and slipped a needle in, then hung an IV of dextrose 10% with normal saline.

"Have some dinner," she muttered as she strapped his legs and his middle. "You need it." A queer pity quivered through her at his defenselessness. She was sure he wasn't used to being helpless. Her fingers lingered on the band she'd tightened around his diaphragm. When they began to curl against his muscled abdomen, she jerked her hand away and quickly prepared a syringe of meperidine and promethazine.

"Dessert." She smiled at her joke. The narcotic and the antinauseant would let him sleep for a while and would relieve some of the pain from his bruised ribs. Later when he woke, maybe she could find out some information about him—who he was, how he'd been hurt, why he was so afraid.

She sat down in the chair beside him and dozed.

***

Rider Savage felt better than he had in years, maybe in his whole life. He was floating on a cool cloud high above the earth where nothing could reach him, nothing could hurt him. He liked it up here. He felt clean and new, a part of the cloud.

Here there were no wire leads feeding him hours of detailed history about the Deviants, those twisted quasi-humans who called themselves skipworths. The computers had fed him more information than he'd ever wanted to know about how Deviants could get inside your head and suck out your soul, how they burned out the brains of children if they got close enough, how they were plotting to take over the world and kill everyone who wasn't one of them.

But something was wrong. Something didn't belong. With a wrenching lurch of his heart that sent adrenalin pounding through his veins, he realized what it was.

Feelings. He wasn't supposed to have feelings. He was a killing machine, intent only on one objective—to search out the one person who was responsible for the Deviants. It was his only purpose, and a cold, killing hatred was his only emotion. It was why they called them tanks, a play on the acronym TAINCC. Tanks from the TAINCC.

He eased slowly toward consciousness, testing the space around him with his trained senses, trying to figure out where he was. The place was bright and dry, so it wasn't the alley.

It wasn't heaven either, but it wasn't the slimy, unyielding tangle of leads and wires that made up the Total Acclimation and Immersion Neuro-physiological Conditioning Chamber. The TAINCC, where he'd left the last of his feelings and all of his memories.

He'd exchanged them for the cold hatred that would allow him to accomplish his mission—this mission he'd volunteered for, this mission to find and kill the woman whose progeny had destroyed his life.

He was an emotionless machine, programmed to kill. So why was he shivering with fear, burning with anger, and why was there a deep, almost familiar sensation inside him that he couldn't quite identify?

Wincing at the shock of pain his movement caused, Rider thought of the last conditioning session. That time, instead of sucking out his memories, the grueling seventy-two hour session had imbedded in him the information he'd needed to accomplish his mission, to eliminate his target.

Then before he'd even had a chance to recover from the trauma, he'd been hurled through a dark, eerie tunnel—a journey so bizarre, so frightening, it still made him cramp with nausea to remember it.

At the end of the tunnel he'd slammed joltingly into a solid wall. He thought he had died. When he was able to move, agony shrieking through every muscle, breath stolen by the stabbing in his ribs and the pain in his head, he'd wished for death.

Everything had been cloaked in darkness. He hadn't been able to get a grip on reality, hadn't been able to move and breathe at the same time. Even his hatred for the Deviants, which he'd counted on to sustain him through this suicide mission, hadn't helped. All he could do was lie there, racked with pain, shrouded with helpless anger.

When he'd finally been able to form coherent thoughts and see without everything swimming around, he hadn't recognized anything. Wherever he'd landed, it was a dismal, earthy place, totally unlike the stark whiteness of the TAINCC. Odors and sounds assaulted senses made raw by pain. The nauseating smell of rotting flesh, the grating, irritating sound of shoes crunching on asphalt, the murmur of machines humming all around him. Stones and grit bit into his face and his palms. Cold seeped into his bones like water into a dry sponge.

He'd drifted in and out, dreaming disturbing images like memories from his past while unconscious, enduring the unfamiliar dinginess of the world around him while awake.

Just when he'd thought he would die at last, an angel had walked by and he'd reached out, defeated, to beg her to take him with her to heaven, or at least walk with him part of the way to hell.

The angel must have taken pity on him. She'd brought him to a place of clean, white odors and dry warmth—it might not be heaven, but it was a good substitute.

The last thing he remembered seemed more like hell.

No. The last thing he remembered was her, standing in the misty rain, saying *"I can't leave you, you hurt too much."*

Or was there a newer memory? A memory of gentle hands

brushing his cheek, loosening the buttons of his jeans, loosening the bonds of his conditioning. He remembered the delicious fullness in his loins, then the searing, nauseating agony in his thigh. He remembered stopping her, before she uncovered his shame.

Adrenalin shot through him again. That was it. The familiar sensation. Feelings. Nothing had ever felt as good as his angel's hands on him. Soothing hands, healing hands. Hands that comforted his fear and eased his pain. Hands that made him feel things a tank shouldn't feel.

Rider clenched his jaw, reminding himself of his mission. He needed to get out of here, wherever here was, and find his target. He pushed away the unfamiliar emotions before they triggered the nausea conditioned into him, and concentrated on what he knew.

The person he was looking for was a physician, so he needed to find the medical care facilities. That would be a good start.

He stirred, wincing against the pain, and prepared to push himself upright.

Hello," the angel said, cutting into his thoughts, her voice soothing and musical, with a teasing note in it. "You've had a good, long nap. Maybe you can talk to me now that you've had some lunch."

He squinted at her, frowning as she gestured toward a pole with a bag of liquid hanging from it.

Lunch? He hadn't eaten, had he? He couldn't remember the last time he'd eaten. His gaze followed the line of the tubing from the bag to his taped wrist. They were feeding him through his veins, like they'd done in the TAINCC.

Disgust rippled through him. It was what he'd hated most about their damned conditioning—being invaded by the wires and tubes.

He took his gaze further, down to where a clean white sheet covered his lower body. A dreadful realization seeped into his hazy brain as he shifted his leg and felt the smooth fabric of the sheet against his bare skin. Naked. So now she knew.

He gritted his teeth against the burning sensation in his thigh as he glanced back at her face, steeling himself against the contempt reserved for the criminals and rejects from society who were conscripted by the government for the TAINCC. But she just watched him, a tiny smile on her lips.

It took a minute for his brain to adjust. He'd been conditioned but not really prepared. He was in the past, centuries before the TAINCC. No one here knew about tanks. Still, his face grew hot, embarrassed that she'd seen the mark, even if she didn't know what it meant. He snapped at her to cover his humiliation. "Where am I?"

His voice came out creaky, like one of the old wooden doors in—in what? He didn't know what he'd been thinking of, but the angel was speaking, and he concentrated on her voice.

"You're at the Street Clinic. What happened to you?"

"Accident," he said automatically. He tried to sit up and realized that his middle was taped so tightly he could hardly move. "Clinic?"

She nodded.

Clinic. So that was why the tube was in his arm. His body tensed with apprehension. Maybe he could find out something about his target, or at least find out where the medical care facility was. "Can I leave now?"

"No." The angel's mouth widened in a larger smile, as if at a private joke.

Rider's eyes were drawn to her mouth. It was a nice mouth, with a vulnerable lower lip. An uncomfortable sensation tickled the back of his throat as an echo of emotions he wasn't supposed to have rippled through him, and the burning in his thigh reminded him he couldn't afford to look at a woman in any way other than how she could help accomplish his mission.

"No," she continued. "I want to watch you for a while, until you're back on your feet. Were you mugged?"

"Mugged?" He was going to have to concentrate harder. His brain was still foggy, and the words she used made no sense.

"Did someone attack you?"

"Some *thing*," he muttered, wincing as he remembered the brick wall rushing at him at light speed as he emerged from the long, dark tunnel of time. He squeezed his eyes shut for a moment, then glanced at the angel. "When?" he asked.

"When what?" she asked, bending her head over his wrist where the IV needle was inserted, and touching the bandage with a tentative finger. Her touch sheared his breath. His gut tightened, and the imprint on his thigh burned. What the hell?

He searched his brain for an explanation. Hadn't the TAINCC conditioned all that out of him? The irony was he couldn't even tell if the feeling was desire or fear. Sometimes there wasn't much difference. "When can I leave?"

"Oh. As soon as you can stand up by yourself."

"I can do that right now, lady." Rider turned over on his side and prepared to push himself upright. When he stretched out his right arm he felt a ripping pain, and the angel cried out sharply.

"Oh, no! Stop!"

She grabbed his wrist with quite a bit of strength, stealing his breath again. He couldn't remember anything that compared with the touch of her cool fingers on his skin. They were like a balm, soothing him, drawing out the pain.

Rider let her pull him back to lie on the table. As soon as he was flat again, the lights quit whirling quite so madly around his head. Maybe he would indulge her for a while, let her think he wasn't quite ready to get up. As the room quit spinning, the rending pain in his wrist returned.

"Look what you've done. You've ripped your arm open. Now I've got to restart the IV in your other wrist." She glared at him, then turned back to the bloody wound, gently wiping gore away from the torn flesh. "If you try that again, I'll have you put back in restraints."

"Just who the hell are you, lady?" Rider growled through clenched teeth. One part of him wanted to jerk his arm away, to stop the treacherous feelings her touch evoked. But another part of him craved the comforting yet disturbing sensations.

"I'm the doctor, Mister!"

Rider closed his eyes. The Street Clinic. The doctor. A cold resignation warred with anticipation inside him. He remembered something else from the TAINCC. His target was a doctor, so he had to search the med care facilities, but he'd been warned about being examined.

It could be dangerous, they'd told him. *If you're discovered, you will be dissected like a lab rat.*

What had they done to him that would tell a twenty-first century physician he had come from the future? Incompetent bastards! He was at risk of being exposed because they couldn't get their damned machines calibrated enough to send him into the past without slamming him into a brick wall.

It might be a little rough. You might be a little shaken up. Nothing to worry about, though. You'll be fine.

Fine, hell! For all he knew, he was supposed to be dead

now. After all, there was no communication after transfer. He'd signed on for the ultimate one-way trip, five hundred years into the past. A bitter amusement curled his lip. Well, maybe one of the two ultimates—if you counted death.

They'd explained it all to him. Once he was back here, he was on his own. There was no return. No second thoughts. The only way they could know if he had completed his mission into the past was if the future changed. And he was only the third tank ever sent back successfully, and the only volunteer. They'd blown up several poor bastards before they'd given up on sending metal back.

The first two must have failed, though, because the Deviants hadn't disappeared. So they'd sent him.

He laughed, then gasped as his messed-up ribs ground against each other. He was probably the first one who'd made it alive.

Damn big responsibility, Rider, old man. A frisson of fear rippled up his spine. He was stranded in this godforsaken time.

He needed to get out of here. He needed to figure out what to do, but right now, he couldn't even sit up. He felt like he'd been drugged, and he was damned tired. Too tired to run. Too tired to care.

But not too tired to be affected by the emotions the do-good doctor's touch was eliciting from him. He searched inside himself for the cold hatred that was supposed to sustain him.

"You want to tell me your name now, Mister?"

Rider squinted one eye and took a long, slow breath full of the strange, spicy scent and enticing aura of femaleness that wafted from her like perfume and played hell with his conditioning. "No."

"Are you going to start that crap again?"

"Crap?"

"That 'no' crap! I'm tired of your monosyllabic answers. I practically saved your life. I, at least, ought to rate more than 'no'."

"No, ma'am."

Her eyes flashed with golden fire, and her lips twitched. Something tickled the edge of Rider's brain like a memory, a very important memory, but it flitted away as fast as a dream upon waking.

"How about this one, then," she continued, "and I dare you to answer 'no' to it. Would you like something to eat, so I don't have to restart that IV?" She crossed her arms and stared triumphantly at him.

He still thought she looked like an angel, although he'd never heard of an angel with black curly hair and eyes like a cat. Still, even if he was in heaven, his stomach rumbled just like it always did when he forgot to eat.

He glanced down at his bandaged wrist and up at the IV bag. "Yes." Anything to get rid of the tubes.

"Hallelujah! We have a 'yes!' I'll be right back."

Rider watched her leave. She took the spicy scent and the disturbing sensations with her. Good, because when her big bright eyes were on him, he had trouble remembering why he was here.

What was it about her eyes, anyway? A twinge of nausea reminded him that he wasn't supposed to notice people except in terms of his assigned mission. For tanks, there were only two types of people—targets and everyone else.

His target. He had to get out of here. Once these people started asking questions, running tests, they'd realize he wasn't one of them. They'd find out he'd been enhanced with stero-vitamins and conditioned into single-minded resolve. Then, at best, he'd be executed. At worst, he'd be caged and studied like an animal.

Sadness and regret tried to worm their way into his consciousness—more of the feelings that should have been sucked out of him in the TAINCC. He tamped them down with the cold hatred, and took his first good look at his surroundings.

Things actually weren't much different here than in his time. He was lying on a table covered with a sheet. A real wooden desk and chair were the only other furnishings. There were two wooden doors, one through which the angel doctor had disappeared. The other was open and led into a bathroom.

So much wood. That was different. He wondered if the doors creaked like the door to his office in the History Building. His office. He tried to concentrate on that thought, but it evaded him.

As his angel came back in with a big glass of yellow liquid and some fragrant, pie-like things on a plate, he decided as soon as he ate, he'd escape. After all, he couldn't locate his target if he was locked away like a barking mongrel. He sipped tentatively at the liquid. Orange. The taste evoked a haunting image of bright sunlight, bright hair.

Distracted by his odd thoughts, he drank the juice down in a few huge gulps. "What's that?" he said, nodding toward the plate.

The angel looked at him as if he'd lost his mind. "Pizza," she said carefully.

"Oh." Pete-sah? What in the hell was pete-sah? He tried to appear casual and uninterested as he studied the plate. He'd been briefed on preferred eating habits and local favorites, but he couldn't remember a damn thing right now. His brain was fuzzy, his ribs hurt, and she had brought her woman's fragrance and soothing presence back into the room with her.

He lifted a piece of the 'pete-sah" to his mouth, but the pleasant fragrance turned nauseating, and he dropped it back onto the plate, shuddering.

"What?" Angel-doctor looked puzzled. "Is it bad?" She sniffed. "It's just left over from lunch."

He stared at the triangle. "Flesh..." he whispered, gagging on the word.

"Flesh? You mean meat?"

"Meat?"

"Yes, meat. Pepperoni, sausage, ham—meat!" Her amber-green eyes assessed him with all the analytical coolness of the researchers who handled the TAINCC. "I think maybe I'd better see about getting you to the hospital. You need a CT scan, or an MRI. You may have some internal swelling in your brain."

"No!" he shouted, close to panic. He couldn't let them examine him. He had to stop making mistakes. The bastards had told him he was totally prepared. Had they forgotten to mention these people ate meat? Or had *he* forgotten? "Look, ang—doctor, it's okay. I'm fine. I just don't —"

She observed him as if he were a specimen under a microscope. "Oh," she said slowly. "You're a vegetarian."

"Vege... right." So, at least everybody didn't eat flesh. Maybe he wouldn't starve.

"I'll order you a veggie pizza. Meantime you need to sleep."

"Look, I..." Rider gestured vaguely toward his legs. "I don't seem to have any clothes on. What if I need to...?"

Angel-doctor chuckled. "Don't worry. You're catheterized," she tossed back over her shoulder as she left.

Rider lifted the sheet, knowing and dreading what he was going to see. Catheterized. Sure enough, another tube invaded him, this one so personal, so intimate—had she done it? His body tensed, and the catheter jerked as a vivid image of her gentle hands on him flashed across his vision and a flutter of nausea made his mouth go dry. As soon as the vision rocked him, his damn thigh started burning like fire.

If the angel doctor had catheterized him, there was no doubt she had seen the imprint on his left thigh that bespoke his rank. But then, she had no idea what it meant to be a tank.

He closed his eyes, fighting the nausea and anguish made worse by the compelling image of her touching him.

She had no idea that tanks were the lowest of the low. Convicted felons, murderers, traitors, whose only choice—other than death by lethal implantation—was to agree to enter the TAINCC, to be turned into killing machines for the government.

Because where he came from, the imprint of the dagger made him an outcast. The dagger told anyone who got close enough to him that he was a tank. And tank meant murderer.

Murderer. Something in his brain rebelled at that name. He wasn't a murderer. He hadn't been conscripted; he'd volunteered.

He was the only volunteer in the program, and the only tank with a college degree, an IQ above 140 and a personality profile without any major aberrations.

They'd considered dogged determination and a fascination with games that offered impossible odds as assets, not liabilities.

No wonder they'd sent him back as soon as they'd thought it was even marginally safe. He had two unbeatable qualities. Brains, and a very good reason to want to see the Deviants dead.

He was no murderer. He was an avenger. The Deviants were the murderers. Anger and hatred bubbled up in him until he thought his blood might literally boil. He didn't even stop to wonder why the anger was hot and not cold.

Deviants. Depraved mutants who penetrated your brain, leaving you soiled and violated. Deviants, who stopped at nothing to attain their ends, not even the murder of an innocent woman.

A vision of a tall, blonde woman sent a pang through him harsher than the ache of his broken ribs. His wife—murdered by the Deviants.

He was shaken by the strength of his anger and grief. Was this why the other two tanks had failed? Had their conditioning broken down, allowing dangerous emotions to get in the way of their mission?

Well, emotion wouldn't get in his way. He had an advantage they hadn't had. They had been condemned criminals. Their hearts weren't in it. He, on the other hand, had a personal motivation. The Deviants had killed his wife. He didn't know why they'd wiped his memories of her, but they'd left the important thing—they'd left his determination to avenge her death. All he had to do was get out of here, find and eliminate his target. It should be easy.

THREE

Kristen brought the veggie pizza into the exam room, but her patient was sound asleep. She sat in the wooden desk chair, the smell of the cooling tomato sauce pungent in her nostrils, and watched him.

He was an enigma, this man who wouldn't tell her his name, who had some sort of implant in his right eye and a strange tattoo on his thigh, who got inside her head like no one ever had except her brother.

She rubbed her temples, thankful he was asleep. He'd fallen asleep about fifteen minutes ago. She knew, because until then she'd been assaulted with more anger and hatred than she'd ever experienced in her life. Anger strong enough to muddle her brain, hatred so deep it was like a cancer growing inside him.

Right now, he wasn't even dreaming. Kristen rolled her head, stretching the tendons in her neck, welcoming the respite. She didn't need his feelings intruding. She was having enough trouble with her own.

Feelings unbecoming a doctor.

She'd never in her life experienced what she'd felt while examining him, preparing him for the IV. Thank God he'd been unconscious and Moira had been busy with the Medicaid files.

Catheterizing him had shaken her faith in herself as a doctor. Despite her determination, despite her training, she'd found it impossible to remain detached while she performed that most intimate of procedures. His steel-banded belly, his magnificent thighs, his overwhelming maleness, had affected her like she'd never been affected before. Ever. She'd been jolted to her toes by the tremors of raw desire that had rocked her when she'd touched him.

She'd never reacted that way. Not in all the years of internship and residency, not in hours of emergency room work. The human body was a smoothly functioning machine, and she was fascinated with its function. Her life's work was to repair that machine when it failed to function properly.

She had always been proud of the fact that her empathic response to people didn't affect her professionalism. When she slipped into the role of physician, the empathy that made it so hard for her to simply walk down a street became a tool, an asset, that aided her in diagnosis and therapy.

How disgusting that all her control, all her training, could puddle into a fiery pool of lust when she performed a mundane procedure on a dirty, battered refugee from the streets, a procedure she'd performed dozens if not scores of times in her career without a blink.

Even as she berated herself, she found her eyes traveling over his naked torso yet again. The sheet had slipped down, and the slight curve of one muscled hip was exposed where the fabric slanted over his loins. As many male patients as she had seen in various stages of undress, none had ever made her feel this way.

Her fingers curled, wanting to touch his smooth skin that hid tendon and muscle as her gaze slid downward. A few more inches, and the tattoo on his thigh would be exposed. Her mouth went dry and her body thrummed with an unfamiliar, aching need.

A colorful, stylized dagger, its steely point aimed right at— with an effort, she tore her gaze away from his pale flesh and her thoughts away from his body. She focused on his face.

His grim lips were relaxed and slightly open, and Kristen could hear his shallow breaths. His nose was thin and straight. His startling eyes were closed, his lashes thick and long against his cheeks. He had a high forehead, and his hair, still dirty but dry, was a light brown with hints of gold.

His face wasn't classically handsome. It was too angular, the planes too harsh. His cheeks were almost gaunt. His mouth, though wide, was almost too thin. But all his flawed features together made up the most beautiful face she'd ever seen. She fought the urge to smooth out the lines that ran from his nose to the corners of his mouth. She clenched her fists to keep from touching his lips.

As she watched, his nose twitched and his eyes opened. She steeled herself against his intense blue gaze. When he focused on her face, his wary confusion wafting toward her, she smiled. "The veggie pizza is here. Think you're ready for some solid food?"

"Yeah." He sat up gingerly, his brow furrowed, his jaw clenched.

"Amazing! Another 'yes'!"

He looked at her sidelong, and she shook her head as she handed him a slice of pizza and a napkin. "Never mind. If you keep that down, I'll take the IV and the—catheter out."

"Keep it down?"

"If you don't regurgitate, vomit, throw up."

"I get the picture," he muttered as he nibbled a tiny bite of the pizza, his expression reflecting wariness. His eyebrows shot up. "Not bad. Is there any more of that juice?"

Kristen fetched him a glass of juice, delighted that he was acting more human, thrilled that the food hadn't caused his empty stomach to rebel. As he polished off the wedge of pizza and drained a second glass of juice, she ventured another question. "You want to tell me your name now? Or is it still a state secret?"

He shot her a glance filled with suspicion and fear, and shook his head. "No."

Fine. He could refuse to talk, but she wasn't going to make it easy for him. She didn't know what he was so afraid of, but she was going to do her best to find out and help him conquer it if she could. "No, you won't tell me your name, or no, it's not a state secret?"

His mouth quirked so slightly she wasn't sure she could really call it a smile, but it gave her a peculiar satisfaction deep inside.

"Rider."

"What?" Her heart leaped. What had he said? Rider? Was that a name?

"Rider."

"Rider? Your name is Rider?"

"Yeah."

"Great! I'm so glad to meet you, Rider." Kristen sat up just a little straighter. How much more did she dare to ask at this point? His gaze was still wary, but she thought he'd relaxed a little. He was obviously feeling better after having eaten some solid food. "Well, Mr. Rider..."

"Just Rider."

"Well, Rider," she amended quickly, "do you think you could tell me a little about your eye?"

Dropping the last crust of pie back onto the plate, he frowned at her. "What about my eye?" he asked, easing back onto the table.

He sounded confused, but he'd sounded confused about most things since he'd awakened. She pressed on. "Come on! I've never seen anything like it. I've never even heard of anything like it. Did you have a detached retina? Is it some sort of optic muscle replacement? I've never seen a prosthetic like that in the eye. Where did you have it done?"

His arms were rigid at his sides and his eyes were closed, but as she finished speaking, he opened them to narrow slits and squinted at her. "I don't have any idea what you're talking about. I've never had anything done to my eye."

It was Kristen's turn to be confused. He sounded sincere, but she was so sure there was something there. She shrugged. Maybe she'd get Bill to look at it. He'd had more experience in eye surgery than she had. She'd only done one rotation in ophthalmology.

Rider was still watching her. "I ate my supper, Doctor," he said. "You going to keep your promise? I want to be awake for the withdrawal of the catheter, since I missed the insertion."

Kristen gasped at the embarrassed thrill that rushed through her at his words. Her face burned and she stiffened. "You know, *Mister Rider*, I could make that experience very unpleasant if I wanted to."

He grimaced and laid a fist on his belly. "Yeah?" he growled. "And you could make it very pleasant, too, I'll bet. Couldn't you, Doc?"

She recoiled. "You're despicable! I'll have Doctor Maxey take care of you when he gets in. I'm almost sorry I found you."

His face darkened ominously, and he muttered something too low for her to hear.

"What?"

"I said you should be. Never mind. I apologize for the crudity." He laid his head back and closed his eyes. "Why do you think there's something wrong with my eye?"

"There's something in there. It could be scar tissue, I guess, but it looks more like some kind of implant. Are you sure you haven't had surgery?"

"Surgery?"

She studied his face. It didn't reflect his feelings. He was good. He'd obviously had a lot of practice hiding his true emotions from the world. But he couldn't hide them from her. He was afraid, deathly afraid of something, and overlaying the fear was sadness and a chill emotion she could only describe as hate. "Sure. You could hardly have forgotten it."

"Yeah, well, I must have."

His voice held a note that Kristen couldn't quite identify, but as she laid her hand on his arm she had no doubt about his feelings at that moment. No doubt at all.

"I'm sorry," she whispered, suddenly overwhelmed by the

depth of pain and grief and paralyzing fear rippling up her arm and into her heart.

"For what?" he demanded, shifting restlessly and grunting when his sore ribs stabbed him.

"I didn't mean to bring back painful memories. I was just interested in the technology."

"Memories?" He gazed at her, his eyes as hot as blue lasers burning into her soul. He made a sound like a laugh, but his mouth grimaced as he pressed on his midsection. "There are no painful memories, Doc. None at all. No memories. No feelings. Nothing."

"That's not true," she whispered, wanting to cry, wishing she could take away his anguish. How would she bear it? She wanted to help him, but she was afraid she couldn't stand under the weight of his pain.

Still, she had to try. There was something there, something inside him that called to her. He needed his memories, distressing as they were. He needed his emotions—his anguish, his anger, even his fear. She wasn't sure how she knew, but she knew.

"The memories are there, Rider," she whispered. "And the emotions. They're just buried awfully deep."

His anger slashed through her, and the shock made her jerk away.

"What the hell do you know about it?"

She picked up the pizza plate and the wadded napkins, anything to avoid looking into those eyes again. She made her voice deliberately light. "I'm the doctor. I'm supposed to know these things."

He grabbed her arm, pulling her close, assaulting her with his anger.

"You don't know a damn thing, Doc. Not a damn thing! And that's too bad. Because if you knew what was good for you, you'd keep your nose out of it. Now, I've got to get out of here, so get me untangled from all this stuff!"

His grip sent spasms of fear and rage through her nerve endings. She felt like a convicted felon must feel when the executioner throws the lever, sending electric current gushing through the wire leads to destroy him. "Let go of me, Mister. I can call for help, and you'll be in jail for assault."

He spoke through clenched jaws. "Yeah, right. Me lying here injured and trussed up, and you standing there all cute and pouty. Just get me untangled!"

"Fine! It's none of my business if you want to walk out of here half dead." She welcomed the surge of her own anger, a candle-flame next to his inferno, but still something she could focus on.

"Damn right it's not. Anyhow, I walked in here half dead."

"Three-quarters, and you didn't walk, I carried you."

"You? Hah!" A moue of bitter amusement twisted his mouth, but his eyes still burned with rage.

"I did! Ask Moira!" Kristen couldn't keep her voice from quivering. "In fact, I'll send her in here to get you untangled."

As the image crossed her mind, she couldn't help chuckling. "That'll serve you right!"

"Wait! What do you mean?"

Confusion and fear commingled within him as she turned away. His mobile face didn't show it, but inside he seemed lost, bewildered by his surroundings and by her. She frowned. She really had to quit picking up strays. If any one of them were ever dangerous, it was this one. "Good night, Rider, I've got to go."

"Doc! Wait a minute." She turned around to see him sitting up gingerly, breathing shallowly through his mouth to keep his ribs from aching. "I told you my name, but you never told me yours."

Kristen stared at him as she felt the anger and fear that boiled inside him, fear of something so dreadful she couldn't imagine it, anger that he couldn't control the fear. Pity suffused her.

"Come on. I got a right to know who saved my life, don't I?"

Kristen shrugged, choosing to ignore his sarcasm, and walked back to the table. She held out her hand. "I'm Doctor Kristen Skipworth."

Hot adrenalin streaked through him, leaving his limbs quivering, his mouth dry. He felt the blood drain from his face, felt his fingers and toes grow numb as his body pulled the blood into its core, trying to protect itself from the shock.

Kristen Skipworth. The name hovered in the air like a storm cloud, echoed down the corridors of his brain like footsteps in an empty chamber. His gut twisted in revulsion.

He recoiled from her outstretched hand. Kristen Skipworth. The latest best guess of the best researchers had traced the problem back to her. The entire problem.

Somehow he'd known all along that she was special. If

he'd been paying attention, he'd have realized what his battered brain had tried to tell him.

It was in her eyes. Those amber-shot jewels should have
warned him who she was. All the Deviants had those peculiar
gold-flecked eyes. The electric charge whenever she touched
him should have told him she was doing things to him no human
being should be allowed to do to another.

Why hadn't he recognized her? The blow on his head must
have screwed up his brain's wiring or something. Yeah, something like maybe he didn't want his angel doctor to be the ultimate enemy, the target.

"Rider?"

Her trembling voice buzzed in his brain like the temple leads
in the TAINCC. He should have known. How had he been so
lucky? So lucky, and so damned *unlucky*! He forced himself to
focus on her Deviant eyes.

"Rider? Are you okay?"

A wisp of cloud brushed his forehead. No, it was her hand.
He jerked his head away, welcoming the searing pain the movement caused him. He needed the pain to keep his focus, to
keep his mind off her angel face, her gentle soothing hands, her
trusting, treacherous eyes.

"Talk to me!" she demanded, and he made himself listen to
her, made himself look at her. *The Mother of all the Deviants.*

He had trouble focusing. Her image kept fading to another
fainter one. Another beautiful face, this one framed with blonde
hair. Mari. His wife. His throat contracted, and his eyes burned.

This woman had killed his wife. Her descendants were
murderers. Slowly his wife's image faded, and he was staring
at the Mother of All the Deviants again.

Hot blinding hatred sucked the last dregs of strength from
his quivering limbs. He stared helplessly at her, digging deep
inside himself for the protective cold resolve, for the conditioning, hating himself for the fear and pain he couldn't block.

He had a job to do. He wasn't supposed to react with
heated anger. A shudder racked him and he drew a long breath,
trying to ignore her scent, concentrating on his mission—his
reason for being here.

He could do it right now. He could kill her. She was close
enough for him to wrap his fingers around her pretty neck and
snap it with no more effort than snapping a twig.

FOUR

Rider Savage stared at the Mother of All the Deviants. Something wasn't right. Something in her amber-green eyes paralyzed him.

He flexed his fingers slowly, willing them to move, willing his body to act like the weapon it had been conditioned to be. His fingers weren't cooperating, though. They moved like old, arthritic fingers, creaking, the joints rubbing together agonizingly.

The eyes watching him clouded with worry. He tore his gaze away from her. She was a Deviant. She'd get inside his head if he let her.

A violent wave of nausea ripped through him, and he welcomed it. It was a relief after the confusing emotions she evoked in him. He'd kill her all right. But killing her wasn't enough for him. First he wanted her to know why she was dying, wanted her to feel all the pain her descendants had caused down through the centuries.

His gut spasmed, and he swallowed hard. Then quelling his revulsion, he forced himself to grasp her hand in his, wincing at the anticipation of a blinding wave of nausea that never came. He stared at their clasped hands, his bruised and scraped, engulfing her smaller, smoother one.

Her touch rattled his brain. Instead of increasing his sickness, multiplying his hatred, her touch soothed his beat up emotions. Her fingers were cool and light. Her skin exuded peace and caring.

He slowly raised his gaze to hers, using all his strength to dredge up enough hatred and anger to make his voice quietly menacing as he squeezed her fingers. "How do you do, Kristen Skipworth. I've been sent from the future to kill you."

Through the hand of the man she'd rescued, Kristen was bombarded with more conflicting emotions than she had ever sensed from one person. She felt an intense burning hatred overlaid with deep sadness and wary yearning. She carefully extricated her fingers from his steel-hard grip, finding it more difficult to wrench her gaze away from his. The look in his eyes was murder, but her senses gave her an entirely different message. She sensed a conflict in him that was tearing him apart.

She tried to equate the confusion with his incredible words as she studied him. His blue eyes had looked perfectly rational until the crazy words had spilled out of his mouth.

It was really too bad. Too bad that such a lovely body had to house such a sick mind. Strange, though, at the same time, because as irrational as his words were, what she sensed within him wasn't the chaos of a psychotic brain.

She'd worked with mentally and emotionally disturbed patients during her residency. She'd always come away dazed and confused. It was almost impossible for her to touch them, the bedlam inside them was so strong. It would be hours before she could rescue her brain from the anguished chaos in theirs.

As muddled as his emotions were, Rider didn't evoke the chaos of psychosis in her. Oh, he was baffling, with his intense eyes and his anger and despair, but she was having a hard time convincing herself he was psychotic.

Disturbed, definitely. Possibly paranoid, maybe even mildly schizophrenic.

She blinked deliberately and pulled her gaze from his as she berated herself. Get with it, Dr. Skipworth. He said he had come from the future. That had to rank right up there with being kidnaped by aliens. He was psychotic. Definitely.

"That does it," she muttered, dropping her gaze. She couldn't avoid it. She had to admit he was mentally unstable.

"What?" His voice held a note of barely controlled panic.

"We've got to get you to a hospital, now." She turned toward the door, and almost screamed when he jerked her back around to face him.

She had thought his grip was relentless before. Now the bones in her forearm rubbed together from the pressure of his fingers. She clenched her teeth. "You're hurting me. Let go!"

"No."

"Damn it, let—me—go!" She locked gazes with him again, setting her jaw against the combined pains of her arm and his ribs. Physically, she was no match for him, but she had help.

"Moira!" she called, her voice steadier than she would have expected, her gaze never wavering from his. "Moira, could you come in here a minute?"

A flicker of deadly amusement lit his face before he opened his hand. "You win, Doc," he said wryly just as Moira came through the open door. "This time."

"Yes, Dr. Skipworth?"

"Moira, would you please remove Mister Rider's catheter, and discontinue the IV. He would like to take a shower. And could you find him some clothes, please?" Kristen flashed Rider a triumphant smirk. "Unless you'd prefer to go to the hospital like that?"

If the tiny object imbedded behind his pupil were a weapon, Kristen thought as she left the exam room, she'd be dead now. She shivered, remembering his words and the reasonable, even tone. *Hello, Kristen Skipworth. I've been sent from the future to kill you.*

Sitting down at the desk, she picked up his chart and began writing. Rider. Just Rider. She wouldn't be surprised to find that he'd escaped from a psychiatric hospital.

Too bad he was crazy. Bill and Moira were right. She always managed to find them—the ones who were kidnaped by aliens, like that poor man last month, or the woman who swore she was carrying Elvis' baby.

It was too bad. Kristen shook her head, wishing she could forget the feel of his silky rough skin under her fingers, the profound effect his naked body had evoked in her. He was a gorgeous psychotic.

Still shocked by his effect on her, Kristen wrenched her brain away from unprofessional thoughts about his body, back to practical matters, like writing progress notes for John Doe, now Rider, just Rider.

Patient is a well-nourished white male, approx. 35 y/o, in good health. Presented with minor contusions, possible hairline fracture of one or more ribs, some deterioration of muscle tone due to lack of nourishment and dehydration.

Alert, responsive to stimuli. Possibly delusional. Rule out paranoid schizophrenia, psychosis. No sign of substance abuse. Ingested approximately 500 ml of orange juice and 90 gm of pizza. IV and catheter removed. Recommend immediate transfer to Midtown General for psychiatric evaluation.

After suffering the indignity of having the catheter removed by Moira, Rider was at least grateful he could move around. When the nurse pointed the way to the shower, he wrapped the sheet around him and gingerly fled to the solitude of the tile-lined room.

He closed the door, noticing the faint creak as it moved on its hinges. His hands lingered on the painted wood surface.

There was so little wood in his time. Trees were an endangered species.

The roughness and grainy texture of the wood felt familiar and seductive under his fingers. His office in the History Building.

He hated this part of their damned conditioning. He hated not being able to remember mundane things, like his job.

He'd been a teacher—no, a historian. No, definitely a teacher. He remembered lecturing in front of a room full of bored young faces.

His legs quivering with weakness, he stepped into the sterile whiteness of the shower stall. He unwrapped the bandage around his ribs, groaning at the increased pain as the stiff gauze came off. He grabbed at a chrome rail as more unwelcome memories raced through his brain like a vidlink.

Marielle frowning at him, her fingers manipulating the knobs of an ancient radio...

The room awash with green light...

He gripped the chrome with both hands and pressed his forehead against the cold tile, trying to force the memories into cohesion, but every time he'd grab onto an image it would dissolve like a snowflake.

Grabbing her as she collapsed, hugging her to him, trying to hold the life in her by force of will... the heat from the blaster still in her body... death sucking her away...

Waves of sickness washed over him. He rolled his forehead against the tile, fighting the horrible images, but wanting them, too, because as bad as they were, at least they were his.

Why didn't they let him keep his memories? Why didn't they use the memory of his wife's murder to motivate him?

Even as the thoughts formed, he understood the argument against them. A cold, unfeeling predator would be more effective than a hotheaded, grief-stricken man.

Stop it, he screamed silently. Tanks don't think. Tanks don't feel. They just kill.

He thrust the wisps of memory away, dredging up the detachment conditioned into him, and surveyed the room.

The white, unrelenting chill of the tile reminded him of the TAINCC's prep room. He shuddered as he inspected the apparatus on the walls.

In the prep room, he and the other trainees had been forced to stand at attention with goggles protecting their eyes while spigots spewed icy chlorinated water at them from all directions, cleansing them for immersion in the conditioning chamber. For several moments he stood rigid, his eyes squeezed shut, waiting for the lone spout above his head to turn the gush of chlorinated water on him.

When nothing happened, he squinted at the shiny fixtures on the wall. The red dotted handle had HOT written on it. The blue dotted one said COLD. He looked at the spout. A drop of liquid gathered on its lower edge.

Rider touched his forefinger to the droplet and touched the droplet to his tongue. Water! Pure, clean water!

He tentatively turned the handle marked HOT. Water began to trickle from the spout, water that smelled like rain and quickly turned warm, then suddenly hot. He yanked the COLD handle, sending an icy spray into his face. After some cursing and manipulating, he finally had a wonderfully warm flow of water raining down on his head.

He raised his face to the purifying stream. How long had it been since he'd had a real shower with real water? Had he ever?

Yes. Once he'd taken showers, gone to work, owned a car. Once he'd had a real life. Once he'd been a person, not a tank.

Marielle, dressed in unrelieved black, the signature uniform of the underground... No!

How did his memories of his wife get mixed up with a vision of the perverted Deviants who killed her?

A blinding nausea gripped him. Gut-wrenching, sickening fear stripped the vestiges of memory away, leaving him shaken and weak.

He gripped the chrome rails and let the water massage the back of his neck while he forced his brain to focus on his mission. He'd been sent—no, he had volunteered—for this suicide run for one reason and one reason only. To kill Kristen Skipworth, the Mother of all the Deviants, the progenitor of the bastards who'd killed his wife. The sickness and fear began to dissipate as he concentrated on that fact.

He hadn't killed her yet, but that was only because he'd been so battered and weak. He was already better. Amazing what a little food and rest could do.

The water beat rhythmically, comfortingly on his temples, on the tense muscles in his neck. After a few seconds he threw his head back, opening his mouth to let the warm stream sluice out the bitter taste of grief.

As the water began to cool, he quickly washed his hair and soaped his skin, carefully peeling away the bandage on his temple, rinsing the filth of the streets and the centuries down the drain. He slung wet hair out of his eyes and stepped from the steamy cubicle.

Fluffy white towels awaited him, another luxury he'd forgotten. After the TAINCC, they'd always been sprayed with more chlorine water then buffeted with dry, stale air, as if they were some kind of living utensils in a giant washing machine.

Dressed in worn jeans, a little loose but long enough, a white tee shirt, and some sort of cloth and plastic shoes with thick, soft soles, Rider rubbed the steam away from the mirror and looked at his reflection. The gash on his temple looked nasty, but the swelling had gone down, and his head no longer hurt. He stared into the intense blue eyes that stared bleakly back. A gap-toothed comb lay on the lavatory, so he combed his hair back from his face.

Damn, he was skinny! When had he lost all that weight? He touched his cheek where a shadow outlined his cheekbone, then looked at his bicep. He'd lost too much muscle in the past—how many days? Three? Five? Without the stero-vitamins, he'd soon be scrawny. And it was for damn sure the food here wasn't ennutriated either!

He caught his own gaze again and smirked. Not like he'd have time to get fat. One way or another, he probably wouldn't be around long enough.

FIVE

A rap on the door startled Rider. He whirled and crouched into attack position.

"Mr. Rider?"

It was the nurse. He took a long, harsh breath, easing out of the crouch and gingerly relaxing his arms. When would those damned ribs heal?

"You okay, Mr. Rider?" The voice came muffled through the thick door.

"Fine," he said shortly. "Be right out."

"The ambulance will be here in a minute."

Rider tensed. Ambulance. So the pretty little doctor was determined to turn him over to the dog catchers.

What sick twist of fate had put him right in her path? They had been so careful to explain to him how resourceful he'd have to be to find Kristen Skipworth. He had spent hours in the TAINCC while electrodes attached to his temples fed him information about this era of history. He'd even been told they were meat eaters. He remembered now. It was just that he'd been caught off guard when she'd put the pizza in front of him. His nose wrinkled at the memory of the smell of burned flesh.

It should have been done by now. He could have broken her neck with one flick of a wrist, there in the alley. He closed his eyes and tried to picture how it would happen. Her as-yet-unborn children, dissolving one by one, down the centuries. Even the ones who had killed his wife. It was a satisfying picture, if a slightly grotesque one.

But he hadn't. When he'd touched her ankle, he'd been buffeted with a sensation so alien, he hadn't been able to put a name to it, but it was all tied up with clouds and heaven and feeling good. And it was part of the reason he'd allowed her to bring him to the clinic. He'd been so hurt, so tired, and touching her was the best thing he ever remembered.

A moment of weakness, that was all. The sensation was probably hunger.

Now, because of his weakness, he'd given her enough time to call the dog catchers. He looked up at the small, steamy window above the toilet, then back at the door.

"Sorry, Doc," he whispered. "I'm not going to a med care facility, to be locked up and dissected like a dog."

Guilt sliced through him. Where had guilt come from? His

conditioning, no doubt. It was probably guilt from even thinking about escape instead of keeping his mind totally on destroying Kristen Skipworth. The TAINCC was quite effective in implanting things like total loyalty to the system and unreasoning concentration on the mission.

And his mission was to destroy Kristen Skipworth, not to run away. How in the hell had he managed to latch onto her so fast? He'd been reaching out for an angel to help him get into heaven, and he'd caught his prey.

He looked in the mirror again. There should be no emotions inside him anymore. But somehow, there was that alien sensation tied up with the angel doctor that went so counter to everything he'd had imbedded in his brain in the TAINCC that it made him gag. He swallowed hard and took a long breath.

What was that smell?

His nostrils twitched, and he took another breath, this one carefully shallow.

Benzofenfluramic diacetyltrialamine. BeeDee. The most dangerous chemical ever invented. The unique odor of rotten bananas and old urine triggered visions Dante would have been proud of.

Red, blinding explosions. Agonized screams.

His conditioned lightspeed reflexes kicked in. Without stopping to consider why he would smell BeeDee five hundred years before it had been invented, Rider glanced once at the tiny sealed window above the toilet, dismissed it as a means of quick escape, threw open the door and ran out—right into the waiting arms of two burly men in white.

One grabbed him while the other brandished a white coat of some sort with ties hanging from it like fringe.

"Look out! Let me go!" Rider shouted, struggling to free himself from the man's grip. "Get out of here!"

The white coat twisted Rider's arm up behind him. "Take it easy, bud," he said, pinning Rider's other arm to his side. "You're okay. We're just going to get you all dressed up."

They thought he was crazy, a barking mongrel. They were the dog catchers.

When the second man approached, holding out the white garment, Rider braced his back against the man holding him and kicked up with both feet, sending the second man sprawling against the wall. Then Rider dropped his weight, ignoring the searing pain in his twisted shoulder and the pain in his side. When the man behind him overbalanced, he kicked his feet over his head and connected with the man's skull. The ache in his shoulder lessened as his attacker let go and fell to the floor.

The second man was straightening up and the one he'd just kicked was groaning, so Rider took off down the hall.

His angel-doctor was standing in a doorway staring at him as if he were a rabid dog.

"Doc! Get out! BeeDee!" He grabbed her with the passing thought that he'd be damned if he'd let her die before she knew why she was dying. He pushed her resisting body ahead of him.

"What are you—wait—Moira!" Kristen screamed, but Rider ignored her.

In the waiting room, the nurse was talking with a woman and a little boy and she looked up, shocked, as Rider and Kristen crashed through the door.

"Get out!" He screamed, pushing Kristen ahead of him, not waiting to see if the others obeyed him.

Outside, through the muted darkness of early evening, he saw the ambulance waiting, its engine running. He paused and gestured toward it. "Can you drive one of these, Doc?"

She stared at him, eyes wide as mini-disks. She shook her head slowly, as if she weren't quite sure what he'd said.

He wasted a precious few seconds considering her. Surely she knew how to drive these big, internal combustion vehicles. If they worked like solar cars he'd be able to drive it, but if not....

"I think you're lying, but we don't have time to find out." He skirted the back of the vehicle and dragged her away from the clinic.

"Stop! Let go of me! What are you doing? I'll have you arrested!"

Rider heard Kristen's babble without sorting it into words as he ducked into a dark alley and turned, pulling her tight up against him and clamping a hand over her mouth.

Relief flooded him. She was safe. He'd gotten her out in time. He ignored the fleeting thought that if he hadn't pulled her to safety his mission would be accomplished in a very few minutes.

"Come on, come on. Get out," he muttered, watching the door of the clinic, his heart pounding, every muscle cramped with tension as he waited for the explosion. It wouldn't be more than a few seconds, judging by the overpowering smell of the BeeDee.

Moira and the woman and child came through the door.

"Get away from the clinic!" he whispered desperately, cringing in anticipation of the blast he knew was imminent.

Kristen was rigid as death in his arms, her limbs quivering with resistance. She struggled, grunting and moaning behind his hand. He could only imagine what she was saying.

His eyes never left the doorway as he waited for the two men in white to come out, already knowing it was too late for them.

Suddenly, a horrific explosion rent the air, its searing blast knocking them backwards with its force and lighting the alley with a black-red light that tore through the air like violent thunder.

Rider fought to keep his grip on his prey while he recovered his balance. "BeeDee," he whispered, shuddering.

He couldn't see anything through the smoke and debris. Behind the clinic, where the explosive had probably been placed, red and yellow flames flared then quickly died down as he watched.

BeeDee was relatively clean, for an explosive.

Pain ripped through his hand.

"Shit!" She'd bitten him. He almost smiled as he jerked her arm behind her, eliciting an angry cry. At least she wasn't a whiner. He admired her courage. She was brave, tough when she had to be.

A thought tickled the edge of his consciousness, almost a memory. He stiffened, but before he could explore the turn his thoughts had taken, he was jolted back to the present by the sudden pain of a small foot stomping on his.

"Hey," he grunted and jerked on her arm.

"Ow!" she groaned. "What did you do? Where's Moira? Oh my God!" Her whole body began shivering as the wail of the sirens split the air and voices shouted incoherently over the noise.

"Shut up, Doc." He bent her arm just a little further up her back, drawing a quiet cry from her. "Don't move, or your arm will break."

She fell quiet and her body, though still trembling, no longer resisted him. He breathed a sigh of relief, but didn't let up the pressure on her arm.

He needed some time. Time to figure out where the BeeDee had come from. Time to wonder why he'd pulled her out of the clinic, rather than just running. Part of his brain reminded him that he didn't want her to die that easily. He wanted her to understand why she was dying.

Rider wondered why his reasoning, which seemed sound, didn't fit with his emotions. He was too relieved. Saving her felt too good. It was almost as if the act of saving his angel doctor had healed something inside him, had canceled out some of the fear.

Where had his conditioning gone? It seemed like every time he touched her, a little more of the armor the TAINCC had built around him was stripped away.

"Where's the fire?" a jolly voice echoed through the alley as a car door slammed shut. Then there were other car doors, other voices, footsteps crunching on asphalt. As screaming fire trucks pulled around to the back of the clinic, Rider took several steps backward. Dragging Kristen with him, he glanced behind him down the dark alley.

"Where does this go?" he whispered in her ear.

"I don't know. Let me go!" Kristen began to squirm in his grip. "I can scream!"

He efficiently sent another ripple of agony down her shoulder through her body, knowing from experience exactly how much it hurt, though he was careful not to really injure her. "Oh, yeah? Try it."

He waited for her to draw a breath, then right in the middle of it, he tugged a bit more on her arm. The breath exploded in a gasp of distress.

"I said, where does this alley go?"

"It—comes out on—Lombard," she grated through clenched teeth.

"Where are your quarters, Doc?"

"My quarters?" She sounded genuinely bewildered.

Oh, yeah. Quarters were what they called them in his time. "Apartment, house. Where you live."

"Ha, no way!" she spat.

She drew in a long breath as if preparing to scream, so he gave her another taste of broken shoulder. Then he felt around in her jeans, making a determined if futile effort to ignore the enticing curves underneath the denim, and tugging on her arm again when she tried to kick him.

In her back pocket was a slender wallet, and in her front pocket was a set of keys, which he hung on his finger by the ring while he flipped open the wallet. A license of some kind and a picture I.D. No address. Good picture, though.

He worried a slip of paper out with two fingers. Some sort of invoice, with her address. "Damn," he breathed. "You live on Lombard. Why didn't you say so, Doc? Come on."

Without loosening his hold on her arm, he gently propelled her ahead of him.

"Hey! You!" A voice boomed behind them.

Rider stiffened, then pushed her faster. She stumbled, running, urged on by his brutal grip on her arm. His ribs hurt abominably as he ran.

"Hey, over here! After them!" The voices were closer, and beams from flashlights stung their heels.

He ducked into the shadow of a building and slipped inside a utility door, pulling Kristen up against him. "Don't make a move, Doc, and I'll let up a little."

She nodded, the movement wafting her warm, spicy scent toward him. That scent drew disturbing visions before his eyes and gave him a decidedly uncomfortable tightness in his loins. The imprint on his thigh burned like fire, and a tickle of nausea lodged in his throat. He shook his head and eased off the pressure on her arm.

Sucking in a sharp breath, she carefully flexed her shoulder, but to her credit, she didn't try to run or cry out.

Footsteps crunched near them and voices were lowered to urgent whispers. After a while, the footsteps retreated.

"Which way?" he asked.

"Which way what?" Her voice was edged with panic, her breath still coming sharp and fast. She occasionally rubbed her arm as if she wasn't quite sure it would work.

"Come on, Doc. Don't go stupid on me. I've got a good cure for stupid."

"You're crazy if you think I'm taking you to my apartment." She twisted her neck around to look at him. "What did you do to the clinic? Is Moira dead?" Her voice broke a little on that question.

He swung her around and gripped her shoulders. "I said which way?"

She lifted her chin. His admiration for her grew along with his irritation. She was either very brave or very dumb. He didn't have time to consider which. He had to rest, had to have some time to figure out what was going on.

He shook her. "Where, damn it?"

Fear widened her eyes as she stared at him, her lower lip trembling slightly.

Rider had to tear his gaze away from her mouth. It was too vulnerable, too tempting. He was just about at the end of his patience and his strength. Slowly, deliberately, he ran his hand up her arm and past her shoulder to caress the nape of her neck, ignoring the stinging in his thigh and the stirrings in his loins.

"I could kill you with a flick of my wrist," he whispered, his heart racing. He demonstrated with a quick, harmless motion. She winced and gasped, but never took her gaze from his.

"Go ahead," she said. "It's what you came for, isn't it?"

A wrenching nausea closed his throat. "Damn right it is," he grated, clenching his jaw against the pain and sickness. He tightened his fingers around her neck, pleased when she stiffened.

"Then do it," she said through lips white with tension, her eyes watching him sharply. "But I'm not taking you to my apartment. I'm not a fool."

He forced a harsh laugh. "Oh yeah?" he asked, his voice cracking, his fingers paralyzed, refusing to obey his will. What was the matter with him? He wanted to kill her—needed to. So why couldn't he?

She stood rigid, her eyes squeezed shut, waiting like a doomed empress for execution. Her bravery made him ashamed, and his whole being resisted the feeling. He searched for anger to wash out the sensation of her touch.

He flexed his fingers, and she flinched. Then he flipped her wallet open in front of her eyes. "Take a look here, Doc. Forty-four fifty-three Lombard, Apartment Seven. Shouldn't be too hard to find, should it?" He turned her around and wrenched her arm up her back again. "Let's go. Just two lovers out for a late stroll."

She moaned softly as he prodded her forward. At the edge of the alley, he found a street sign that read forty-four hundred Lombard.

"Well, how about that," he whispered against Kristen's hair, ignoring her scent that was tied up with poignant longing somewhere deep inside him. "We're even on the right block." He bent her arm just a little more. "You ever tried to catheterize somebody with one arm, Doc?"

"Okay!" she gasped, her voice strained and small. "Okay. It's that building there. Please!"

He let up just a little and guided her across the street and into the building. They climbed the steps to her apartment, she leading the way and Rider struggling up each step behind her. Between the ache in his ribs and his head, the exhaustion of days of starvation, and having to keep a death grip on her arm, he wasn't sure if he would make it without passing out. If she had any sense, she'd figure out how weak he was.

He executed the last steps in a near stupor, and so was caught off guard when he almost stepped on a cat.

Kristen gritted her teeth against yet another jarring pain. She was so dazed, so confused by all that had happened, she couldn't even tell if it was his pain or hers. Each time he'd prodded her by tugging just a bit harder on her arm, she had thought she would pass out. With each step he took, the pain in his side stabbed her as efficiently as it stabbed him. And under it all, like an underground stream, ran the anger and fear.

When Sam yowled, Rider jerked backward and snapped into a crouch so fast she was taken aback, his arms up in a peculiar gesture which, combined with the menacing look on his face, terrified her. His cobalt eyes glittered madly as he glanced around without moving his head.

She ought to be doing something, she thought. If he didn't hurt so much, if he weren't broadcasting his every sensation to her like radar, maybe she could put her thoughts into some order.

Maybe she should run. She gauged the distance to the stairs. She'd have to run past him, but he didn't look like he could catch her right now. While she was trying to decide what to do, Sam jumped into her arms, startling her. She buried her nose in his soft fur, swallowing a disgusting urge to cry.

"Put it down."

She looked up, sensing a terror from her captor that was ridiculous, given the circumstances. "This is my—"

"I said put it down." He leaned against the wall, his face as gray as the faded paint, his eyes filled with horror and anguish.

"What's the matter with you?" Kristen gasped, a dizzying haze blinding her. She clutched Sam and swallowed against the dreadful sickness. It was coming from him, all of it. She glanced at him, propped against the wall, his body shivering and his face ashen. He was about to collapse.

Gathering every shred of will she could, Kristen did her best to shield herself from his emotions. She bit her lip and shook her head, trying to shake off the haziness, trying to force herself to think coherently. Rider coughed and gagged, and splayed his fingers on the wall for support.

Tearing her gaze from him, she glanced at her apartment door. He was between her and the stairs, but she was closer to the door, and on the inside of that door was a deadbolt and a chain. A few feet beyond was a telephone—a telephone that could bring the police to cart off this psycho. A telephone that could tell her if Moira was okay. A telephone that could link her with someone sane.

But the door was locked and Rider held the key. Her gaze dropped to his right hand fisted against his rib cage, her keys protruding between his fingers. He had closed his eyes, breathing shallowly.

Kristen assessed him. He was almost unconscious and suffering from shock. She knew, not only from his appearance, but because she could feel the blood in her own body pulling in, pooling in her body core, trying to protect her from the sensations his body was broadcasting.

Her fingers and toes were growing cold and numb, her heart rate was speeding up—all symptoms of shock, and all coming from him. She breathed slowly, deeply, using the calming techniques she'd often instructed panicked patients to use.

Carefully, never taking her eyes off his face, she stretched her arm up and retrieved the spare key from over the door facing. Not original, but then she didn't have much worth stealing anyway.

Ignoring a strange compassion for the sick man that tried to push past her good sense, she slid the key into the lock and turned it.

Slipping through the door, she slammed it shut. She reached for the deadbolt. Just as she was about to flip it, Rider crashed through the door and fell on top of her, his weight knocking the breath from her lungs. She gasped and struggled, but he easily pinned her hands.

"Don't give me any trouble, Doc," he grated through clenched teeth, his body heavy on hers. "I'm not having a good day."

Sam darted across his back and he cried out, every muscle in his body cramping.

With a peculiar satisfaction, she felt the deep shudder go through him, saw the pale horror on his face. "I don't—believe it. You're—afraid of—cats?" she wheezed, wishing he'd take his considerable bulk off her.

He shook his head. "Shut up." His voice cracked, and sweat ran down his face to soak the neck of his tee shirt.

Kristen felt sadness and regret through his body. She couldn't look away from his anguished gaze, and somehow, through it, she saw a glimpse of the man he might have been— brave, honorable, but weighted down with loss and sorrow.

"I'm sorry," she choked, struggling to breathe against his weight. "I've lost someone, too." She wasn't even sure why she said it.

He recoiled, his eyes lit with the insane glitter that frightened her so. "You—Deviant!" he spat in her face. "Get the hell out of my head! I ought to kill you right now!"

Kristen turned her face away, but still his rage and hate blasted her, as strong and blistering as the heat from the explosion.

The explosion! Had he caused the explosion? But then, if he had—if he were trying to kill her as he kept saying, why had he jerked her outside, away from danger?

"Who are you?" she whispered, but he wasn't listening to her.

A terrible fear began to build inside her. She hadn't really believed him. Not even when he'd put his fingers on her neck and forced her to tell him where her apartment was. She wasn't sure what she'd thought she was going to do, but now she knew with a sick certainty that he wasn't just another harmless kook she'd picked up. He really was going to kill her. She felt the conviction, the dogged determination that drove him past exhaustion, past pain, past everything good she sensed inside him.

She'd gone too far this time. She'd finally rescued a stray who had turned on her.

He gripped both her wrists in one hand and yanked them over her head, sliding his other hand underneath her nape. His eyes were glazed, his breathing shallow and fast as his fingers tightened around her neck.

"Kill you right now," he whispered, sweat dripping off his face onto hers. He squeezed until Kristen thought her neck was going to snap. She closed her eyes and clenched her teeth, truly afraid for the first time in her life.

She centered herself, searching for the calm inside her that made her a good doctor, and tried something she'd never tried before with anyone, even Skipper. She tried to connect with Rider, to reach inside him, down past the unyielding determination, down to where he lived, tried to touch his soul with compassion as he touched hers with hatred.

His whole body went rigid and he rolled off her, clutching his middle, curling up like a fetus. The agony that gripped him seared through her, even after he no longer touched her. She took quick, shallow breaths, trying to minimize the tearing pain.

She couldn't move. She was paralyzed by his pain and terror, so she closed her eyes and flowed with it like she'd tried to teach her cancer patients to do. She focused her attention on the man beside her.

Had she succeeded? Had she reached something within him? It was a strange notion, that the empathy she struggled with every day could be turned around, could become a tool, a weapon. Of course, everything about this whole insane experience was strange, to say the least.

She had never known anyone who affected her like this fugitive from a mental ward. His every emotion ripped through her like her own. She could no more separate herself from him than she could separate her soul from her heart.

Skipper had been a part of her consciousness, closer to her than any other person, but now, this man Rider was insinuating himself into her more deeply than Skipper had ever been. Rider was becoming entwined with her soul.

Skipper had told her that when she found her soul mate it would be like finding the rest of herself. She had protested, saying she didn't know how anyone could be closer than he, her brother, but Skip had been insistent.

"You'll know," he'd said. "You'll know. I can't wait until you find him. I can't wait until you unleash all that love you've got so bottled up inside you, hiding from the pain of the world."

But Skipper was gone, and Kristen had never found the love he'd promised would be hers. Now this crazy bum who wanted to kill her was drawing her to him like no one she had ever known, and she was powerless to break the link that joined them.

And somehow, she knew she could use that link. Something had happened in those few seconds when she'd desperately tried to touch his soul. When she'd tried to turn aside his hatred, to find something inside him besides the pain and devastating sorrow.

She knew him. Deep inside, she'd found the man he had been. How she knew baffled her, but she knew. The crazy bum who'd kidnaped her and threatened to kill her was a good man, a decent man.

She laughed at herself.

He was lying next to her, his hatred soaking her like his sweat, and she was counting his good points! Kristen swallowed hard and forced herself to keep in mind that she was being held hostage by a self-acclaimed assassin.

Rider clenched his teeth and waited for the wave of pain and nausea to pass. He knew she was watching him. He could feel her gaze. If she had a weapon she could kill him now, while he was paralyzed under the weight of the pain in his gut. That knowledge sent fear ripping through his frame.

He found a small part of himself that wished she would. Death might actually be better than the netherworld in which he'd existed since he'd volunteered. Hadn't it been his motive? Wasn't it a suicide ride, this trip to the past?

So why did it scare him so much to think about it? Why didn't he just get it over with and get on with his own death? He had nothing to live for, back here, hundreds of years before his own time. Nothing and nobody. All he had was his mission, to wipe out the Mother of all the Deviants.

He glanced through narrowed eyes at the subject of his thoughts. She lay next to him, small and helpless, her body rigid with fear, her eyes squeezed shut.

God, he hated her! But right now, the overwhelming feeling inside him wasn't hatred, it was confusion. Things were happening too fast. The clinic, the cat, the mysterious way Kristen's touch seemed to banish all the conditioning and leave him feeling better than he could ever remember. The way she could get inside his head and mix up his thoughts.

He flexed his hands, the numbness of shock and nausea in his fingertips, and remembered the softness of her vulnerable nape with the damp hairs curling there. He needed time to figure out what was happening to him.

He didn't have the luxury of time, though. Someone was trying to kill his angel-doctor, and he'd be damned if he'd let them take the pleasure of killing her away from him.

A stray thought flitted across his brain too quickly to catch. Just like the shadow of a thought that had emerged when the clinic exploded.

The explosion. What the hell had happened at the clinic?

All he could remember was his panic—the driving need to get out of there as fast as possible. He blessed the TAINCC for the training that had allowed him to overpower the two dog catchers so easily. They'd looked strong, with their bulky muscles, but as he'd known it would, his agility and knowledge of leverage and balance had beaten their sheer strength.

After all, when you've sparred for months with specially constructed robots, mere flesh and blood men are a piece of cake.

He pulled his thoughts back to the seconds before the panic had sheared his breath and cramped his muscles. Where had that blinding urgency to get out of the building as fast as humanly possible come from? His nostrils twitched in remembrance.

BeeDee! He had smelled that deadly chemical. Smart plastic. Rider knew a lot about it, he and his fellow trainees, for an excellent reason. They'd been forced to test it.

Thank God he'd been involved in the beta testing, not the alpha.

BeeDee was a binary plastic explosive that could be programmed by its mass. It had taken a lot of experimentation and more than a few blown off arms and legs in the alpha testing stages before they had gotten the pattern perfected.

Once you mixed the two components together, BeeDee was set to explode. The amount of malleable plastic determined the number of minutes, or in some cases seconds, before detonation, and the only problem with it was its characteristic odor.

Yes, he knew a lot about BeeDee. Especially the fact that, at the time he was ready to go, BeeDee hadn't been stable enough to be trusted on a time-transfer.

Yet there it was, in the clinic. And he'd been right about the odor, too. By the time its distinctive odor was that strong, it was within seconds of detonation.

There was only one explanation for the presence of BeeDee in the Street Clinic today. Someone else from the future—from farther in the future than his time—was trying to kill Kristen Skipworth.

SIX

Rider felt her move. With only a shade of slowdown in his reflexes, he whirled and pinned her to the floor again. "Where you going, Doc?" he hissed.

"I—feel sick," she muttered, avoiding his gaze. "I need some anti-nausea tablets."

Somehow he knew she was lying, but the idea of tablets that might ease his engulfing sickness sounded very good. "Get me some, too," he said. "And don't get any cute ideas. I could..." He stopped when his brain warned him of the blinding nausea that still lurked in the back of his throat.

"I know. Kill me," his angel doctor said wearily as she pulled herself to her feet.

He forced himself upright with the determination born of long hours in the TAINCC. He grabbed her arm, as much to keep himself from collapsing as to turn her back around to face him. "That's right. You're catching on. But it's beginning to look like I'm not the only one."

"What?" Her eyes widened in alarm, then quickly narrowed. "You mean somebody besides you wants to kill me?"

"Crash the crap, Doc."

She lifted her chin and gave him a chilling look. "There's no one in the world who would want to kill me."

Not in this time, he started to say, but he just tightened his grip on her arm and whispered in her face, "Then what do you think happened to the clinic?"

He watched with satisfaction as her haughty expression crumpled into a bewildered frown. "I don't—I don't know. Maybe a faulty gas line?"

"Yeah? Then why didn't it keep burning?"

The bewildered frown deepened, and Rider had the sudden inane thought that she was older than he'd estimated. She looked like such a waif, all wide eyes and pouting lower lip, and the delicately curved cheek with its youthful roundness. But with her brow creased in worry, with her mouth turned down in puzzlement, he revised his thinking. She could be as old as thirty.

Had they told him how old she would be? If they had, it was something else he didn't remember.

He watched her mentally run through the possible explanations for the explosion, her mobile face reflecting her every thought. Rider's fingers twitched to wipe the furrows away from her forehead, to smooth the lines, lines he was helping to deepen. His gaze strayed to her mouth and he almost lifted a hand to push the frown into a smile, but there was nothing he could give her to smile about.

She stared at him, chin lifted, and his heart constricted again in admiration. She'd been threatened, almost blown up, and still she faced him defiantly. He thought, as he had before, that either she was the bravest person he'd ever known, or the stupidest. Or maybe there was a third possibility. Maybe those amber-shot eyes could see inside him. He shuddered at that thought. Maybe she knew something about him he didn't even know himself.

He dragged his thoughts away from their disturbing turn with an effort. He couldn't think of her as anything but the target. The target he would eliminate. "I asked you a question," he said quietly. "Why do you think the clinic blew up?"

She shrugged, then moaned at the movement of her shoulder. "Short in an electrical wire? A smoldering cigarette? A—a—what?" she shouted when he laughed.

"Lots of reasons, huh? Lots of reasons the clinic would just blow up. You don't buy it. I can see it in your damned Deviant eyes."

She twisted her arm out of his grasp. He could have held on, could have broken her arm rather than let her go, but he relented, and stifled the thought of why he would worry about breaking her arm even as it surfaced.

"Well, then you tell me," she said. "What did cause the clinic to blow up?" She looked at him, frowning again. "Did you?"

He gleaned a modicum of triumph from her question. Maybe if he could convince her he was telling the truth, he could... He stopped, confused by his thoughts. What did he want to do? His only job was to kill her.

The ache started to grow again in his gut, and this time it was all tied up in a sadness he couldn't explain to himself. Gritting his teeth, he forced the thoughts away—he didn't have time for self-pity. He concentrated instead on how the BeeDee had gotten planted in the clinic. He felt better immediately. Any thoughts of protecting his angel-doctor played hell with his conditioning and brought on the searing nausea that accompanied any thought counter to the TAINCC's mission. *His mission.*

"Well, did you?" Kristen asked again.

Rider focused on her face. "No, Doc. I didn't plant the explosive. But somebody did. Somebody who had access to a weapon that hasn't been invented yet."

Her wide eyes appraised him unblinkingly. "Hasn't been invented yet? What are you talking about?" Then her eyes narrowed. "Oh, yes, excuse me for forgetting. You're from the future," she said sarcastically. "So you're saying there's someone else from the future after me, too?"

Nodding curtly, he grabbed her again and dragged her over to the kitchen counter. He dropped heavily onto a counter stool without relaxing his hold.

She laughed shakily. "I do declare," she drawled in a strange, broad accent. "How in the dickens did I get to be so popular? Why, just the other day I was saying to Sue Ellen, 'Sue Ellen,' I said, 'there's just no excitement around here whatsoever' and now I've got all kinds of strange folks trying to kill—" She grunted as he twisted her arm.

"Anybody ever tell you you're a pain in the ass, Doc? Now where are those anti-nausea tablets you mentioned?"

"They're in the bathroom." She looked pointedly at her arm, which was encased in his fingers. "If you could let me go..."

"Why don't we get them togeth—Shit!" he exploded as the cat jumped at Kristen's chest. He barely checked himself in time to avoid breaking the animal in two, and possibly the Doc as well.

"Get that thing the hell away from me!" he shouted, backing away from Kristen as she cradled the creature in her arms.

She clutched the cat to her, watching him with narrowed eyes. Her gaze darted between him and the cat, and he could almost read her mind. She was considering how much time she would have if she threw the cat at him. It was written plainly on her face.

"Don't even think about it, Doc," he hissed. "I don't like cats, but I could damned sure kill it and you before you could get out the door."

She threw the cat at him.

The animal yowled as he stiff-armed it and dove blindly for Kristen, groaning at the pain in his side. His wrist brushed her leg, and he groped in the air until his fist closed around her ankle. She fell with a thud.

Rider jumped up and wrapped his fingers around her neck, drawing her upright. Her eyes were huge and wet with panicked tears. She took a shaky, sobbing breath.

"I told you not to do that," he whispered, tightening his fingers around her neck, but as he did, his hand began to shake, and the nausea returned as visions assaulted him. Visions of a spacious, bright apartment, with a vidscreen and a portable comlink and an old transistor-type radio. Visions of a pale, worried face framed with dark blonde hair. Visions of a kitten...

"Why are you so afraid of cats?" she asked in a small, quivery voice.

He realized he'd loosened his grip on her neck. He tightened it again and shook her slightly. "Would you shut up about the damned cat?" His voice cracked. "She had to go back after the damned cat." Back after the cat? Where had that come from? He had a flashing vision of a gray kitten, stretching lazily.

Mari reaching to pick the kitten up as a ribbon of green light shot toward it, leaving a smoking lump of flesh...

All this, all the pain, was because of Kristen Skipworth. His fingers twitched on her soft, vulnerable nape, but a fluttering of nausea in his throat made him stop and take a huge breath.

Not just yet. He wouldn't kill her yet. He wrenched his gaze away from her neck, concentrating on her eyes instead— those unmistakable golden eyes that identified a Deviant. Another disturbing thought tickled at the edge of his brain, but he lost it as Kristen spoke.

"Who went back after the cat, Rider?" Her voice was soft, compelling.

He glared at her, terror shearing his breath. "You damned Deviant! Stop getting inside my head!" He suddenly couldn't stand to touch her any more. He gritted his teeth and dragged her back toward the kitchen counter, away from the door.

"I didn't! I can't. You said it." Her amber-green eyes reflected a bewildered apprehension.

He stared at her. Had he said the words aloud? He wasn't sure. "Yeah, well. Just stay out of my head, understand?"

A frown creased her forehead. "What are you saying?" she asked softly. "You think I can read your mind?"

Her eyes were wide. She appeared genuinely puzzled. Did she really not know what he was talking about?

"That's what skipworths do," he grated.

Her eyes widened even more, and a look of real horror crept into their depths. "Skipworths?"

"Yeah. Skipworths. Deviants."

"The people you call Deviants are people with my name?" She backed up against the counter like a cornered victim, her hands behind her.

"Yeah, Doc. What about this don't you understand?" He sighed and closed his eyes wearily. "Five hundred years from now, your descendants are trying to take over the world with their perverted mind invasion. It's filthy, disgusting." He clenched his jaw against the pain of memory. "And it was skipworths who murdered my wife."

"She died when she went back after the cat," Kristen said softly.

He could choke the life out of her right now, squeeze her throat until her hurtful words stopped evoking the horrible images—images of burning flesh lit by green light, images of Mari crumpling in his arms. The sensations were overwhelming, and he wanted to give her some of them, wanted to transfer as much of the pain and horror to her as he could.

"Yeah," he said, forcing his mouth into a slow, deadly grin. When he did, her gaze dropped to his mouth, and she shuddered. She was afraid of him. That was good. He was glad he wasn't the only one afraid here.

"She died, the cat died, and very soon, Doc, you're going to die." Even as he said the words, he realized he didn't quite believe them. His heart pounded and his breath caught at the thought of killing her. He doubled over, clutching his gut, coughing and gagging. He was sicker than he'd ever been, sicker than death.

Why was he reacting this way? He wanted to kill her. *Needed* to kill her, but his fingers wouldn't do it. His brain wouldn't even contemplate it. What had happened to him? He was a tank. He had no feelings. Where was the cold fury that was supposed to sustain him?

He cringed as another wave of sickness flowed over him. He gagged again, unable to get a breath, gasping, searching in vain for the icy nothingness.

Kristen the doctor, the paragon of professionalism, couldn't move. Her hands were frozen on the edge of the counter. She clenched her jaw while sweat drenched her pain-racked body, knowing all the while that her torment was only an echo of his, and the compassion she'd tried so hard to tamp down came welling up into her throat, almost choking her.

He was psychotic, delusional, and he believed he'd been sent from the future to kill her. He had the strange notion that people called skipworths had murdered his wife. He was one for the textbooks all right, so what kind of twisted logic made her feel sorry for him? She should grab a frying pan and knock him unconscious, then call the police, or just run as fast as she could to get away from him.

With a huge effort, she peeled her fingers off the counter and backed toward the cabinet where she kept the pots and pans.

"Don't—even think about it," he grunted, startling her.

She glanced at him. He was still doubled over. Had she been that transparent? It was almost as if he'd read her thoughts.

He dragged himself upright, using the counter as a support. Kristen backed away, but once again he pulled strength from some bottomless storehouse inside him and sprang at her, too quick to avoid.

"Let's get some medicine, Doc," he said, grabbing her arm and twisting it behind her.

He wrenched her sore shoulder, making her gasp.

"Couldn't you work on—the other shoulder—for a while?" she muttered through clenched teeth, wanting to scream in frustration. She was being held hostage by a man who could barely stand. Threatened by a man so sick he was turning shocky.

She strained against his hold on her arm, gritting her teeth against the hot streak of pain, but he just laughed. That laugh was worse than his pain. It made him look like a demon from hell.

"This is a very efficient hold, Doc, and it works better the second or third or tenth time, when the tendons are swollen and sore. If you move against me, you'll dislocate your shoulder." Her breath caught as his fingers tightened around her wrist.

"Okay," she said quickly. "Sorry."

In the bathroom, he let go of her arm, and she sobbed when she tried to move it. Flexing it gingerly, she found the anti-nausea tablets and opened them.

"You first," he muttered, and he didn't take his eyes off her as she swallowed two of the tablets.

She knew they would make her sleepy, but they'd work the same on him, and maybe, just maybe, she could stay awake longer.

"Let me see it," he said, gesturing toward the bottle.

She put it in his hand, visualizing the directions as he read them. "One or two tablets every six hours for nausea and vomiting."

He gave her a searching look, then took the pills and swallowed them without water.

"You should probably take three," she said, "given your larger frame."

He shot her a disgusted look. "Right. I think I'll stick with two, like you. After all, you're the doctor."

Kristen sighed, resigned. It would take about ten minutes for the drug to kick in. Then, in his exhausted and debilitated condition, he'd surely fall right to sleep, and she'd have no trouble sneaking to call the police and the hospital.

He knotted a fist against his stomach and groaned. "Could we get some food now?"

"Sure. Coming right up." Back in the kitchen, she opened the refrigerator, her rigid apprehension dissipating into anticipation. Maybe she could play on Rider's peculiar sickness. She hadn't been able to figure out what was causing it, but she thought she had a pretty good idea of what might aggravate it.

"Let's see," she said casually. I've got ham..." She turned to look at him innocently.

"Ham?" His eyes narrowed suspiciously.

"Sure. You know, aged, cured pig."

His pale face turned positively green, and he emitted a choked groan.

"Oh, I'm sorry," she cooed, her diaphragm fluttering with swallowed laughter. "I forgot you don't like meat—flesh. How dumb of me." She'd better be careful, though. After everything that had happened, she could easily become hysterical, and she didn't think her captor would like her roaring with laughter at his expense. She bit her lip and composed her face into a mask of feigned innocence.

"Doc," he croaked. "I'm not doing real well, but I'll bet I've got enough strength to wipe that simpering little smirk off your face."

His deadly quiet voice sent terror racing through Kristen's veins. "Sorry," she said meekly. She would probably do well to avoid provoking him until the he fell asleep. "There's some eggs. Can you eat eggs?"

Rider's eyes blazed like topaz in his ashen face as he nodded. "Chicken eggs?"

She laughed a little nervously. "Sure, chicken eggs. What do you have in the future, soy eggs?"

His face didn't change.

She shrugged, wincing as the movement hurt her sore shoulder. "Bad joke. How about if I scramble some eggs and make you a salad? I think the lettuce is still okay."

"Fine."

Kristen silently begged the drug to hurry and kick in. How long could it take? All she had to do was keep him happy until he got sleepy. Unfortunately, she wasn't a bit drowsy, and she'd taken the same dose as he had.

She broke lettuce into a bowl and set it in front of him with a fork and some low fat salad dressing, but he ignored the dressing and ate the greens piece by piece with his fingers as he watched her. Then when she gave him the plate of eggs and toast and poured him a glass of water, he wolfed down the food so fast she was amazed he didn't immediately regurgitate it.

She was yawning and his head was drooping by the time he'd finished. He grabbed her arm, sending the bitter taste of hatred and fear rippling through her. "Bedroom."

Finally, he was getting sleepy. Maybe he'd lie down, and she could call the police. "I need to do the dishes first."

He gave her a disgusted look. "Knock it off, would you? Let's get this straight, okay. You stay with me. All the time. You don't do the dishes. You don't do anything. All you do is stay with me and do what I tell you. Got it?"

Kristen made an involuntary noise of distress as he grabbed her arm roughly.

"What did I say, Doc?"

"I stay with you," she parroted hoarsely, tears burning her throat. It was ludicrous. He was debilitated, half-conscious, and he was threatening her and ordering her about. What was wrong with this picture?

He dragged her into the bedroom while she fought to keep the hope and anticipation out of her face. Once she got him into bed, he wouldn't be able to stay awake, then she could get away.

He let go of her arm. "Get undressed."

Kristen stared at the man who thought he'd been sent back from the future to kill her. Her heart pounded, and her temples throbbed with terror. What was he planning? Wasn't it enough that he'd threatened to kill her, almost broken her arm, kidnapped her? "No," she said resolutely.

"No? Doc, did you forget the plan?"

She shook her head, her chin high. His deadly quiet voice sent chills through her. She had to bite her lip to keep it from quivering. He sounded ruthless, like he would stop at nothing.

She'd been afraid of him before, like one is afraid of the unknown. But now, he was coalescing into a very known danger. Now she was limp with a terror that she'd seen the other side of too often. She'd treated girls and women who'd been assaulted. She'd lived their nightmares.

But in her arrogance, she'd always thought she was protected by the very empathy that made her understand their horror. She'd always thought no danger could get close to her without her knowing it. Now she realized the fallacy of her reasoning.

She'd been somehow distracted by the feelings Rider evoked in her. She'd forgotten he was a crazy man who could harm her. For some reason, the things he threatened and the sensations she gleaned from inside him conflicted, and she'd made the mistake of believing what she felt, rather than what he and everyone else kept telling her. It was dangerous to pick up strays.

And now, she had done it once too often. She'd let danger get too close. She'd invited it, and now she was going to live—or die—to regret it.

He pulled her up close to his face, which was dark with some dread emotion—rage, or hatred, or who knew what. It took all her will to keep her gaze steady as the hot lava of his emotions washed through her, emanating from his hand on her arm.

His lips stretched back against his teeth. "I said get undressed."

"Please," she said, trying to keep the shakiness out of her voice. Trying not to sound like a victim who has already given up. Terror engulfed her. She could feel her body quivering with adrenaline response. What would she do if he raped her? She wasn't sure she could survive the physical and emotional assault of that ultimate violation.

"I won't do anything, I promise," she whispered, unable to look away from his burning gaze. "Please don't hurt me."

"Do it," he grated, swallowing hard.

Sweat popped out on his brow, and she felt the sickness in him again. It gave her a thread of hope. She gathered every vestige she could find of her doctor's imperious voice, hoping he wouldn't hear the quaver she knew she couldn't completely squelch. "You need to sleep. I'll just be in the other room."

He grinned again, sending freshly honed shards of terror through her diaphragm. "Like hell you will. Get undressed. I hope you don't think, even if you do think I'm crazy, that I'm dumb enough to go to sleep and leave you to run away?" He laughed, a harsh sound that grated on Kristen's nerves as painfully as his sore ribs punished her side. "Take off your clothes. Now!"

She shuddered at the cold threat in his voice and, despite her determination, she sobbed aloud.

His eyes flickered downward over her body. "Look," his voice was soft and strained. "I'm not going to hurt you. I could have killed you already. And believe me, I'm in no condition for anything else."

His voice had changed, softened, and against her judgment, despite her fear, Kristen had a strange urge to believe him.

"Now, come on," he whispered soothingly, as if he were talking to a child. "Get undressed. Otherwise, I'll have to tie you up."

That decided her. She wouldn't have a chance if he tied her up.

With shaky hands she unbuttoned her jeans and slid them down her legs. Then she slid her knit shirt over her head. Once or twice she glanced at Rider, but he was purposefully keeping his eyes averted. She climbed into the bed in her bra and panties, hovering in the far corner, away from his hard, imposing body, praying she wasn't wrong, praying he'd been telling the truth.

"You've got to move closer. Not much. I don't particularly want that lovely little body touching me any more than you do. It's—distracting. But come on." He reached over and grasped the nape of her neck and pulled, gently but firmly, until she was forced to scoot toward him. He stopped the pressure when her torso was about three inches from his.

He relaxed, but he didn't loose his hold on her nape. His

forearm rested against her neck as she lay on her side facing him. It wasn't terribly comfortable, but it wasn't unbearable, either, so she finally relaxed a bit.

He lay, eyes closed, half on his side and half on his stomach. Kristen let her gaze roam over him. The white flesh of his arm and shoulder rippled with long, steel-corded muscles, just like his chest and belly. The weight of his forearm against her neck and jaw were at once strangely soothing and disturbing. She didn't like the conflicting emotions his touch evoked in her, the fear and the compassion, the mistrust and the urge to believe him. She didn't like knowing how angry he was, how much he hated her, how badly he hurt deep inside himself. She didn't like feeling his fear.

Kristen couldn't ignore the battle within her own heart. She couldn't reconcile her reaction to this crazy bum. The sensations he evoked in her were a mixture of attraction and revulsion.

His essence, so open to her, was a return of the link she had shared with Skipper and had thought she'd never experience again. But this link was with a psychopath who wanted to kill her.

And there was another problem, too. Why did this maniac kidnapper stir feelings inside her she barely recognized? Feelings she'd never before experienced?

Why, when he was probably the most dangerous man she'd ever encountered, was she so compelled to trust him, to believe in his outlandish lies?

Why was his touch, even as it threatened her, so deliciously disturbing to her senses?

"You might as well settle down," he said without opening his eyes. "Even asleep I'll be able to feel you tense up before you make a move, and these fingers can snap your neck in two seconds." As he spoke, his fingers tightened on her neck, and she felt the nausea that welled in the back of his throat. The fingers relaxed into what she might have imagined was a caress, were it not for his ominous words.

The caress continued, though, after the echo of his words had faded. His fingers moved in a circular motion on her nape, massaging out the knots of tension, rubbing the soreness created by the past hours of fear. Kristen relaxed against her will, soothed by his gentle touch.

"You can relax, Doc. I swear I won't hurt you," he whispered, then grimaced in pain. "Not yet."

What was the matter with her? A psychotic had made her a promise, and she was willing to stake her life on it. His agony was so real, his sadness palpable.

She couldn't shake her conviction that he was a decent, honest man. If she'd ever been right in her life, she knew she was right about this. There was no rational explanation for his bizarre behavior, no way his outlandish story could be true, yet all that was inside him was sincere.

Despite her fear, despite the danger, she wanted to help him, protect him, heal him of the wrenching pains that racked him. And that wasn't all she wanted. There was something else, something that was growing with each hour she was forced to be with this obviously demented man. Something she'd only read of, dreamed of, fantasized about.

Deep inside her, a sleeping beast was stirring. A dear beast. A sweet, savage beast that terrorized her in ways that this real man, with all his threats, never could.

Rationally, she knew what was happening. Her doctor's mind diagnosed her reaction easily. But the diagnosis was so alien, so frightening, that her conscious mind fought it with all the weapons at its disposal: logic, rationality, determination.

Logically, she couldn't be sexually attracted to a man who threatened to kill her. Rationally, she knew he was crazy, his claims of coming from the future couldn't possibly be true. It was probably the Helsinki Syndrome—the inclination of kidnap victims to become infatuated with and dependent on their kidnappers. It was a known phenomenon, although she'd never heard of it beginning this quickly. Well, she would just have to stay calm and rational, and avoid the syndrome until she was rescued.

SEVEN

"So where in the future do you think—do you come from, Rider?" Kristen said, her voice straining with tension.

He'd almost been asleep. She could tell by the soft, even breaths that escaped through his slightly parted lips. When she spoke, his eyelids twitched open, and he smiled.

He'd frowned, he'd smirked, he'd grinned that awful demonic grin, but this was the first time he'd smiled. Logic, rationality and determination fled when Kristen saw that smile. His eyes, as cold and hard as glacial ice, melted into warm tropical pools, surrounded by soft brown ferns of lashes. His mouth turned from grim lines into the most inviting lips Kristen had ever seen, and the lines in his face vanished as if they'd never been there.

Once again she thought she caught a glimpse of the man underneath the pain and craziness—the man he might have been. The man who had lost his wife to people he called by her name, the man who had told her he could kill her and had saved her life instead. She thought inanely that she could love that man.

How strange, when all her life she'd been repelled by safe, normal men whose thoughts and emotions revealed insincerity and duplicity. She'd never been able to ignore those inner sensations enough to date, much less fall in love with any of them. But now she was actually admitting to herself that she could love this psychotic self-acclaimed murderer because he *felt* safe? She was beginning to fear for her own sanity.

His gaze was on her lips as she licked them nervously. "Well?" she said, more harshly than she had intended as she pushed away her strange thoughts.

"Where in the future?" A few of the lines returned to his face and the smile faded, leaving a pale ghost of it behind. "A long way, Doc. Several lifetimes away. Why?" The azure eyes narrowed. "You trying to believe me?"

"Tell me about it."

His eyes widened and his brow furrowed.

What the hell was she doing? If she'd just shut up, he'd be asleep in minutes. But her heart argued with her logical mind. She really did want to know what he thought. She wanted to hear him talk about traveling through time.

It would help her understand psychotics, she reasoned, arguing with herself about the stupidity of talking to him when what she wanted was for him to go to sleep so she could escape. It would be useful for her practice—if she lived to practice. "What did it feel like? Did you have a time machine?"

He closed his eyes, and a bitter smile twisted his mouth. "Time machine? Not exactly. I was in the TAINCC, all trussed up as usual, and the next thing I knew I was falling down a dark well." He shuddered. "Then I slammed into a brick wall. Literally."

Kristen watched him, lulled by the warmth of his fingers on her nape, soothed by the gentle calm that seeped out of him through his touch. She had never experienced anything as comforting as his fingers caressing her neck. When had he become so calm? When had she?

"How did they do it, send you back in time?" she murmured.

"I don't know, Doc. I'm just the weapon. If they could have sent the robots, they would have."

"Robots?" she gulped. Her heart fluttered. Now he was really beginning to sound crazy—as if he hadn't before.

"Sure. You've heard of robots, haven't you?"

Kristen nodded, moving her head against his fingers. "Well, yes," she said skeptically. "I've seen science fiction movies and read books. So why wouldn't they send—robots? It would make sense, wouldn't it? They'd be almost indestructible."

Rider sighed, and Kristen remembered how tired and sore he was.

"Yes. It would make a lot more sense. There's only one problem," he said lazily. "Metal won't travel through time. It acts like gold in a microwave. Flash and burn."

Kristen stared at Rider, trying to absorb what he was telling her. He looked like a man—a beautiful, battered man—but just a man. And he was telling her things no rational person would believe. He was telling her about the future.

"How many years?" she asked again, closing her eyes as his fingers found a sore spot of tension in her neck.

"Five hundred."

"Five hundred? Years?" A rumble rippled through him, as if he'd laughed. Her eyes flew open. He was watching her warily, a ghost of amusement still touching his mouth.

Five hundred years! Five hundred years ago, Columbus

had just landed in the New World. Five hundred years ago a lot of people thought the Earth was flat. What did people five hundred years from now think?

She looked at Rider, seeing him for the first time as a man who could have been alive five hundred years in the future. Science fiction stories notwithstanding, he didn't look any different from men today. Unless she considered that his face and body were far more attractive to her than any man she knew in the present. Her face burned as she remembered touching him.

Then a flicker of amusement rippled through her. She was considering his outlandish story as true. She was held hostage by a crazy man who thought he'd traveled through time, and they were lying in her bed discussing it calmly.

Still, it was an appealing thought, to talk to someone who knew what it would be like five centuries from now.

"Tell me about it. What's there? Do we find a cure for AIDS? Is the world still as mixed up as it is now?" Kristen actually began to get excited. It was all a game, sure, humoring him, but what a concept! What if you really could look into the future? A pang of regret and grief stabbed her heart. If you could see into the future, could you change it? She thought of Skipper. If she had known ahead of time, could she have saved him?

"AIDS?" He shook his head. "No. Around the middle of the twenty-second century, AIDS almost wiped out Africa, but they got a handle on it finally. Now there are better treatments, longer life expectancy, even better quality of life, but no cure yet. No cure for the common flu, either." He closed his eyes, his fingers still making their lazy circles on her neck. "The world will probably always be mixed up. It's really not that much different."

She watched him, seeing his mobile face across a landscape of white sheets, feeling the sincerity and honesty that beat within him like his heart.

It was new to her, this total communion with another person, this certainty that, whoever he was, wherever he'd come from, Rider was honorable and good. And he believed in himself. He believed what he was saying.

"You're not telling me much," she whispered. "Why don't you eat meat?"

His eyes flew open in real shock. "Meat? Do you have any

idea how many acres of grain it takes to support one cow? How many people could live off what you people feed one cow so you could eat its flesh and drink its milk?" He coughed and swallowed hard.

"You don't have milk?"

"We have soyamilk. It's ennutriated, like everything else."

"Well, you still have to feed the cows, don't you? What do you do with them?"

He laughed. "There are a few in zoological preserves. Like horses and chickens—and pigs." He shot her an amused glance. "And I guess if you were warped enough, and had enough credit, you could eat their flesh, or have real chicken eggs every day. But it's too expensive. The world's too crowded to raise animals for food."

His voice buzzed with drowsiness. His fingers on her neck slowed. "Did you convince yourself, Doc?" he whispered. "Am I for real?" His heavy-lidded eyes caressed her face like his fingers caressed her neck. His mouth was quirked in a quizzical smile.

"I don't know," she said, licking her lips. His eyes flickered downward, and she sensed desire welling up within him. She moved her hand to cover the exposed tops of her breasts even as her nipples hardened just from his glance. Her face burned and panic lanced through her. She tried desperately to think of something to distract his gaze from her nearly naked body.

"Why do you want to kill me?" Her voice cracked on the incredible words.

His face changed like a light going out, and his fingers tightened ominously on her neck, sending faint cramping waves through her muscles.

He laughed harshly. "Why? You haven't understood anything I've said, have you?" He shifted his gaze to a place over her left shoulder. "No, of course, you haven't. You still think I'm barking. You could easily die never knowing." He looked back at her and stabbed her with the cobalt shards of his eyes.

"But I want you to know, Doc. Kristen Skipworth." He spat her name as if it were a foul piece of food. "Skipworth. Deviant." Dark anguish clouded his face, and her throat burned with nausea. Nausea dulled by medication, nausea from him.

He closed his eyes and his fingers relaxed, beginning the circular massaging that so soothed and disturbed her.

"Conditioning. The conditioning must be breaking down."

He turned over on his back and threw his arm over his eyes, but not before he'd insinuated his other hand under her neck to keep the gentle pressure that reminded her she was his hostage.

"They scrub you 'til you're raw, then put you in the TAINCC, where all the good that was ever in you is sucked out and only what they want you to know is left. That's why it's so much easier for poor bastards like me who didn't have any goodness to start with."

Kristen's eyes stung with tears. Wherever he had come from, whatever delusions he had brought with him, he'd been hurt. Hurt so badly she wasn't sure he could ever recover from it. His anguish was numbing.

And she knew he was wrong. There was goodness in him. She'd known that since the first time she'd touched him. The goodness, the decency were there. He'd just buried them too deeply.

"So they get you all conditioned, 'til you think you'll never have a real emotion again. And you're glad, because emotions are awful, much worse than anything they did to you in the TAINCC." His voice was muffled by his arm, but Kristen heard every word, and each one of them etched itself on her already sore heart.

"Don't..." she whispered. *Don't tell me this. Don't make me feel for you. It hurts too much.*

"Something's happening to their damned conditioning, though. From the time I hit that brick wall, there's been something wrong. Every time I woke up, cold and starving on that slimy street, there was something there, easing the pain, giving me hope. Then, when I touched you, you drew out the pain..." He stopped and swallowed hard. "It was almost like a healing. For a while I hoped... Do you know how frightening it can be to hope?" His voice quivered and died.

She brushed his arm away from his face, trying to see his eyes. "I'm so sorry," she said. "I'm so very sorry."

He pushed her hand away and leaned up and over her, pressing her back into the mattress, his glittering eyes dark and unreadable.

"You," he spat. "You're sorry? You perverted...Mother of all the Deviants! I'd love to take that pretty little neck between my fingers and snap it." His fingers tightened on her neck, sending a lance of panic through her.

She lay there, pinned under him, accepting the assault of his anger, unable to move, even to blink under the force of his unwavering hatred.

"Tell me," she whispered, her heart thundering in her ears, his thundering against her breast. "Tell me what I did to you. I don't understand what they did that was so bad."

"They killed her. You were the start of it all. Your spawn killed my wife. The stupid, fucking cat. The Deviants killed them."

Kristen watched him, fascinated.

He'd started out so certain, so enraged, but as he talked, his voice became less vehement, as if he couldn't remember everything. As if he'd been reciting a poem by rote and forgot his lines. He shook his head in confusion, and when he did, a drop of something wet fell on her cheek. A tear, or a drop of sweat? Did it matter?

"H-how? Why? Even if it's true. Even if these Deviants are my descendants. What did your wife do to make them kill her?"

He squeezed his eyes shut, as if he were trying to conjure up a fading image. "I came home late. I caught the last shuttle. It was our—anniversary. But Mari..." He swallowed hard. "Something was wrong, something had happened. We had to get away." His words trailed off. He'd forgotten Kristen was there. "She went back after the cat. We could have gotten away, but she went back..." He stopped. Tears welled in his eyes.

Kristen touched his face, wishing she could wipe away the hurt, stop his tears. "Why did they kill her, Rider? What had she done to them?"

He stared at her, his eyes glistening. "I don't know. I don't know. It's what they told me," he whispered uncertainly.

His fingers pressed against her throat, choking her, and he shook his head like a wounded deer, trying to shake off the pain, shake off the haze, shake off the smell of death. His eyes focused on her. He looked startled, as if he'd just remembered she was there.

His fingers moved on her neck again, and panic speared through her.

"I will kill you. I will," he muttered desperately.

Kristen swallowed the acrid saliva that his nausea brought to her mouth. The sensations from his fingers, his body touching hers were more confusing than the worst psychotics she'd ever tried to help. Her brain was awhirl with pain and anger, regret and fear, nausea and engulfing sorrow.

"I'll kill you," he whispered, his blue eyes burning like lasers into her soul. "As soon as I can."

***

Rider was dreaming, and his dreams weren't making him sick. At least not very. He dreamed that a curly-haired angel had detached herself from the heavenly host and joined him on his cloud.

She was curled into his side, resting her cheek on his shoulder. This must be heaven, he thought, pulling her sleep-warmed body closer to his until he could feel her all along his length. He buried his face in her hair.

The angel murmured something, and he turned her face up so he could see her mouth. Her pouty lower lip looked so inviting, he had to kiss it.

When he touched her angel's lips, she made a soft whimper of protest, but her fingers clutched at the sparse hairs on his chest, so he pulled her closer, molding her body to his like warm clay. He tangled his fingers in her hair and urged her lips open with his tongue. She gasped and allowed him access.

He'd never tasted anything so sweet as the angel's mouth, never touched a body so soft yet firm. Her knee bent, and he pushed his leg between her thighs, her heat searing his skin.

Somewhere, divorced from the exquisite pleasure of her body against his and her sweet mouth yielding to his kisses, he noticed a metallic tang in the back of his throat, and a faint burning in his thigh, but even that couldn't override the sweet throb of his erection pressed against her.

The other angels discretely left them alone as he deepened his kisses and his hands roamed her shoulders and back, down the curving lane toward her buttocks, and up again, to trace her ribs. Then God turned the lights down low, and Rider and his angel were alone in heaven.

He lifted his head to look down at her, his fingers tracing her mouth, her nose, her eyelids. He thought she was the most beautiful angel he'd ever seen, and she smelled like he'd always thought heaven would smell. All clean and spicy and bleachy-white.

"Angel," he whispered. "Doc?" The word falling from his lips without his conscious knowledge startled him into full wakefulness.

This wasn't heaven. It was a small, hot bedroom. And he wasn't on a cloud with an angel, he was in a pile of tangled bedclothes with the Mother of all the Deviants. His gut spasmed, but not very hard.

Still, even if she was the Mother of all the Deviants, she felt very good pressed up against him. How long had it been since the softness of a woman had touched him? How long had it been since he'd had a full erection without the accompanying agony?

Damn them and their conditioning, he thought, even as pain wrenched him again. They couldn't get anything right. What he'd told Kristen was true. It had been a lot easier living without the memories, without any hope. But that had been before she'd touched him.

This desire that was seeping out from under the conditioning, this hope that was worming its way into his heart, hurt far more than anything they'd done to him in the TAINCC.

She stirred against him and snuggled in closer, turning her face invitingly up to his. With a faint nausea causing sweat to bead his brow, he lowered his mouth to hers, and almost cried out when she responded.

She opened her lips. When he drew her closer, she opened herself to him, lying slack and ready against him. His whole body throbbed with need, with long forgotten desire.

He thrust his tongue deep into her mouth and splayed his hand on her buttocks, pressing her hard against him. A flash of remembrance gave him a freeze-frame of a blonde woman all in black, and a wave of agony streaked through his belly.

Kristen moaned at the sharp twinge in her stomach. Her eyes flew open and encountered an intense blue stare. She was dazed, still caught in the netherworld between sleeping and waking, still bound to sleep by the dregs of her dream.

What had she been dreaming? Certainly of blue eyes. Blue eyes and pain and sweet desire. She closed her eyes again and curled her fingers against his chest, seeking the comfort and exquisite yearning that had suffused her just seconds before.

He thrust her away roughly. "What the hell do you think you're doing?"

"I'm sorry," she stammered. "I was asleep. I don't..."

He pushed his hand up under her hair and clamped his fingers around her neck, sending pain shivering through her muscles. Fury burned like pure oxygen in his eyes. "Did you do that?"

"D-do what?" She closed her eyes against his rage, but he grabbed her jaw and shook it.

"Look at me," he growled through clenched teeth. "Did you do that?"

Tears of fright welled in her eyes and ran down her cheeks. "Do what? I don't know what you mean. Please!"

His hot breath burned her face. His fingers bruised her jaw. "Deviant! Stay out of my head, damn you!" He shook her jaw again, and she cried out. Then he pushed her away as if she were hot and rolled off the bed. "And keep that enticing little body away from me."

He went into the bathroom and splashed water on his face.

Kristen hadn't moved. She watched the bathroom door cautiously, waiting to see what he was going to do next. Her head was whirling.

She looked toward the living room. Why wasn't she running? Why was she acting like a starry-eyed school girl about this man who swore he'd kill her? A thrill of need rippled through her belly as she recalled his kiss. He had kissed her, then he'd accused her of trying to get inside his head. He'd caressed her, then he'd grabbed her jaw hard enough to bruise it.

He said her descendants had killed his wife. He said he was going to kill her. So why did she have this overwhelming urge to protect him, to keep him safe, to—

She shook her head sharply and moved slowly toward the living room door. Just as she crossed the threshold, the phone rang.

She jumped, then lunged through the door, desperate to answer the phone, to hear a voice other than his deadly quiet one, but an efficient, painful grip on her arm stopped her cold.

"What's that?" he demanded.

"It's a telephone. Don't you even have telephones? I need to answer it."

"Like hell."

It rang again, and Kristen glanced at him, but he wrenched her arm a fraction of an inch higher. "I said leave it."

Her heart sank clear to her toes. "But somebody might be looking for me. Bill. Or Moira, if she's still—alive? You've got to let me answer it." She moved her arm a little, but his grip was relentless. "Please."

He twisted her toward him until his face was mere inches from hers. The electric blue eyes flashed a warning. "Doc, you haven't been paying attention."

She gave up as the answering machine clicked on and her recorded voice spoke into the air. "You've reached Dr. Skipworth. We're not available right now, please leave a message after the tone."

"Kris! Where are you?"

Moira! Kristen wanted to cry, to laugh in relief. Moira was okay. She'd gotten out of the clinic in time.

"The police want to ask you some questions about the explosion. Are you okay? If you don't call me soon, Dr. Skipworth, I swear I'm going to tell them your gorgeous bum kidnaped you. Call me!" The machine clicked as Moira hung up.

Kristen looked triumphantly at Rider. He'd have to release her now. The police were looking for her.

He frowned and let go of her. "Why don't we have some more of those chicken eggs?" he asked softly.

She rubbed her arm and sighed with irritation. "You must be from outer space. Don't you realize the police will be here any minute? They're looking for me."

"I said I was from the future, not outer space."

"Wherever."

"Come on. Let's go to the kitchen, what do you say?" His voice was as casual as a friend's. It didn't belong to the man who'd been calling her a word that seemed to be the worst insult he knew—Deviant.

Kristen stared at him. Definitely psychotic. Where were the damned police, anyway? "Chicken eggs?" she said, trying to sound as casual as he. "Uh, sure. Listen. I'll fix something while you take a shower."

"I don't think so, Doc," he said, pushing her ahead of him toward the kitchen. He stopped, looked back at the telephone, then reversed his steps and yanked it out of the wall. The bell clinked in brief protest as he tossed it on the floor.

Kristen stared in despair at the frayed wires, then at him.

He didn't have a shirt on, and a few drops of water glistened on his face and chest. Her body, which had betrayed her as she slept, wasn't finished with its treachery. The sight of long muscles rippling under his skin reminded her of how warm and rock-hard those muscles had been pressed against her. And that wasn't all that had been hard, she thought, her face growing hot, her insides going soft and liquid. She quickly averted her gaze, looking down at herself.

She'd almost forgotten she was dressed in her underwear. She swallowed. "Could I, could I get dressed first?"

Rider's eyes flickered over her body, then back up to her face. "Yeah, you'd better," he said, and reversed direction, pulling her back into the bedroom.

She searched in her dresser for clean underwear. "You'll let me take a shower, won't you?" she asked casually, thinking if she could stall long enough, surely Moira would send the police.

"No," he said, reaching around her to push the drawer closed.

Kristen turned to find him much closer than she had gauged. Her breasts, covered by the tiny wisp of lace that was her bra, brushed his chest and he recoiled, his gaze traveling over her body, his mouth set in a frown.

"You can't take a shower. Get your clothes on. You're too distracting like that." He bent over and retrieved her shirt and jeans from the floor and tossed them to her.

She had just finished tying her shoes when he clapped a hand over her mouth. She squeaked in protest, but his fingers tightened and he whispered in her ear. "Sh-h-h. What was that?"

Like she could answer him with his hand crushing her mouth. What she'd like to do was bite him, but all she could manage was a bare negative shake of her head.

"Sh-h-h."

Then she heard it. Usually when she heard sounds at night, she assumed it was Sam, prowling around the apartment, scratching at the door. It was one of the benefits of having a cat. She'd quit worrying about things that went bump in the night.

But this sound was definitely metal scraping against metal. Someone was trying to break into her apartment. The police!

Rider's voice was as quiet and deadly as a snake's hiss. "What did you do? Who is that?"

Again, all she could do was shake her head.

He pulled her back against him. The hard body that she'd found so tempting a few minutes before was now cold steel and threatening. He twisted her arm behind her back and whispered again. "How do I know? How can I trust you? I was asleep. Did you call the cops? Or the dog catchers?"

She kept shaking her head, kept straining against his hand until he loosened it enough for her to speak through pain-numbed lips. "Of course not," she whispered desperately. "How could I? You had that death grip on my neck the whole night."

He turned her around and stared into her eyes for a long time. She stared defiantly back, daring him to call her a liar, trying not to be affected by the doubt and fear behind his cobalt eyes.

"Then who is that?" he whispered.

Kristen shook her head. "I don't know. Maybe the police. Moira said she'd call them if she didn't hear from me."

Suddenly, the noise stopped, and Rider was as rigid as a corpse.

"What?" she started, but he grabbed her around the waist and shoved her toward the bedroom window, where Sam was sitting on the sill.

"Get out! Go! Now!" he shouted and vaulted through the open window, dragging her over the casement with him. She almost fell before she could get her footing on the old iron fire escape.

"Sam!" she cried, but Rider didn't even stop. He stepped on the spring-loaded stairs and jerked her up against him as they began their slow descent to the ground. As the stairs squeaked to a halt, a deafening explosion blew out the side of her apartment.

Kristen dove off the fire escape, covering her head with her arms. Hot sparks and shattered glass rained over her. The he jerked her upright and dragged her to the other side of the road. Rider pulled her close and wrapped his arms around her, pinning hers to her sides.

It was probably a good thing he was holding her so tightly because her legs were wobbly and she couldn't take a full breath. She gasped again and again, trying to breathe.

He pushed her face into his shoulder, his hand cradling her skull gently. "Breathe slow and easy. You're hyperventilating, Doc. Don't you know the cure for that?"

"My—apart—ment. Sam—what—did you—do—" She huffed against his shirt.

"I was just going to ask you the same question," he said softly in her ear, "until I smelled the BeeDee."

"The what?" She pulled her head back to stare at him.

"BeeDee. Didn't you smell something up there? Just before the explosion?"

Kristen tried to calm her panicked thoughts as her gasps
quieted to normal breathing. Had she smelled something? "Sickeningly sweet? Like rotten bananas?"

"Got it in one, Doc."

Kristen looked up at the building, where her window had
been. "Sam," she whispered.

Rider hadn't relinquished his hold on her, but now he pushed
her gently away and pointed to an alley.

"Sam!" She started after her cat, but Rider jerked on her
arm.

He pulled her up against his unyielding body until she could
feel his breath on her cheek. She wanted to duck away from
the unrelenting fury in his gaze.

"Leave the goddamned cat!" he spat and grabbed her jaw.
"Don't give me any trouble, or I'll break your jaw." He let go
of her jaw but not her arm, and she had no choice but to follow
him, stumbling as she tried to keep up with his longer, faster
strides.

By the time they stopped, blocks from her apartment, her
muscles ached and she heard the sirens wailing. Naturally, he
wouldn't want to be around when the police came. They'd ask
questions about the explosions.

The explosions. Kristen twisted around until she could see
his face. "How'd you know?" she asked.

"Know what?"

"About the explosions? That's the second one you've pulled
me out of." She shivered, not just from the cold. "And, Mister
Rider from the future, if you're so intent on killing me, why do
you keep flubbing it? It would make a lot more sense to leave
me *in* the building when it exploded." It was getting ridiculous.
A man from the future who claimed to be intent upon killing her
had saved her life twice.

"Don't give me any ideas." His eyes were blue as glacial
ice, and his voice was like a deep freeze.

"Give you any ideas? Look, if it's not you who keeps blow-
ing up these places, then who is it?"

Rider slumped, and his hold on her shoulders slacked. She
felt a stab of compassion when she saw his face turn bleak
with despair.

"I don't know," he said. "BeeDee wasn't perfected when
they sent me back here. So it's got to be somebody else from

the future." He looked toward her apartment building, then down at her. "Somebody else who's trying to kill you."

Kristen stared at him, openmouthed. "Somebody else? You were serious? You think somebody else from your time is trying to kill me?" She laughed shakily and shook her head. The things he was saying were too bizarre, too confusing to be believed.

"That's just it. Not *my* time. BeeDee was too dangerous when I left. They would have sent it with me if they'd been even remotely confident it wouldn't blow up on the trip." He pushed his hands through his hair and narrowed his eyes at her. "Listen to me, Doc. These guys are from farther in the future than I am."

Kristen shook her head angrily, helpless against a logic that was no logic at all, but must be a very deep-seated psychosis. Or the truth.

"No. You can't ask me to believe all this." She twisted her hands together. "First you, then the explosions. Now you're telling me they're coming from farther in the future than you? No. No." She felt like she was being spun in a circle. She was dizzy with it all. "No. I can't believe that."

She closed her eyes and reached for the professional calm she kept inside her. She was drowsy from the promethazine she'd taken, and almost sick with fear, but she dredged up enough calm and assurance to keep her from falling apart. Sighing, she peered at Rider.

He was exhausted. The few hours sleep they'd managed to catch hadn't been nearly enough to take the edge off his weariness. His face was gaunt, his eyes dark-rimmed and bright with pain. She could probably deck him and get away, he looked that tired. But, right now, it was all she could do to stay upright. She couldn't even lift her arms.

"Doc! Look out!"

Rider's grip tightened desperately as Kristen looked up. Blinding headlights rushed at her just as Rider threw her sideways. She landed hard, rolled, and found herself lying up against a set of concrete steps. Her head pounded where it had hit the bottom step, and her chest convulsed as she tried to breathe.

She opened her eyes and found herself staring up into eyes as black as midnight, peering brightly out of a hooded garment of some indefinite color. An odor of unwashed flesh sifted through the haze that enveloped Kristen.

She pulled herself up into a crouch and shook her head.

"Oughta watch where you're going," the derelict croaked, waving a hand hardly covered by the remnants of a tattered wool mitten.

Kristen squinted at the owner of the voice, trying to focus enough to tell if it was a man or a woman. Something tickled at the edge of her memory.

"Yep. Cars can be dangerous. 'Specially when they speed up. But then, so can houses. Houses don't speed up, though." The voice cracked on a discordant laugh. "You know, the electric company don't never knock. They just read the meter and leave."

The figure sank back into the shadows as Kristen's head swam and her arms and legs gave way. She wanted to sink down onto the damp sidewalk and go to sleep, and to hell with people from the future who wanted to blow her up.

Then a hand touched her cheek with amazing gentleness, and Rider was bent over her. When she looked up, his gaze searched her face while his fingers traced a spot on her cheek that was beginning to burn. Kristen felt a tenderness emanating from him that was so counter to anything she had gleaned from him before, she hardly recognized it. Tenderness and concern. Was all that for her?

"Are you all right?" he asked breathlessly.

She nodded, still finding it hard to breathe. "Wh-what happened?" she stammered.

Rider shook his head and looked in the direction the car had taken. His brow was furrowed, his mouth turned down in a frown.

She took his outstretched hand as she looked at the deserted street down which the car had disappeared, then turned toward the other end of the street. The streetlights were haloed with haze, their brightness barely able to penetrate the thick fog.

Turning back to Rider, she saw that his shoulders and arms were smeared with dirt, his face was smudged and drawn. What had the old derelict said? She wiped her face and pushed her hands through her hair, trying to force her brain to think. It was important, she was sure. Something about cars and houses.

"It sped up," she whispered, staring at him. His face didn't change. The furrowed brow, the bewildered frown stayed as his gaze searched hers for understanding.

"Cars speed up. Houses don't. It came around the corner, then sped up." She wanted to shake him. He was staring at her stupidly. "Rider. Come on. That's what the woman said." She pointed at the steps. "She was right! It sped up when it saw us."

The lines between his brows got deeper. He looked toward the building. "What woman?"

"That—" Kristen stared into the shadows, but she couldn't see anything. She shrugged. "There was somebody there. I don't even know if it was a woman. I think she was pretty crazy, but she was right about the car. It tried to kill us."

When Kristen said the words, their impact hit her with all the force of a blow. She dropped onto the curb, her legs no longer able to hold her up.

"Someone tried to kill us," she whispered, listening in awe to her own voice. If she said it three times, or thirty, or three hundred, would it make more sense?

"That's what I've been trying to tell you, Doc. Now, come on," Rider said, pulling her upright. "They'll be back. We've got to get out of here."

Kristen leaned against him, waiting for her arms and legs to stop acting like jelly. "Why?" she whispered, wanting to cry. "Why are they trying to kill me?"

Rider wasn't listening to her, though. He was concentrated on something else. She looked up at him, then in the direction of his gaze. A car was bearing down on them. As soon as she saw it, she heard its rumble. Rider pulled her back into an alley too narrow for a car to get into. The car slowed down for a brief instant, then sped up again.

She heard the sound of the engine recede, then slow.

"Run, Doc. They're turning around!"

She ran.

EIGHT

Kristen and Rider ran for hours, ducking from one dark alley to another, avoiding the busy streets, zigzagging too fast for a car to follow. Kristen couldn't think. All she could do was force one leg forward, then the other, jerked along by Rider's hand clamped on her wrist. Miraculously, she kept her feet under her. Air burned in her lungs like hot gas, and her side hurt.

Suddenly, she was jerked sideways between fetid garbage bins, into a cramped space. She fell against a hard, warm body, which rumbled with a groan as her weight hit him.

"Damn, Doc. Take it easy," Rider gasped. "These ribs are still sore."

She was wedged between his legs, her buttocks up against the juncture of his thighs, and her shoulders resting against his broad chest. His chest heaved with his labored breath. Frosted puffs wafted in front of her face. Her own breath whistled in her throat.

"Sorry," she started, when he hissed.

"Shhh!"

They crouched there, ludicrously positioned against each other like dogs in heat, her backside so close to him she felt the throb of his tightly constrained passion. The sensation was so powerful that she gasped.

His breath warmed her cheek as he whispered to her in a muffled, strained voice. "Close your eyes. They reflect. And try to stay still, please."

The amused desperation in his voice made her face burn with embarrassment.

She squeezed her eyelids together and turned her head toward his collarbone, breathing in the warm redolence of his skin. His palm cradled her forehead gently as they waited.

The time stretched to eternity while they sat, joined more intimately than Kristen had ever been to anyone. Once, foot-steps crunched menacingly near as someone passed. She didn't move, didn't even breathe, and whoever it was finally passed by.

"Good girl," Rider whispered in her ear, so faintly she hardly heard him over the beat of her heart. His hand on her forehead was as comforting as a mother's, his hardness against her bottom more disturbing than anything she'd experienced since she'd found him

Still she sat there, surrounded by Rider, her insides churning with emotions she had no name for, more confusion than she'd ever known. She was being held hostage in an alley by a murderous psychopath, and yet she felt safer than she'd felt since Skipper's death.

It was unthinkable that this man who threatened to kill her was the first man to stir desire in her. She, who had thought her empathy would never allow her to get close enough to a man to experience love and lovemaking, was having erotic fantasies about a deranged killer.

The night eased toward dawn while Kristen alternated between an exhausted doze and a throbbing strain she was sure no tranquilizer could fix. Rider was similarly affected because his hand would relax against her, the hard pressure on her buttocks would ease, then he would jerk, and the throbbing tension would increase.

She was awash with his feelings and her own. Each time he stirred to wakefulness, his body tensed with unwanted need, and his gut cramped with nausea. Because of his reaction to it, she knew his desire was unwelcome. She understood. She was a physician. It was her job to understand these things.

His reaction was just the physical response of a male body in close proximity with a female, she reasoned. Of course. That was all. The reaction was innate, programmed by aeons of DNA selectivity. The DNA would survive. Constant, unrelenting sexual desire had been programmed into the species to assure survival.

Thank goodness for her scientific background. Kristen blessed her professional objectivity, while at the same time she wondered why it kept failing her.

Because it *was* failing her. Miserably. Even if his feelings were unwanted, accompanied by disgust and even nausea—how flattering—hers were not.

As much as she'd like to pretend she was unaffected, even disgusted by the betrayal of her body, the truth was she was savoring each distressing moment, just like a school girl in the throes of her first crush.

His slightest movement, the tiniest shift of his body, brought a new height of awareness to her. She sat there, surrounded by his heat and his hardness, while her mind and body went through each nuance of awakening like a pubescent adolescent. Physically, she'd been through it all years ago, but reliving it now, she was suffused with a sweet agony she'd never known back then.

Then she'd been too frightened by the changes in her mind to pay much attention to the changes in her body. It was during puberty that her empathic abilities had blossomed, and those sensations had overridden the more simple, less bothersome sexual maturation of her body.

Now, in the space of a few hours, sheltered and safe in the arms of a deranged bum, Kristen experienced all the sweet kindling of sexual response that she'd never quite achieved during adolescence. Emotionally, she flourished as she had physically fifteen years before.

So she sat imprisoned, sheathed between his hard thighs, her skin alternately burning with embarrassment and heated with desire. She wondered if he could feel her heat, if he knew how her body was reacting to him.

Finally, ready to scream from the unreleased tension inside her, Kristen whispered, "Why'd we stop here?"

He sighed, his diaphragm rising and falling against her back. "I didn't know where to go, and I couldn't go any farther."

Her heart contracted at the defeated tone of his voice. "You saved my life."

Suddenly, giggles erupted from her belly. "You came from the future to kill me, and you've saved my life—what—three times now? Why? If you're who you say you are, and if my great-great-great-grandchildren did what you say they did, that doesn't make a lot of sense."

His body wrapped around hers became rigid, pain and nausea warring with exhaustion inside him. "Could you shut up?" he growled, even as he responded to her again. He moved involuntarily, and she pressed backward into him, savoring his heat, his hardness.

She had no idea where her instinctive reaction to him came from. She had never, ever reacted like that before. No one had ever gotten close enough.

The few men she'd dated had telegraphed their insincerity, their selfishness to her through their touch, and those sensations had always effectively tamped any desire she might have felt.

But Rider's touch was very, very different. Kristen shook

her head. None of this made any sense. All she knew was she'd never felt anything as incredibly erotic as his body wrapped around her, his sex pressed hard against her.

She moved again and heard the deep groan that rumbled up from his chest. The vibrations against her back stoked unfamiliar yearnings inside her. She leaned her head back against his shoulder.

Her heart pounded as his breath quickened. His hand caressed her throat, and his thighs tightened around her. Then, as her heart sped up and her insides melted, his hands moved lower to gently trace and cup her breasts, and his mouth sought hers.

She arched her back to reach his mouth, pressing her breasts into his hands, her nipples seeking his warm, searching fingers. Something sweet and alien happened deep within her and she gasped.

The sound seemed to bring Rider back to his senses, because his body went rigid and he withdrew.

Breathless, bereft, and embarrassed by her abandoned response to him, Kristen said caustically, "Could we move now?"

A ripple of laughter rumbled through her companion. "Sure, Doc," he drawled, deliberately tightening his thigh muscles around her again. "What's your pleasure?"

Hot desire lost the battle with embarrassment as she flushed, burning her skin against his hand. She tossed her head, trying to rid herself of his suffocating, wonderful clutch. "Let me up, you—you..." she hissed, squirming against him.

"Whoa," he gasped. "Stop elbowing me in the ribs. Shit!" He grabbed her arms and thrust her from him. "Doc!" He shook her until she stopped squirming.

No matter how angry she was at him for causing this disturbing yearning to rock her, no matter how painful his injuries were, she had enough sense to know that he could hurt her if he wanted to.

"Doc, you listening to me?"

She nodded, trying to see his face in the darkness. Any playfulness was gone. He was totally serious. Suddenly, after hours of sitting behind garbage bins, the odor of rotting food gagged her. She wondered how he had stood it, since the smell of even fresh meat made him sick.

"I can't figure out how they keep finding us." The weary confusion in his voice worried her. "We need to find someplace safe. Where can we go?"

She lifted her chin and stared at him. Red streaks of dawn were beginning to sneak into the shadows, outlining the harsh planes of his face like a pen and ink drawing.

Kristen wrenched her thoughts from his sculpted beauty and reminded herself that he wanted to kill her. Or at least that's what he kept saying. "We? Wouldn't I be pretty stupid to tell you if I did know some place safe?"

He shrugged. "What are you going to do?"

"What I'd like to do is overpower you and knock you out, then go to the police."

He wiped a hand over his face and gave her an exasperated look between his splayed fingers, amusement dancing in his eyes. "The police. Right. What would you tell them?"

"I'd tell them—I'd say that you..." She stopped. What would she tell them? That she had rescued a bum from the street who was sent from the future to kill her? That she almost believed him because she could *feel* that he believed it himself? And now apparently someone else was trying to kill them both? "Oh."

"Yeah, 'oh.' Where, Doc? Is there anyplace we can go?"

She put her hand on his arm, not so much for support, but to test him. To see if she could glean anything from him that might reassure her. He watched her suspiciously, but he didn't move away.

He was tired and hungry, and his ribs hurt. Other than that, the overwhelming sensation was of worry, with a vague bewilderment lingering.

Something whizzed past her temple with a strange, reverberating whir. Before she could react, a second whir seared the skin on the top of her hand. She cried out in pain. As Rider grabbed her and shoved her back into the alley, she caught a brief glimpse of a dark figure holding something that looked like a weapon.

Rider wrapped his arm around her waist and ran, forcing her to run with him. She could barely keep up, and several times her feet left the ground as he carried her along. Her hand burned like fire, but she hardly had time to think about it.

"Who was that?" she huffed.

"Tank," Rider muttered, stopping at the end of an alley to glance briefly behind him.

Kristen looked back, too, but there was no one behind them.

Yet.

"Weapons..." Rider had a bewildered scowl on his face.

"What?"

"They've got blasters."

"Blasters?" She gaped at him. "Blasters? Like *Star Wars* or something? Come on, Rider."

This was really getting ridiculous. Okay, so she couldn't explain the two explosions. Okay, so there was somebody after them. But she drew the line at Star Wars and blasters. "What next, Mr. Rider from the future? Robots?"

"It could happen," he muttered, grabbing her hand and holding it in front of her face. Kristen looked for the first time. A streak of white, puffy blisters surrounded by reddened skin ran across the back of her hand.

"Blaster burn, Doc. It barely skimmed your hand. You know what it can do in a direct hit?"

She shook her head, swallowing hard as her brain assessed the seriousness of the burn. Second degree. No sign of charred flesh like third degree burns, but those blisters were going to give her a lot of trouble over the next several days.

Rider grabbed her jaw. "Listen to me. A direct hit burns a hole right through anything but metal. You could be seeing the sidewalk through your hand right now."

She shuddered, feeling his sincerity in his touch. "I can't believe this. It can't be happening."

"It's happening, Doc. We need a place to go."

When he touched her, she believed him. But that was just hormones and her traitorous empathy trying to cloud her judgment. At the very best, Rider was psychotic. At worst, there were people five hundred years in the future who wanted her dead so badly, they were sending killers with blasters after her.

"Don't touch me," she snapped, pushing his hand away. "You're confusing me." She looked behind them, then back at him. "Who wants me dead?" she said, cringing at her own irrational words, at her meek tone. "Who sent you? Who sent them? Why?"

Hot tears welled in her eyes, and she clenched and unclenched her fists, stretching the burned flesh of her hand. Her heart fluttered, her breath caught. "Why?" Somewhere in the rational part of her brain, she noticed the hysteria in her voice.

He must have heard it, too, because he grabbed her shoul-

ders and shook her. "Come on, Doc. Use that doctor's brain.
Don't bark out on me like a mongrel."

His touch sent urgency streaking through her. She concentrated on his voice, on his intense blue eyes.

"Think about it." He glanced down the alley. "Damn, we
don't have time for this. Think about what I told you. When I
left, the technology that would allow them to send weapons
back here was at least a year away, maybe more. I know this,
Doc. I was in on the testing.

"Metal caused the damn machinery to explode. It couldn't
be done. This guy had a blaster—and blasters are metal. That
means at least a year from now I won't have killed you, or
there'd be no reason for them to still be after us."

"A year from now?"

"A year from my time, in the future. Here, it's still now."
He gave her a quick look, then shrugged.

Kristen stared at him, trying to make sense of his words. It
was too much to comprehend. A year from now he still hadn't
killed her? A year from now, unnamed people from some un-
imaginable future five hundred years away were still trying to
kill her right now, today?

"You're here now, and a year later, they're here now, too?"
It was too much. She couldn't grasp it.

"That's time travel," he said, shrugging. "They can set you
down anywhere, any time... well, close," he added wryly.

Rider's eyes changed, turned pensive, as if he were considering all the implications of his words for the first time, too.
He shook his head slowly, his eyes squeezed shut. Kristen could
feel the bewilderment in him, and the urgency.

Behind them, down the alley, she heard a noise. "What do
you say, Doc? Me, or him?" He jerked his head toward the
sound.

They could go to Skip's house. As soon as the thought
surfaced, she tried to quell it. She hadn't been there since he'd
died, and she didn't want to go now. But there was nowhere
else they could hide.

As her heart screamed in protest, she pointed. "This way,"
she said. "We'll go to Skip's house."

"Skip?" Rider asked suspiciously, even as he dragged her
down the street in the direction she'd pointed.

"My brother."

"Your brother."

Kristen looked at him.

His eyes were narrowed in suspicion.

"Yes, my brother. He's dead, all right? Is that safe enough for you? He's dead, so he can't be much of a threat. At least, in my time that's true," she added sarcastically.

She wanted to cry. She was tired, confused. She didn't want to be forced to confront Skipper's house. It was too soon.

Rider's gaze assessed her. "Why do you think your brother's house is safe?"

She shrugged wearily. "I haven't been back to his house since he died." Her voice broke a bit. She didn't want to go now.

"Okay." He sounded unsure. "Lead the way. But, Doc." He jerked her around to face him. "Don't go the easy way. We need to lose this guy. How far is it?"

"Where are we?" She squinted at the street signs in the early morning mist, then sighed. "We've been running in the right direction, but it's still a long way."

"How far?"

"The hard way?" She shrugged, trying to figure it. "Probably eight, ten miles. His house is out toward the bay."

Rider ran his fingers through his hair and wiped his face with his hands.

He wasn't sure he could make it. Kristen saw that in the slump of his shoulders, in his drawn white face. If his strength failed him, she wouldn't be able to make it alone.

So she squared her shoulders and put her arm through his, sending up a prayer that she was doing the right thing. Oh, and as an afterthought, a quick prayer that Rider wasn't psychotic, because if he was, then so was she for believing him.

"Come on," she said, trying to send confidence and strength to him through her touch, confidence she didn't have, strength she was fast losing. Some of her determination must have transferred itself to him, though, because he seemed to rally.

He wrapped an arm about her waist and propelled her forward, into the misty morning.

Kristen kept them to the back alleys and side streets as much as possible. Cars passed occasionally, and each time they would crouch behind a garbage bin or in the shadow of a building, but the cars drove harmlessly by.

There were homeless people too, curled up on steps, huddled in alleys, their desperate eyes following them. Kristen steeled her mind against their desperation as best she could. Between her own and Rider's, she had quite enough to deal with right now.

The sky had brightened considerably by the time they reached Skipper's house almost three hours later.

Rider was as close to collapse as he'd been when she'd brought him into the clinic. His head lolled on his neck, and his breathing was labored. His skin was clammy. She was afraid he was going into shock.

She maneuvered him up to the front door, then stopped. "Oh, no!" she breathed, despair and weariness nearly undoing her.

Rider raised his head. Through his arm, which clutched her shoulder for support, she felt the cramping in his muscles, the sudden tension that gripped him. "What?" he whispered.

"Locked. I don't have the key." Tears stung Kristen's throat. She couldn't go any more. She was too tired. She had no keys. Nothing. "We came all this way for nothing."

He stared at her. "The key..." he muttered, then let go of her to reach into his pockets.

When he pulled out her key ring, Kristen sobbed in relief. "You had them. I forgot."

He fitted the right key into the lock and turned it. "After you, my dear," he muttered as he opened the door.

Kristen just stood there. Could she walk into the house where Skipper had lived? Could she stand to feel the echoes of him again, after all this time? She still remembered the instant he'd died, the moment in time when his presence had gone. It had been like a physical blow. She'd been dictating charts, and she'd dropped the microphone. It was so intense—that sudden absence of sensation. Between one second and another, Skipper was gone.

Then the echoes had started. Echoes in the hollow corridors of her heart. She'd known what they were, but knowing didn't make it any less painful to endure. Would faint echoes still be lingering in his house?

Rider stood there like a concierge, his arm out in a gesture of welcome. "What's the matter?" he asked, peering at her.

She just shook her head, still staring into the darkened interior of the room. "I don't know if I can," she whispered.

He took her hand and pulled her in with him and closed the door.

"No!" Panic suffused her, blocking out everything else. She fought him, pulled against the hand clutching hers so tightly, beat at him with her other hand. "No, no, no!"

"Hey!" He caught her and flipped her around so his arms were around her from behind, pressing her wrists against her breast, scraping the burned flesh of her hand. She was pinned against him, unable to move.

"Look. I really don't have a lot of strength left," he whispered in her ear. "So could you stop throwing a fit and tell me what's the matter?"

"Skipper. He's..." She stopped. Rider still held her firmly, but she no longer fought him. She shut her eyes, testing the air, testing the room, testing for Skipper. There wasn't much there. Skipper was gone. The little she did glean from the atmosphere in his house was good. A feeling of welcome, of peace. She went limp in Rider's arms.

"It's okay," she said. "I'm sorry. I'm fine. I just haven't been here since he died."

Rider's hold relaxed. "How long?"

"Two years. He died two years ago." A lump tried to form in her throat, but she swallowed it.

"Yeah. Not hardly long enough, is it?"

Something in his voice made her turn around and look at him. His eyes were brilliant blue with fatigue and pain. His arms hung loosely around her shoulders, and she felt his grief.

"You lost your wife two years ago?"

"Probably closer to three," he said flatly. "Time loses its meaning after a while in the TAINCC."

Kristen nodded, her sadness melding with his. "It can lose its meaning if you're not in the TAINCC, too."

He stared at her as if trying to search for something in her eyes. "There's something about you..." he whispered, his gaze traveling from her eyes to her mouth and back.

Kristen closed her eyes and relaxed, leaning in toward him, lulled by the tender sadness and wary desire she felt inside him.

He stiffened, dropping his hands from her shoulders and averting his gaze. "Think the shower works?" he said curtly.

She almost overbalanced when his supporting hands left her shoulders. It was so jarring, the way he could abruptly withdraw from her. "Everything's still on. I pay a maid service to clean it twice a year." She shrugged. "I was thinking about selling it, but..."

Rider looked around, assessing the layout of the house. "Who knows about this place, Doc?"

She thought for a minute. "Skip had a lot of friends. Unlike me," she said with a little laugh. "He could handle a lot of people around—he loved it. There were guys and girls always coming over. That's why I finally got my own apartment." It had been too noisy, living in the house with Skip. People had always been drawn to him, had seemed content just to be around him. And they all broadcast their every emotion to her, until finally, drained, she'd moved into her own place.

Rider's voice brought her back to the present. "You didn't answer my question."

She heard the faint threat in his voice, had no doubt that he could gather enough reserves of strength to twist her arm one more time.

"Probably no one I know. And Skipper's friends—well, it's been over two years. None of them ever call me." She thought about a couple of his friends she'd tried to date. They thought she was weird.

It had always irritated Skipper that she isolated herself. He was just the opposite, and while he had tried to understand her discomfort around people, he never really could.

"Hey, Doc. Your comlink get caught in a loop?"

She looked at him, catching the quirky smile on his face that turned her heart upside down. "My what?"

"Never mind. Which way is the shower?"

"His bedroom and bathroom are through there," she said, pointing. "I'm going to see if there's any canned food. You might—you might check his closets for clothes."

Kristen steeled herself for the chore of digging through Skipper's pantry. But like coming into the house, the reality wasn't as bad as her anticipation. It actually comforted her to be here, to see his things meticulously laid out, so unlike her own jumble of an apartment. She smiled as she touched the row of cups hanging on their little cup hooks underneath the cabinets, then winced as she saw her blistered hand.

In the pantry, she found a stock of canned foods. There were several kinds of soup, two canned hams, and a various assortment of canned vegetables and meats.

She heated vegetable soup, carefully keeping her burned hand away from the heat, and opened some asparagus and new potatoes, which she tossed with a jar of marinated artichoke hearts for an impromptu salad. After a longing gaze at the canned ham, she decided not to offend Rider's sensitive nose by opening it.

Just as she set the dishes on the table, Rider emerged, his hair damp and clinging to his skull and his lean body encased in a pair of sweatpants she recognized as Skipper's.

He hadn't put on a shirt, and his beauty assaulted her like it did every time she looked at him. Even bruised and scraped, his body looked perfect to her. There was a huge, inflamed scratch across one shoulder. Kristen crossed to him and touched the raw skin, drawing a quick breath at the ribbon of desire that whipped through her when she touched him. "I should put something on that," she said. "It's going to be sore."

He put his hand over hers. When he did, her heart sped up, and she felt like she'd had the breath knocked out of her.

"It's not as bad as your hand," he said softly.

Her gaze was caught by the mesmerizing blue of his eyes. She licked her lips and he frowned, his gaze dropping to her mouth. Through his skin, she felt the heat of arousal burning in his belly.

"I—I made us some food," she stammered, pulling away.

For a brief moment, he held her hand imprisoned beneath his, but then he finally relented.

It was probably exhaustion that made her vulnerable to his every touch. Exhaustion and the irritating way he broadcast his feelings to her like sonar.

He dropped into a chair and ate heartily. Kristen ate, too, but it was an effort. She was so tired she could hardly keep her eyes open.

Rider was apparently having the same problem. As soon as he'd finished, he pushed the chair back. "Doc. I have no idea what's going on in that pretty head of yours, and I'm not going to ask you if I can trust you because I wouldn't know if you were lying. I guess you can trust me, though, since I apparently won't have managed to kill you by the time they've perfected the transfer of metal through time."

His eyes were heavy-lidded with drowsiness. "I've got to have some sleep. If you call the police or the dog catchers while I'm out, then so be it. I don't think I give a damn anymore." He shrugged, an odd look of regret shadowing his face, then got up and left the room.

NINE

Kristen sat at the kitchen table for a long time before she roused herself and glanced at the clock. Ten o'clock. She'd almost lost track of time. As near as she could tell, the explosion at the clinic had happened early Friday evening. Then they'd escaped her apartment sometime probably after midnight.

She pushed her hands through her hair and sighed. Just a few hours, and within that time she had come to be a fugitive, linked by danger to a man who claimed to be from hundreds of years in the future.

The really absurd thing was, she was beginning to believe him. And even more ridiculous, she trusted him. His emotions were more open to her than anyone she had ever met, other than Skipper.

Every pain, every emotion, communicated itself to her through his touch, and sometimes just his glance. She was exhausted from his anguish, and the sadness and fear that lay on his heart. There were other, sweeter feelings, too. The tenderness he exuded when he touched her, the desire he tried to deny. Yes, she was linked to him by more than danger and chance.

Her thoughts kept coming back to the physical attraction. She wasn't immune to it, not by a long shot, but she had never been able to endure more than kisses before. She'd always been repelled by the casual attitude of the kisser—and sometimes the calculated, planned seduction. They'd been so shallow, those few men who had tried to come on to her.

Nothing like Rider. Whatever he was, whoever he was, he was sincere. Whether he was a refugee from a loony bin, or a killer from the future, he believed in himself. There was something very reassuring about that.

There was something else that gave her a measure of reassurance, too. He genuinely cared about her. She had felt it in his fingers when they caressed her nape, denying the threat of his words. She had tasted it in his lips.

Kristen started. Had she fallen asleep? She sighed and stood. She needed a shower, too, and a long, undisturbed nap. With a poignant smile she remembered she'd kept some clothes here at Skipper's for late nights when they were working on his research.

She unearthed a pair of jeans, a tee shirt, and some underwear in the guestroom. Holding up the jeans, she measured them against her. If she hadn't gained too much weight in the past two years, she could still fit into them. She'd started toward the bathroom at the end of the hall before she remembered the front door.

She threw the deadbolt and put on the chain, then went back toward the bathroom, passing Skipper's room where Rider was stretched out on the bed, his breathing soft and even.

For a moment she stood in the doorway and watched him sleep. He was so tired, so hurt. Her heart melted at the sight of him. In sleep, with his features relaxed and his lashes resting against his cheeks, he looked like such a little boy. Gazing at him, she hoped he'd had a good childhood, because it sounded like his adult life had been hell.

She turned toward the bathroom, then back toward the bedroom. Maybe she would take her shower in Skipper's bathroom. After all, she'd nearly been blown up twice, almost been run over by a car, and been shot by a *blaster*, all within the past twenty-four hours. Maybe she'd rather have somebody between her and the outside world, even if he was sound asleep and crazy to boot.

She quickly showered and towel-dried her hair, taking care to protect her blistered hand. Then she wrapped it with gauze and slipped on Skipper's bathrobe. With its softness against her skin, she got another lingering echo of her brother. She was reminded of him telling her to trust her senses.

"When the right man comes along," he said, *"you'll know it. I'll know it too, I'm sure, because the whales will probably start screaming their heads off."*

Smiling sadly, she walked out into the bedroom. Rider was sleeping peacefully, his breaths even, his limbs relaxed. Kristen looked longingly at the empty space beside him in the bed.

It had felt so good to lie next to him in her bed. It was a sensation she'd never experienced, that of sleeping next to someone, of knowing the other person was there even if you weren't touching.

And his dreams...

Kristen shivered, remembering the vestiges of his dreams. Somehow she had moved closer to him in her sleep, and his dreams had gotten mixed up with hers. Something about angels and clouds and good, good kisses. Were the kisses part of the dreams? Or had the dreams been born out of the kisses?

Her head nodded, and she caught herself. She was almost asleep on her feet. She really didn't want to sleep in a room by herself, especially the guest room, which was in the front of the house where people might be able to see into the windows, or break in.

No, if she wanted to sleep, she probably should just curl up on the edge of Skipper's bed with Rider. Just for a few minutes.

She lay down next to him and closed her eyes, comforted by his presence, feeling his cautious relaxation, his wary comfort. He still hurt. She could tell, even though it was nothing compared to the wrenching spasms that had gripped him earlier. Now her senses told her it was more of a dull ache, behind the bruises and scrapes, beneath the exhaustion and the sore muscles. Good. The anti-nausea pills were working.

Carefully, not wanting to disturb him, she shifted, curling up inside Skipper's robe, finding a comfortable position for a short nap—just a short one, before she tried to sort out her feelings about this man who had dropped out of the blue, perhaps literally, and disrupted her life.

With the passing thought that if she really wanted to, she could still call the police and make up a plausible story, she dozed.

Rider tensed. He lay very still without opening his eyes for an instant until he realized that the sound he had heard had been the pad of soft footsteps across the carpet. The movement had been the sinking of a slight body into the bed beside him, and the odor that was now tickling his nostrils was the clean-washed smell of his angel doctor. He hated the fear that engulfed him every time he woke up, and the unwelcome desire that seared him every time he looked at her, or thought about her.

What was it about her scent, her essence? Was he remembering his wife? With that thought came a dizzying pain and a faint breath of nausea.

He clenched his teeth and forced himself to endure the memories, such as they were. His wife.

Marielle. The name evoked a vision of dark blonde hair, a dazzling smile, and a pleasant, spicy scent. He closed his eyes and tried to capture a vision of his wife. Black leather pants and jacket? Could that be right? And some kind of night vision goggles?

His gut spasmed again and he gave up, wiping sweat from his face. He was getting her mixed up with the Deviants, somehow. That was their underground uniform. He wasn't sure how he knew that, he just did.

He wiped the disturbing thoughts out of his head and turned his attention to his angel doctor. He breathed deeply of her newly washed skin, her damp hair. She was curled up on the edge of the bed, engulfed in a big terry cloth robe. Her hair was curled around her face like a halo, fitting for an angel. Her eyelashes were spiked with dampness and dark against her pale cheeks.

The slender column of her neck disappeared into the terry cloth much too soon for his taste, but pink toes peeked out from the bottom of the robe, and they were enough to set his blood on fire, to increase the pressure of his erection against the slick fabric of the sweat pants he'd borrowed from her brother. With the desire came the pain—the searing burn of the imprint on his thigh that reminded him of who and what he was.

But even the pain wasn't enough to blot out his memory of the hours spent crouched in the alley, hours during which he'd vacillated between the hatred that gnawed at his entrails and a sweet desire unlike anything he could remember.

He watched her face as she dozed. Her lips were slightly parted, her mouth curled in a winsome smile. He wondered what she was dreaming about, or whom.

Those long hours, with her nestled intimately between his thighs, he'd dreamed about her—about his angel, come from heaven to save him. He'd dreamed she was there, touching him, not as his hostage, not afraid of him, but willingly, nestled against him in a lover's embrace. He'd dreamed she had responded when his body had begun to throb against her.

But he'd awakened to find her tense and shivering, obviously afraid of him, and he remembered why he held her imprisoned there. Then the nausea and the pain and the fear had returned, and he'd been plunged back into the same hell from which he'd tried to escape by going to sleep.

But was it all a dream? Hadn't he been awake when she'd pushed backwards against him and turned her head at his gentle urging to allow him to kiss her? Hadn't she arched her back to press her breasts into his hands, to reach his mouth with hers? Surely he hadn't dreamed that.

He moved cautiously, groaning at the soreness in his muscles, wincing at the sickening pain in his ribcage. But still the sweet desire was strong enough to override the pain and soreness.

This was stupid. He had no right. Still, what difference would it make? He was dead anyway. Death just hadn't caught up with him yet.

He looked at her, and a strange thickness coated his throat. An unfamiliar stinging in his eyes made him blink. She was as good as dead, too. If not he, then someone else would kill her. The thought of her dying made him sad.

As his eyes feasted on her delicate form, he thought about the dark figure holding a blaster. A sleeker, more stylized piece than he'd ever used in training. He'd seen the glint of metal.

They hadn't been able to send any weapons back with him because of something about the magnetic fields created around metallic objects. They hadn't even been able to transfer metal buttons or a watch.

So the only conclusion was that they were still trying to destroy Kristen years after he'd transferred. His eyes stung with a ridiculous relief at the realization that he hadn't killed her by then.

Nausea gripped him and sweat beaded on his brow. What was the matter with him? He hated her! He hated everything about her. She was a Deviant. She was dirty, disgusting. She read minds, for God's sake.

She had killed his wife. Rider clenched his teeth and repeated the words like a litany. She had killed his wife. It was her fault, her descendants. Why was it getting harder and harder to keep his mind on that fact?

He remembered her question. Why? Why had the Deviants killed Mari? Why had they blown a hole in their apartment and stormed in with blasters? He was just a college professor, and Mari was just a housewife.

An image of Mari dressed in the unrelieved black of the Deviant underground flashed across his vision again. He turned his head and squeezed his eyes shut, but the vision didn't fade. She was fiddling with dials on an old-fashioned transistor-type radio.

He pressed the heels of his hands into his eyes, clenching his jaw against a bitter tang at the back of his throat. Where were these confusing memories coming from? Why did he keep getting Mari mixed up with the Deviants? Was it Kristen's Deviant mind, getting inside his head and mixing up his memories?

The picture finally faded, leaving him bewildered and weary. He took a long breath, trying to calm his racing thoughts, and Kristen's scent assaulted his senses. Unwelcome desire began to stir in his loins again.

He tried to force his mind to stop thinking. All he wanted to do was feel. He almost chuckled. That was a switch. Wanting to feel emotions that should have been destroyed.

Their damned conditioning hadn't removed his emotions as effectively as they'd thought it had, so why not make something of what little time he had left.

They were both as good as dead. They were no match for the superior weaponry of the twenty-sixth century and beyond. So what the hell difference did it make if he lost himself in lust for a few minutes?

Quietly laughing at the transparency of his so-called logic, he eased closer to her on the bed. If she didn't want him, if she made even the most token protest, he'd stop. He'd just go shower again, this time with cold water.

He stopped when his body was just centimeters from hers, when his bare torso could feel her newly bathed heat. He breathed deeply, taking in the sight and feel and smell of her.

He wouldn't mind stopping time right there. Even battered as his body was, he couldn't remember ever having felt so good before. Sad as he was, he couldn't remember ever being happier than right now, lying beside her.

But time wouldn't stand still. It moved like a river, continuous, never-ending, and whether he was standing to one side watching it, or plunged into the middle of it, he couldn't alter its course. All he could do was flow with it.

Slowly, so slowly, flowing with the inevitability of time, Rider pulled the sash of her robe loose. Slowly he pushed the fabric off one perfectly rounded shoulder. Still promising himself he could stop, he lifted his head and touched his lips to her skin, tasting the soapy cleanness. His tongue traced a path up the rounded slope of her shoulder toward her neck, savoring the different flavors of her, while his heart pounded like thunder.

She gasped, a tiny sound that barely reached his ears even though they were only millimeters from her lips, and her body tensed. He raised his head and met her gaze, dreading what he would see. The amber-green eyes were wide and questioning, caught by his. He searched them, looking for fear, for disgust, for anything that would force him to abandon his quest, but he didn't find any of those, only an uncertainty and an anticipation that confused and stirred him.

He pushed the robe a little further, until the top of one breast became visible. His breath hissed between his teeth as his eyes took in the flawlessness of her body. Her rounded flesh was pale and blue-veined. As he touched it, he had the peculiar notion he was exploring a virgin land.

Her breath quickened at his touch, and he glanced back at her face to assure himself it wasn't with fright, or worse, with disgust.

When he did, she licked her lips. A quiet growl escaped his throat. She had to know by now what that gesture did to him. With an urgency born of desperation, he pulled her to him and covered her mouth with his, ignoring the burning in his thigh and the faint tickle of nausea at the back of his throat.

Amazingly, she didn't stiffen or pull away. He nibbled at her lips, teasing them, torturing himself, until she parted them. Then he deepened his kiss, pushing his tongue between her teeth, gasping when he touched the soft wetness of her tongue.

He felt the change in her, maybe even before she did. Her body softened, went slack against him. She bloomed. He felt the suppleness of desire in her limbs as he rubbed her nipple gently between his fingers, testing. Testing her, testing himself, knowing with a kind of fear that now nothing either one of them did could stop him. He laid his palm against her belly, feeling her quick breaths, the taut muscles.

She was ready for him. Ready and willing. His erection throbbed against her thigh, so sensitive, so sweet, he thought he might pass out.

He pulled his head back to look at her. Her eyes were heavy-lidded, her lips slightly parted. When he pulled away, her fingers clutched at him.

He didn't want to break the spell like he had in his dream, but he couldn't stand the suspense a minute longer.

"Doc?" It was a question so laden with meaning, so weighted with all his hopes and fears, that his voice nearly failed.

Her gaze was centered on his mouth, and when he spoke, she raised her brilliant, amber-shot eyes to his. She wrapped her hand around the nape of his neck and pulled his face down to hers.

Rider was horrified to find himself almost sobbing as he tore his mouth from hers to push the sweat pants off his legs and push aside the robe that still partially covered her. His breaths were harsh in his throat, his eyes burned.

How long had it been? How long since he'd even cared to feel this way? Once he'd thought he would never want to again. Until he'd been rescued by an angel.

She opened herself beneath him, gasping and arching as his hand moved over her gently rounded belly, then lower, to seek the place where all her sensation was centered. She grasped his arm as if she would stop him, but then she encircled his back and pulled him closer, whimpering and whispering his name.

His questing fingers told him what he'd already known, that she was ready, and so he lifted himself above her, gritting his teeth to keep from losing control, and gently pushed into her.

And stopped.

"Doc?" he rasped. "What?"

She looked at him, a blush suffusing her face with heat that he could feel on his. "I never..."

"God. Oh God," he whispered. "It's going to hurt you." Nothing had prepared him for this. Not her shyness, not her hesitancy. Certainly not the knowledge of her that had been conditioned into him. But these thoughts flitted quickly through his brain and were gone, because her hands around his back moved downward, to cup his buttocks and pull him closer, closer.

Suddenly, he had no more control, and he thrust hard, tearing through the barrier, his heart breaking at her startled cry. He watched her, watched her brow furrow, her lips stretch back against her teeth, her eyes squeeze shut.

"I can stop," he gasped, lying. "I didn't want to hurt you." As the shadow of pain faded from her face, her hands still held him to her.

"Kiss me," she whispered. "I can feel it all when you kiss me."

He kissed her without even wondering what she meant, but as he did, something began to happen deep inside him, much deeper than the physical sensations that were rocking him. Deep within him he felt a bond with her, with his angel doctor, a bond not born of knowledge, or fear, or even intimacy. But it formed a link between them that he was sure not even time could sever.

As he kissed her, she began to move beneath him, in the timeless, ageless dance that all lovers know, and he was overwhelmed by the feel of her surrounding him as his passion grew and exploded. He cried out, and her arms tightened about him as his climax shuddered through them both.

For a long time he lay above her, resting his weight on his arms, just savoring the feeling of being joined with her. They kissed languidly, softly, and Kristen nuzzled his neck as he breathed in the sweet, clean smell of her hair.

"It can be better, Doc," he muttered.

"I know," she whispered, stroking his hair.

"I didn't want to hurt you. I swear."

"I know. I understand," her breath caught a little. "I'm a doctor, remember? I understand these things."

She paused for so long that Rider lifted his head to look at her.

"But the textbooks and my giggly schoolgirl friends didn't tell me how wonderful it feels to bond so closely with someone else. How can people treat it so casually?"

He stared at her as she smiled tearily at him. It scared the shit out of him that he knew exactly what she was talking about. It was what he had felt at the moment of their union. He was sure he'd never known anything like it before, doubtful he ever would again. The tickle at the back of his throat warned him against thinking too much, warned him against feeling anything at all.

His arms were giving out, and he didn't want to look at her shining eyes any more, so he collapsed beside her. He pulled her close and she curled against him, splaying her fingers across his belly.

"Why didn't you tell me you were a virgin?" he asked, stroking her hair.

Her shoulders moved against his side. "It never came up."

"Why?"

"Why didn't it ever come up?"

"Why me?" he asked, knowing the answer. Wanting to hear it. Not wanting to hear it. Thinking he would die if he was wrong. That he'd die if he was right. Swallowing hard against the sick pain his thoughts and emotions evoked in him, he asked her. "Why did you wait?"

Kristen sighed, her warm breath tickling his nipple. "It's hard to explain. When guys started noticing me in high school, I'd go out with them just like all the other girls. They all talked about kissing like it was something wonderful. But when I tried it, I was always repelled by what the boy was feeling."

A dull ache centered itself in Rider's gut, and sweat beaded his brow. Something about her words was eerily familiar to him. Something far, far back in the recesses of his brain, back behind the conditioning the TAINCC had so carefully laid over everything that had once been Rider Savage. He lay still and listened to her against his conscious will.

"See, there's this thing inside me," she continued. "This sense. When I'm close to someone, especially if I'm touching them, I can feel what they're feeling. Sometimes it's almost like I can hear them think."

She laughed a little, her breast rippling against his chest, but her warm, naked body against him was no longer delicious. It was awful, somehow tied up with terror and sadness so profound he thought his heart would burst. He swallowed against the bitter taste in his throat and wished she would shut up.

"It's like I said. I think I was looking for something—something those boys didn't have. A bond, a link. Like when you kiss me, Rider. I can feel what's inside you. I can almost hear your thoughts."

Moaning, he sat up and pushed her away, the nausea overwhelming him, the ache in his gut blinding him. He vaulted up and ran into the bathroom, slamming the door behind him, ignoring her cry of alarm.

He splashed cold water on his face and neck with shaking hands, then stood there bent over the sink for a long time, until the waves of sickness began to lessen.

What was it, the memory that was trying to push its way past his conditioning? He clamped his jaw tight, seeing again the vision of black leather and goggles, and Mari's lovely, smiling face.

His wife was dead, murdered by Deviants.

And Kristen Skipworth was the enemy. The Mother of all the Deviants. It was why he'd been sent to kill her. Bitter nausea gripped him again. He'd made love with her—with the one person he hated most in all time.

He gagged and coughed, then sluiced his mouth out with water, swallowing several mouthsful to quell the last of the nausea.

Glancing at his reflection, he searched his face, disgusted with what he saw. What had he done? He couldn't remember the last time he'd made love with his wife, and now he had betrayed her with the woman whose spawn had killed her.

He held on to his hatred with every shred of will he could muster, because something had gone terribly wrong with his conditioning.

But even more frightening than that, something had gone wrong with his heart. No matter how strongly his brain insisted she was the enemy, worthy only of his hatred, there was something inside him that wasn't quite convinced. No matter how much he hated Deviants, he was having a lot of trouble hating Kristen Skipworth.

TEN

Kristen stared at the bathroom door through which Rider had disappeared. What happened? He had jerked away when she'd wanted to prolong the sweet sensation of lying next to him. She'd wanted to savor his closeness, the smell of his body next to hers, his warmth, his strength, the bond they'd discovered.

She shifted in the bed and winced at the soreness between her thighs. She'd waited so long to find someone like him, who wouldn't repel her with treachery and insincerity. How ironic that when she finally found a man who was honest and tender and good, he was also a lunatic who fancied himself an assassin.

"And not just a local lunatic, either," she muttered, quelling an urge to laugh, a lunatic from five hundred years in the future.

She got out of bed and wrapped Skipper's robe around her, yanking the belt tight. Then she pushed open the bathroom door.

Rider was leaning over the sink, his head bowed and dripping with water, his arms rigid, hands gripping the edge of the sink like a lifeline. He stood with his legs apart, his muscled thighs quivering with weakness.

Kristen couldn't help the knee-buckling wave of desire that flowed through her at the sight of his beautiful, naked body. "Come on," she said softly, putting her hands on his shoulders. They were cold and damp with sweat.

He cringed and recoiled when she touched him, but after a few seconds, he allowed her to lead him back to the bed, where he flopped down and covered his eyes with his arm, his chest heaving, his ridged belly rippling with occasional cramps. Kristen covered him with a blanket and climbed into bed beside him.

"Okay," she said matter-of-factly, using her doctor voice as she tucked the blanket up around his neck and pushed damp hair off his forehead. "Conditioning, you said. I would tend to agree. You react violently to certain stimuli." She counted them off on her fingers. "Talking about your past, talking about your wife, cats, kissing me, making love to me. Yes, I'd say we're certainly talking about adverse conditioning here."

She watched him as she talked. Except for his labored breathing and the slight contractions of his belly, he didn't move.

She wanted to slide down beside him, to pull him to her and hold him until all the hurt and sickness went away. She wanted to make love to him again, because she'd never felt anything as wonderful as kissing him and feeling him thrust inside her.

What she'd told him was true. When he kissed her she could feel it all. Not only her own desire but his as well, beating against her like his heart, coursing through her like her own blood. And underlying it all, she could feel his fear, his sickness, his impotent rage at the things they, whoever they were, had done to him.

She turned back to him and put her hand on his forehead. "Would you like to explain to me," she whispered, "why making love to me makes you physically ill?"

He pushed her hand away then slid his arm under his head. He didn't look at her, just stared at the ceiling. "I hate you," he said calmly, no expression at all on his face.

The emptiness in his voice hurt Kristen even more than the words, and the words ripped through her like a knife through rotten cloth.

"I hate you and everything you stand for. You're a Deviant. The Mother of all Deviants. Your descendants murdered my wife."

His voice trailed off as his stomach heaved and he coughed.

Kristen pulled away, shocked and hurt. She asked, and she'd even expected the words. He'd said them often enough. But what she hadn't expected was the return of the cold hatred, not after the beautiful few minutes they had just shared.

"I still don't understand, Rider. Why? Why would they murder her?"

"I don't know, okay?" His jaw worked tensely, his neck corded with strain. "It's so hard to remember. They've fixed it so I can't remember without getting sick. I don't know why I can remember anything. I'm not supposed to be hampered by emotion. It's a pain in the ass to have feelings!"

He threw her a glare of such unguarded fury that she recoiled. He was like a different man, the antithesis of the man who had held her close and made her feel loved just a few moments before.

"If I could get rid of the damned emotions, I could kill you like I was sent to do." He dragged himself off the bed, pulled on the sweatpants and walked out of the room.

Kristen pushed her hair off her forehead with shaky hands.

He still wanted to kill her.

She was becoming more and more convinced that his preposterous story was true, that he really was from the future, come back to kill her. She tried to remember the science-fiction stories she'd read, about time machines and time warps, about people changing the future by destroying something—or someone—in the past.

Drawing her knees up, she hugged them and stared at the doorway. Had she really just made love with someone who wasn't even born yet? Someone who hated her descendants so badly he'd kill her to destroy them?

When she walked into the kitchen, Rider was standing at the patio doors looking out over Skipper's neglected yard. There was defeat in the air. Even without her empathic sense, she'd have had no trouble figuring that one out. She saw it in the slump of his shoulders, in the dejected curve of his spine.

He turned around and smiled at her, that heartbreaking smile that could knock her off her feet. "I can't," he said, his voice cracking like a teenager's. He shook his head. "I just can't."

She reached for him, her heart melting at his lonely despair, but he held up a hand.

"Don't touch me, Doc. I don't have enough strength right now." He slumped down into a chair.

"What? What is it?" She sat opposite him.

He put his head in his hands and ran shaky fingers through his hair.

Kristen was terrified at the change in him. She'd seen him nearly dead, defeated by starvation and pain. But this—this wasn't external. It was something inside him. He'd given up on something.

"Tell me," she demanded.

"I can't hate you. You caused my wife's death, and I can't hate you. I can't kill you." His face twisted in agony. "They will kill me, but I can't do it."

"Rider, tell me why. What about the conditioning?"

"I don't know. It's not as bad as it was, somehow. Ever since I grabbed your ankle in that damned cold alley, their conditioning's been going haywire."

"I mean why can't you kill me?"

He looked at her, despair and fear in his eyes. "I don't know that either. My civilization depends on me killing you. They say skipworths will cause the end of the world. We've got to wipe them out."

Kristen noticed the hesitancy in his voice, just like she had when he'd talked of similar things in her apartment. It was as if he were reciting by rote. As if he doubted the truth of his words.

His head slumped.

"Come on, Rider." She pulled him up and put his arm around her shoulder, guiding him toward the bedroom. He was right. The nausea and pain that lurked behind all his other emotions were losing strength. Maybe soon he would be able to shake off the conditioning and begin to function normally.

"I'm always putting you into bed, aren't I?" She climbed into bed beside him. "Now," she whispered. "Let's just lie here together and tell stories 'til we fall asleep."

For a moment, Rider's body was stiff and unyielding against hers, but soon his exhaustion won over his wariness and pain, and he relaxed and allowed her to curl into his side and rest her head on his shoulder.

"Tell me why you can't kill me," she whispered against his warm skin.

"You never give up, do you, Doc?" From her vantage point she couldn't see his eyes, but his voice sounded almost light-hearted. She shook her head against his shoulder.

"No. I can't give up. I'm a doctor."

"It's you," he said after a long moment. "This is too good. Too real. There's something about you. Something familiar. Something sincere. I don't understand it. Everything inside me tells me I should hate you. But when I touch you, I can't." He shuddered and pulled her close, as if he wanted to draw warmth from her. "Do you know how long it's been since I could feel anything at all? Since I could even remember anything?"

Kristen wanted to cry. He was so lost, so hurt. So terribly alone. "What did you do, Rider, before?"

"Before? You mean when I had a life?"

He shrugged, his voice heavy with irony. "I'm not sure. Until I touched you the first time, there in the alley, I didn't remember anything except the TAINCC. Then, when I touched you, things started coming back to me. The feel of genuine wood, showering with real water. I think I was some kind of professor. I'm not— " His voice broke, and Kristen felt his overwhelming sadness.

She leaned up on her elbow and put her hand on his face. "Okay. Okay, you're doing good. I don't know much about breaking adverse conditioning, but it's probably like deprogramming a cultist. We'll have to work through it. But you're wearing yourself out. You need to sleep." She kissed him gently on the cheek. His arm tightened, hugging her to him with all his might.

She hugged him back, savoring his crushing strength, wanting to be so close to him they wouldn't know where one of them ended and the other began.

What made her feel so protective, so responsible for this man whom any of her colleagues would label psychotic? What made it so easy for her to believe in everything her logical side reasoned couldn't possibly be true?

Finally she whispered, "I'll make you some cocoa, then you can sleep."

His hand cradled her head, and for an instant he kept the pressure there, kept her face buried in his neck as his breath stirred her hair. Then he relaxed his hold and pushed her away.

"Okay, Doc. Whatever you say. You're the doctor." He smiled, then his eyes drifted closed.

Kristen dressed quietly and tiptoed out to the kitchen, her thoughts still with the man in the bedroom. She basked in the lingering warmth of his smile as she opened a can of milk and made the cocoa.

She felt his quiet exhaustion within her as she stirred the hot milk. Deeper, underneath the weariness, she felt the dregs of his passion.

Closing her eyes, she gripped the edge of the countertop as aftershocks of exquisite pleasure racked her. Nothing she had ever read or heard or imagined had prepared her for the instant when he had invaded her for the first time.

"It can be better," he'd said, and she had no doubt he was right. The pleasure that had built in her after the first shocking pain had been filled with promises of greater joy.

But somehow Kristen doubted anything in the world could equal the sensation of being totally joined with him for the first time. The almost unbearable rapture of bonding with him physically and emotionally was something she would never forget.

When she took two brimming mugs of cocoa back into the bedroom, Rider was sound asleep, and her heart ached to see his face relaxed, his lips soft and vulnerable as a child's. She left his mug on the bedside table, leaned over and brushed her lips against his.

In the living room, she sat down at Skipper's desk and sipped her drink while she tried to make sense of everything that had happened.

If Rider came from the future, and if in the future people who bore her name were telepaths and considered dangerous, then... Kristen shook her head. If she told anyone the things Rider had told her, she would be labeled insane. An overwhelming sense of loneliness engulfed her.

Believing Rider cut a chasm between her and everyone she knew. She would never be able to explain why she believed his ravings about deviants and telepathy. Her belief in him made her as much of an outcast in this time as Rider.

But she'd always been something of an outcast anyway. She'd always been odd. Her strong empathy was unusual, to say the least. Sometimes, if Skipper had really wanted to get to her, he'd call her a mutant, Darwin's latest joke. Kristen had never appreciated his humor.

Why would nature select for the type of debilitating sensitivity she possessed? What purpose could that serve in the struggle for life? All it did was keep her emotionally battered and bruised by the constant barrage of other people's feelings.

But her brother had been obsessed with the idea that she was a new breed of human. *A deviant*? The word evoked horror, connected as it was to Rider's story.

She looked at the deceptively small nylon case on the desk. Skipper had been studying genetics, certain he could isolate a gene that would account for her supersensitive empathy. His original thesis, created years before, had been the empathic link between twins, and the literature was full of stories detailing uncanny links between twins, but there were no documented cases of the type of superattenuated empathy that Kristen possessed.

He'd gotten a grant to research a possible genetic reason for empathy between twins, but as he'd often told her, his real goal was to isolate the gene that he was sure she and she alone possessed. To that end, he'd collected dozens of blood samples from her for testing. More than once she'd laughingly accused him of drinking it, or selling it.

She unzipped the nylon pack and touched the putty-colored computer case inside. He'd always kept all his notes on the laptop—his peripheral brain, he called it. She wondered why he hadn't taken it with him to the lab that last day.

Skipper, I need you, she thought, and even as her eyes misted over with tears, she smiled.

He would love Rider, would dissect him like an insect under a microscope. He'd probably already have figured out whether Rider had truly come from the future, whether he was telling the truth, whether Kristen could really be the "Mother of all the Deviants."

She laughed out loud. What Skipper could do with that!

Her hand on the computer case gave her a strong sense of her brother, the strongest she'd found in his house. The hollow place he'd left in her chest began to throb with loneliness. He'd always been there for her. Her only true friend, the only one who'd understood how awful it was for her to live in the world with no skin.

As she opened the computer her gaze lit on the telephone. Her heart began to pound. She sipped at the cocoa, surprised to find it ice cold, then glanced toward the bedroom. Rider was sound asleep. He'd probably sleep for hours. If she wanted to, she could call the police, or the hospital, have him locked up, with a healthy dose of sedative, before he woke up.

She reached for the phone, then paused. *Come on. What's the problem, Doc?* She reached again, then stopped, confusion washing over her. What did she believe? What did she *know*?

If she called the police, if she told them what he'd been telling her, he would be locked up, probably for the rest of his life, as criminally insane. She didn't think she could stand that on her conscience. Rider locked away? She shivered. It would kill him.

On the other hand, someone did mean them harm. Kristen glanced at the gauze on her hand. Something had caused the streak of blisters across the back of her hand, something that definitely was not a bullet. And something had caused the explosions that destroyed the clinic and her apartment.

Could Rider have engineered those attempts on her life? He'd certainly known about the explosions. Of course, he'd explained about the telltale odor and the metal. He'd said it proved people had come from even farther in the future than he had to kill her. If she told the police that, she'd be committed right alongside Rider.

Kristen put her palms on either side of her head, squeezing. What was happening to her? How could she have made

love with a deranged killer? Why did she even hesitate to call
for help?

After a few moments, she lifted the receiver.

***

Rider came awake with a start. For a moment he was
disoriented and his reflexes brought him upright before he realized where he was.

He was in her brother's house. How long had he been
asleep, and what was the Doc doing? He stretched and yawned,
relaxing his muscles. He felt surprisingly good. The naps were
beginning to help.

There was a cup of dark liquid on the bedside table. Rider
took a tentative sip. Chocolate. Not bad. Too sweet, but not
bad. He swallowed it quickly, thinking more of the energy he
could derive from the sugar and milk than of the taste.

Then he heard her voice.

Instantly alert, his muscles tensed and ready to attack, he
quickly and silently slipped on his clothes, then crept to the door
of the living room on the balls of his feet, glancing in all directions, cursing himself for his weakness, aware that anything
could have happened while he was out.

He'd allowed his loneliness and his need to override his
determination, to get in the way of his mission. His heart lurched
as he thought about his angel doctor. What was the matter with
him? What made him lose all the TAINCC's careful conditioning when he touched her?

Kristen's voice rose, and Rider jerked his attention back to
her, his diaphragm lurching with regret and disappointment.

For a while there, he'd actually thought his angel-doctor
believed him.

She was talking on the contraption she called a telephone,
he realized, relaxing a bit in relief. At least the threat wasn't
imminent. He started to crash into the room and rip the phone
out of the wall, but he paused first, trying to discern what she
was saying.

"No, Moira, I won't. Now listen to me. If you don't call
them off, they're going to arrest him, or both of us. For the last
time, I am *not* a hostage. And I am *not* going to tell you where
I am."

She paused, listening, and Rider leaned against the doorway watching her. She rubbed her forehead with one hand.

"I promise. As soon as I can. Moira, please trust me." She

laughed shakily. "I have no idea what I'm doing, either, but for some strange reason, it feels like the right thing."

Rider straightened and walked over to the desk. She looked up, startled, her eyes wide and bright, her throat working as she swallowed.

"I—I've got to go now. Take care, and t-tell Bill I'll talk to him as soon as I can. No, I'm f-fine. Bye."

Rider took the telephone receiver from her hand and slammed it down on the base, then picked them both up and jerked them out of the wall, garnering a cruel satisfaction when she flinched.

"Have a nice talk?" He propped one hip on the edge of the desk and crossed his arms.

"I told Moira to take me off the missing persons list." She gripped her mug with whitened fingers.

"Why?" He had gleaned that much from her side of the conversation. What he couldn't figure out was why she'd done it. She still didn't completely trust him, that was obvious, and he sure as hell didn't trust her.

He watched her closely. Had the conversation been a ruse, staged just for him?

He didn't think so. She had a glimmer of the telepathic sense she'd passed along to her deviant descendants, but she wasn't trained in deception, she wasn't conditioned to perform impeccably under adverse conditions. He shook his head. If she'd known he was listening to her, she would have been stammering and nervous during the whole conversation, just like she was at the end. She'd never have been able to carry it off that calmly.

He focused on her face. She was watching him apprehensively. "I asked why. Why did you tell her to call off the cops?"

She shrugged, never taking her eyes off him. "I don't know. It seemed easier not having to deal with two sets of pursuers."

"So, have you decided I'm not a mongrel?"

"A what?"

"A barking mongrel. Crazy."

She blinked and looked away. Yep, he was right. She still didn't believe him. So why was she acting like she was?

Her shoulders moved in a small shrug, and she answered his unasked question. "You believe in yourself."

Rider felt like he'd been punched. Her words cut across his heart like a laser. Did he? Did he believe in himself? He'd never thought in those terms. At least not any more. The TAINCC conditioned self-centeredness out of you. The concentration was on the target. Being centered on yourself was a distraction, almost as much of a distraction as desire.

Kristen was still talking, and he had to force himself to listen to her.

"You have no doubt about who I am, or what your mission is."

She looked up at him, and he had to look away. Her Deviant, gold-shot eyes could see too deeply into his soul.

"You *are* confused about how you feel about me."

"Stop it," he growled. "Stop getting inside me like a—like a Deviant." His gut spasmed, and hot sickness washed over him. "Just get the hell out of my head."

Kristen recoiled at his words, shock and hurt on her face. He wanted to reach out and pull her close, tell her he was sorry, but his insides were churning and his brain was whirling. He squeezed his eyes shut and took a long breath.

When he opened them, she was toying with an old-fashioned appliance of some kind. A breeze of familiarity brushed the edge of his brain and knotted his stomach, but when he tried to identify what was so familiar, it blew away. "What's that?"

"What?"

He nodded toward her hand. "That."

"Oh. This is Skipper's computer."

He snorted, ignoring the flutter of apprehension the word computer brought to his brain. "Yeah, right." He grabbed her wrist. "Now, what is it, another type of communications link?"

"You're hurting me. No. It's just a computer." She was prepared to wrench her hand out of his grasp, so rather than snap her wrist, he let go.

He stared at the bulky box. "That's right," he muttered to himself. "The nanochip wasn't invented until twenty-one-oh-one."

"Nanochip?" Kristen stared at him.

He hadn't realized he'd been speaking aloud. "It's a genetically engineered virus that functions as a computer chip. You can build—" He stopped. Kristen's face reflected total bewilderment. "Never mind. So what are you doing with this—computer?"

"I was thinking about looking at Skipper's files. You know,

I told you I hadn't been here since he died. He was working on a project. Looking at the genetics of empathy. Trying to find out if there is a gene that carries empathy."

A gene. A link. A strange hope began to build in his breast. What if her brother was right? What if Rider had stumbled across a way to accomplish his mission without having to kill her? He quelled the traitorous thoughts that rose like the bile in his throat. "Let's look at it."

Kristen shrugged. "I've never been in Skip's computer, and he was always a little paranoid. He had a conspiracy theory about everything. He even thought our parents' deaths weren't accidental. I may not be able to access it." She flipped a switch on the side of the putty-colored box. A harsh grinding and buzzing began.

"What's wrong with it?" Rider asked, eyeing the box. Something was definitely familiar about it, although by the twenty-sixth century every person had a comlink, a tiny voice-activated device implanted in the ear. The idea of having to enter commands with your fingers was unheard of in his time. So why was it familiar to him? And why did it trigger disturbing snatches of memories he couldn't capture and couldn't stop?

"Nothing's wrong with it. It's just booting up."

"Sure is slow." He watched her as they waited for the antiquated contraption to power up.

Her profile was so perfect, so delicate, that it made his heart hurt. She was so beautiful. He swallowed against a faint sickness as his gaze devoured the curve of her neck, the slight upward tilt of her chin, her delicately rounded lips, the short straight nose.

Damn. He was almost beginning to feel human again. Very sick, and major confused, but human.

ELEVEN

Rider's attention was caught by an array of colorful blocks and text windows that appeared on the computer screen. Kristen sucked air between her teeth as she maneuvered the cursor around the screen with a tiny ball embedded in a plastic base.

She clicked on several objects, but nothing happened. She sighed and clicked on another icon. The screen went black, except for a cursor in the upper lefthand corner.

"It dumped me to DOS," she muttered.

"What does that mean?"

"He dumped me out of Windows. He's got protection on all his applications."

"What can you do?"

"I don't know. Like I told you, Skipper thought everybody was out to get us, plus he loved games. He's probably got a password or something. I'll try this."

Rider watched as Kristen typed "HELP."

The computer began to buzz and several lines of text appeared.

"Well?"

"IF YOU NEED HELP, YOU DON'T NEED TO BE HERE. TRY A PASSWORD," she read. "That's what I figured. Come on, Skip, what'd you do?"

She tapped a fingernail lightly on the keys. Her brow furrowed in concentration.

"Password, password. I know this is silly, but I'll try." She typed SKIPPER.

Another line of text appeared. "GIVE ME A BREAK."

"Damn it Skipper. Don't play around," she muttered.

"Try your name."

She looked up at Rider, her brows raised.

He shrugged. "It's not as dumb as SKIPPER."

"Thank you very much." She turned back to the screen and typed KRISTEN. The computer buzzed again and a line of text appeared.

"NOW AT LEAST YOU'RE THINKING. HI, KRIS. IF IT'S YOU, THEN YOU SHOULDN'T NEED BUT MAYBE TWO MORE TRIES. HOWEVER, KNOWING HOW COMPUTER-LITERATE YOU ARE, I'LL GIVE YOU THREE."

Rider laughed and immediately noticed how stiff his face

was. How long had it been since he'd really laughed? "Didn't have much faith in your computer knowhow, did he?" he said, earning a glare from Kristen.

She pushed her chair back. "Look, Mister. Do you want to try it?"

"No way. Go right ahead. You've got three tries."

She pulled the chair back up to the desk and bit her lip, running her fingers through her short black hair. "Password. Three tries. Skipper, this is serious. Come on!"

Rider couldn't take his eyes off her. When she bit her lip, he yearned to be her teeth. His fingers twitched to be the ones running themselves through her silky hair. He had to force his brain to concentrate on the computer.

"Let's go, Doc. What means something to you and your brother that nobody else in the world would know?"

"Birthdays? Favorite color? How should I know? You don't understand. Skipper didn't think like other people. He was so smart—a genius." Her lips curved into a sweet smile of memory as her eyes glazed slightly.

Compassion twisted Rider's insides. "Come on, Doc. Think. Something between the two of you. Something he knew you'd know."

Her eyes focused on his face. Gold lights grew in the green depths. "Whale songs!"

He stared at her. "Whale songs?"

"Sure. You know, the beautiful calls of the whales to each other?"

Rider frowned. "Whales. The ancient sea creatures? I thought they were a myth."

She stared at him. "Oh, Rider. Are they gone? Oh, no." Her eyes filled with tears.

"What? What are you talking about?"

"The whales. Oh, Rider, they're so beautiful, and so intelligent. I've got to show you. I can't believe we let them die!"

"Doc! Worry about them later. Do you think whale songs is the password?"

"It's what Skipper always said my thoughts sounded like. See, I could sometimes figure out what he was thinking. It was almost like words inside me, but he said mine was more like a whale song. A pretty, melodic tune that he would have to try to figure out from the sound..." Her voice trailed off into memory.

Rider put his hand on her shoulder. He wasn't sure if it

was to stop her words that searched out the places inside him where the conditioning had buried his past, or to stop her painful memories. "Try it."

She roused herself and typed the words into the computer. It buzzed and put up a line of text.

"COME ON KRISSY. YOU'VE JUST ABOUT GOT IT. DON'T FORGET. WORDS MEAN NOTHING TO A COMPUTER."

"Damn it, Skip!" She clenched her fists. "What is it?"

"Words mean nothing. What does he mean by that?"

"Computers translate everything into binary. It's all numbers." She looked at him. "Don't you know anything about computers?"

He grimaced. "I'm a tank, remember. I don't know anything about anything. At least, I don't remember," he lied. The trouble was, he was beginning to remember more and more. Her manipulations of the ancient computer had triggered a chain reaction in his brain.

He remembered using an old-fashioned keyboard computer, sitting in a dusty office with pale sunlight streaking in through dirty windows. He remembered staring out the window, thinking about Mari. He shuddered, and clenched his jaw against the disturbing thoughts.

"I'm sorry," she said, wrenching his sore heart a little more.

He stared at her. She always knew when he was hurting. Rousing himself, he forced his thoughts back to the problem at hand. "What would WHALE SONGS be in binary?"

Her eyes lit up. "Let's see. W is the what—twenty-third letter in the alphabet. And in binary, 23 would be—damn it, Skipper. You know I hate binary!" She slammed a fist onto the desktop.

"Careful, Doc. Don't break the computer."

She glared at him. "Like I said, take over any time." She pulled a pad and a pencil from a drawer. "Let's see, twenty-three. Two times four is eight, two times eight is sixteen, two times sixteen is—no. It has to be sixteen." She counted on her fingers. "One, two, four, eight, sixteen. Fifth position. And twenty-three minus sixteen is seven, and seven is less than eight..."

She scribbled on the pad, muttering to herself, while Rider watched the top of her head. She ran her fingers through the mop of curly hair, mussing it and making his heart throb with her loveliness.

"That means there's a zero in the fourth..."

After dozens of scraps of precious paper were thrown in the trash, and the pencil had to be sharpened four times, she sat back and rubbed her eyes and flexed her shoulders. "I think that's it. You want to check the numbers?"

He shook his head. "Be my guest," he said.

Kristen typed the numbers carefully. The computer buzzed and whirred for a long time, then printed a screen full of text.

She read the text aloud.

"CONGRATULATIONS, KRISSY. I ALWAYS KNEW YOU HAD IT IN YOU. I KNOW THIS SOUNDS CLICHED, BUT IF YOU'RE READING THIS, THEN I'M PROBABLY DEAD." Her voice cracked, and she clapped a hand over her mouth. "Oh, God. Oh Skip..."

Rider watched her eyes brim with tears. He couldn't help her, couldn't make it any easier for her to know that her brother had known he was going to die. He touched her shoulder and finished reading the screen aloud.

"I'VE THOUGHT FOR A WHILE NOW THAT SOMEONE WAS TRYING TO KILL ME. IT SEEMED RIDICULOUS, SO I NEVER MENTIONED IT. I WAS AFRAID YOU'D READ IT IN MY MIND, SO I KEPT INVENTING PROBLEMS AT WORK TO KEEP AWAY FROM YOU.

"I DON'T KNOW WHAT REASON ANYONE COULD POSSIBLY HAVE TO KILL ME, BUT I'M PRETTY SURE IT HAS TO DO WITH MY RESEARCH.

"BE CAREFUL, KRISSY. I WISH YOU'D JUST CRASH THE COMPUTER NOW AND NOT READ ANY OF MY NOTES, BUT I KNOW YOU'RE TOO STUBBORN FOR THAT.

"BE CAREFUL. I'LL MISS—"

Rider glanced at her. Her eyes were glued to the screen. "'I'LL MISS OUR SONGS,'" he finished quietly. "I'm sorry, Doc."

She looked up at him, her eyes wet and bright. "I've been so alone since he died. Until..." She blinked, and the tears fell down her face.

Rider was afraid to ask what she meant. The thought twisted his gut and shot pain through his middle, but he couldn't stand not knowing. He had a dreadful notion her answer would change everything.

Her tear-stained face was open, naked, and he read the answer there. Read it, and wanted to lash out against the implications. "Until me? You're the one that's barking, Doc. There's no link between us."

He had to grit the words from between his teeth, the pain was so bad. Because he had the oddest sense that he was lying. He was afraid she was right. Deathly, sickeningly afraid. Afraid because he knew what she meant. He'd felt it, too, and not just since he'd made love to her.

From the first moment he'd touched her ankle, there in the street, he'd known. Through the pain, through the sickness, through the most incredible few minutes of his life when he was joined with her, he'd known.

But knowing didn't stop the agony. Knowing didn't kill the hatred that burned within him for Deviants. He tore his gaze from hers. The Deviants had destroyed his life. Hadn't they?

"Rider?"

He squeezed his eyes shut, shaking his head. Sweat trickled down his face.

"Rider? What's wrong?"

He gulped huge breaths of air and forced the strange thoughts out of his head. "Nothing. What now, Doc?" He nodded toward the computer.

"I don't know." She pulled her gaze away from his with an obvious effort, and stared at the screen. "What does he mean? Someone trying to kill him? He never said anything. Never told me anything! Skipper!"

Rider winced at the naked grief in her voice. "How did he die?" he asked, hating that he had to make her recall it.

Kristen shivered and went somewhere Rider couldn't follow. She sat quietly, lost in some nightmare memory of her own, until he began to worry, but then she spoke, her voice flat and soft.

"He thought he'd found something. He was staying at the lab until all hours of the day and night. He kept telling me how busy he was, wouldn't let me come over, wouldn't see me." She brushed tears out of her eyes and laughed shakily. "I thought he had a girlfriend, although I couldn't figure out why the big secret. I thought maybe she was married or something."

Suddenly, she roused herself and slammed her fists down on the table. "How could I have missed it? How did he shield his mind from me so well? How could I have not known he was afraid for his life? Oh, God, I should have known..." Her voice quit on a sob and she slammed her fists down on the table—again and again.

Rider pulled her up from the chair and held her against him. She lowered her head to his shoulder and kept talking, her voice muffled, her breath hot against his skin. Small waves of nausea fluttered across his brain, but he ignored them and cradled her skull in his hand, rocking her gently against his body.

"The lab exploded," she whispered, quivering against him. He could hear her teeth chattering, he could feel the tremors in her arms where she clutched at him. "It all went up in flames. Everybody said it was inevitable. The oldest building on campus. All the chemicals." She swallowed.

"There were four people inside. It was—really bad. A piece of his—foot. It was his shoe—" She stopped, choking, her fists pressed against his chest, her tears wetting his shirt. "The watch I gave him for graduation—it was just a lump of metal, but I could still see part of the engraving."

She lifted her head, and in that moment Rider would have sworn he was the telepath, so transparent were her thoughts and feelings to him.

"They were nice about it, so solicitous. But the bottom line was there was hardly enough to bury." The words wrenched from her throat were harsh, bitter.

Rider understood that she needed the bitter anger to keep from breaking. He didn't offer her any sympathy or platitudes. She didn't want them. He merely continued to rock her against him like a child.

"I knew when it happened," she went on, doggedly. "I mean the very instant. I was working late at the hospital, dictating charts."

Suddenly, it was as if she didn't want to be touched, to be comforted any more. She jerked away from him and sat back down at the computer, toying with the keyboard.

"He just..." she snapped her fingers, "disappeared. Just like that. All his essence, everything that had been inside me all my life, everything Skipper, was gone."

Rider sat perched on the desk watching her, aching with pity for her. She ran her fingers through her hair again, covered her face for a long moment, then wiped her eyes and looked up.

When she did, her eyes narrowed in suspicion. "What?"

"What?" he echoed, bewildered by her reaction.
"Why are you looking like that?"
"Like what?"
"Like you just realized the world was round or something?"
Rider stared at her. What had he been thinking? He stiffened as the subconscious thoughts coalesced in his brain. "The lab exploded," he muttered.
"Yes, what..." Kristen's face drained of color as her thoughts followed his.
He didn't want to do it, didn't want to show her what his brain had put together while she talked. He didn't want to add to her pain, but he had to. She needed to know. She had to understand just how real, how imminent the threat to her was. "The lab exploded, Doc, just like the clinic. Just like your apartment."
"No!" She clasped her hands on either side of her head, her fingers buried in her hair, as if she could squeeze out the truth if she pressed hard enough. "You're crazy."
"Yeah, maybe. Think about it, Doc."
"I don't want to—I can't—oh. Skip? Murdered?"
She stood and wrung her hands. "Why?" she shouted. "Why is this happening? Who's doing this to us?" She stood rigid in the middle of the floor, helpless, wringing her hands, fisting them, wanting to lash out but having nothing to lash out against.
He grabbed her hands, stopping her. Her anguish echoed inside him as he absorbed her struggles. He held her relentlessly, taking it, until she wore herself down, then he caught her as she crumpled.
Gathering her in, his hand cradling her head, he rocked her back and forth while the sobs shook her body like tiny earthquakes. With each sob, an answering aftershock echoed through him, bruising his heart, flooding him with more sensations than he thought anyone could bear in a lifetime, but he endured them, along with the dizzying nausea inside himself. It was nothing compared to her grief.
She began to mumble against his bare chest, her lips brushing the hairs and sending pulses of desire across his skin. "What did he do? He never hurt anybody. Why did they kill him? He was all I had."
He held her so tightly he thought she might burst. He hated them, hated himself for being one of them. "I don't know, Doc, I just don't know." He winced. The physical pain he had en-

dured in the TAINCC had been easier to bear than the pain of knowing he'd caused her anguish. They'd sent him to destroy her, and one way or another, it seemed that's exactly what he was doing.

"But I'm beginning to wonder the same thing. What did you do to deserve this?"

After a long time, he loosed his grip, touching her tear-stained face as she pulled away.

It was puffy and red as she studied him closely through narrowed eyes. "Rider, did you...?"

She believed he might have killed her brother. That hurt, but he couldn't blame her. He could have killed Skipper. If he'd been sent here to go after her brother, he'd have carried out that mission without blinking. It was her that made the difference.

"No," he said, looking her in the eye, standing under the weight of her mistrust. "No. This is my first trip to your fair city."

"So who did? You're saying some other psychopath from the future came back here two years ago and killed him?"

He didn't even wince at her words. As far as she knew he *was* a psychopath. He understood her reaction. "Yeah. And they obviously realized killing him didn't solve the problem. See the theory is if we came back to the past and eliminated the progenitor of the Deviants, they would all disappear."

Kristen shivered. "So if it had been Skip, then everyone in your time who was his descendant would just sort of dissolve?"

"That's the theory."

"That's disgusting!"

"Yeah. But it didn't happen. So it wasn't your brother."

"Or the theory's wrong."

He gave her an admiring glance. Had they ever thought of that, his brilliant 'employers' from five hundred years away? "That's a possibility, I guess. But it looks like they're not taking any chances. Because they sent me to kill you."

"Why? You've never told me why!"

He shrugged. "Because you're the Mother of all the Deviants." It was getting easier to say the words. It was beginning to sound ridiculous, to think that this lovely, innocent woman with her vulnerable lower lip and golden eyes could possibly be such a heinous criminal.

"Why are they so afraid of me?"

"Because they... Because it's..." Rider wanted to explain how revolting it was to think someone else could read your mind. He wanted to tell her that the Deviants were violent sociopaths who would stoop to anything, even murder, to gain their ends, but he couldn't. He couldn't explain how much he hated the Deviants when he was beginning to feel something very far from hate for this woman who'd supposedly spawned them.

He spread his hands. "I don't know," he said slowly. "I don't know why they're so afraid of you." She was just one girl, hardly even a woman yet. She'd been a virgin. That still rocked his foundations.

"But you say the Deviants killed your wife."

He glared at her, trying to stop the churning thoughts in his brain, thoughts that whirled through so fast he couldn't comprehend them. But like a vid on triple fast forward, occasional glimpses coalesced.

Mari, her brow creased in concentration as she pulled off the headphones and gazed at him, saying, "It's here. They're coming here."

The room awash with green light as a blast caught her, throwing her body backwards, away from him.

He clenched his fists, willing the distressing memories to go away.

"Well, did they?"

He stared at her, incapable of speech as all the assurance the TAINCC had fed him dissolved, leaving him naked and raw, and horribly confused.

The cat turning into a pile of charred flesh on the floor.

"You're not sure, are you?" she persisted.

He growled and held his head between his hands.

The heat of the blaster, still burning on her skin.

"Shut up! Just shut up, why can't you?" he shouted, buffeted by the truth. She was right. He wasn't sure. The memories were too convoluted, the images too confusing, like double-exposed film. He couldn't sort them out.

"You can't kill me."

He shook his head, pain ripping through his gut.

"So what happens now?"

He rubbed his face with trembling hands and tried to force himself to think calmly. "I suppose they could think killing you didn't work, either. As far as I know, they can't look back here and see what's happening."

"Then who's after us? And how do they keep finding us?" She had wrapped her arms around herself, hugging herself with all her might. He saw tendons standing out in her arms and neck.

He stared at her, thinking about the BeeDee, the blaster. "They can send metal back, and they've perfected the most dangerous explosive ever invented."

"Are you sure they can't watch what you're doing?"

He shrugged. No, he wasn't sure at all. He wasn't sure of anything any more. "I'd think they would have told me."

A knock sounded on the front door. Rider jumped, then put one hand on Kristen's shoulder. "Who is that?"

"How should I know?"

He tightened his grip. "Are you sure you didn't tell your friend there on the—whatever it is—where you are?"

"No. You heard me, didn't you? I told her I wouldn't tell her. I told her to call off the police."

"Then who is this?"

The knock came again, more insistently this time, and a voice called out. "Hello? Electric company. Hello. We need to check some wiring."

Kristen grabbed Rider's arm. "It's the electric company," she whispered desperately.

Rider couldn't figure out what the problem was. He looked at the door, then back at her. "Yeah? Well, then, if we don't answer the door, they'll go away, right?"

"No, you don't understand." Her fingers were digging into the flesh of his arm. "It's like the little woman said. They never knock, they just read the meter and leave."

"You're not making any sense." He shot her a glance, wondering if she had snapped from the strain. Her eyes were wide as mini-disks, and her voice was quivering.

"I know." She sounded triumphant. "That's the point."

"Doc, sometimes I think you're the one who's barking."

"Hello? Is anyone home? Open up." The knocks sounded more violent.

"I'll try to explain it sometime. Right now we've got to get out of here," she whispered urgently, closing and locking the computer and zipping the belt pack, which she buckled around her waist. "Come on."

"Fine," he said, shaking his head. He had no idea what she

was talking about, but he could feel the urgency in her when she touched him, and somehow, he was beginning to trust the peculiar feelings he occasionally gleaned from her.

He pushed her through the house to the back door.

"What if there are more than one?" she whispered.

"More than one electric company person? Then we're in big trouble. We'll just have to chance it." He grinned at her.

"Rider, please..."

They slipped out the door. "Is there a way out of this jungle?" he muttered, looking at the two-year growth of grass, weeds, and untrimmed flowers and shrubs.

"There used to be a hole in the fence back here," Kristen breathed. "Skip was going to fix it because the neighbor's dog kept getting into his yard and digging up his flowers."

As they pushed their way through the underbrush, crawling under shrubs, Rider heard a crash behind them. He pushed Kristen ahead of him and turned in time to see a man dressed in a blue uniform with a cap that read "Cable Electric" raise a silver weapon.

"Dive!" he shouted, whirled and plunged into the waist-high brush as the unmistakable whir of a blaster sounded, and a green ribbon of heat whizzed by his head. "Doc!" he whispered. "Stay down. Where are you?"

"Here," she said, very close to him.

He reached through weeds and touched her leg, his hand trembling with relief. "Let's get out of here!"

"Here's the break in the fence." Her voice was ragged, as if she'd been running. He knew how she felt. He was terrified, too.

Another whir and a wisp of smoke beside him told him the man was still shooting. Rider had to admire him for not diving into the undergrowth with them. He was smart enough to wait until they gave their position away, then calmly shoot them.

Rider lost his hold on Kristen's leg as she slithered under the fence. He knew the shrubbery was undulating above their heads, and he heard her tee shirt tear as she pushed under the wire. Good, she was through, he thought as he heard the man moving carefully closer to them.

He cringed, expecting a blaster burn any second, but their pursuer must be holding his fire for a good shot. He found the fence and probed beneath it. He wasn't sure there was enough room for his larger body to crawl underneath. As he pushed against the wire, trying to fold it up, he had a grisly vision of himself caught under it, smoking holes burned into his torso. But at least Kristen was free. He almost chuckled at the irony of that thought.

"Rider, hurry!"

Damn. "Run, Doc! Get the hell out of here." Why hadn't she taken off?

He pushed his way under the sharp wires. Metal scraped his bare skin and caught on the sweat pants as he forced his body through the tiny opening.

Kristen's hands were under his arms, pulling. "Damn it, Doc, I told you to run!" he grated as fire brushed his ankle and he smelled burning flesh and rubber.

Then, miraculously he was free, and he scrambled to his feet and grabbed her arm. The only trouble was, on the other side of the fence was a lovely, manicured lawn that appeared to stretch for miles with no chance for cover.

Rider dropped to his knees again, pulling Kristen with him, flattening himself against the fence.

"Rider! Come on! He's got a blaster!"

He put his hand over her mouth. "Shut up! Wait!"

She gripped his biceps hard, and he let her. He was beginning to understand that she needed to touch him to reassure herself that he was rational, that he had a reason for what he was doing.

Now if only the man was alone. Rider glanced up. The fence was at least eight feet high. He wondered if their pursuer would expose himself by climbing over the top.

TWELVE

Rider waited, his breath harsh in his throat, his back stinging from scratches, his ankle burning like liquid fire. He closed his eyes, willing himself to be calm, to think coolly, rationally. He searched within for the calm resolve of the TAINCC.

Sure enough, he heard their attacker scrambling under the fence. In the one quick glance he'd had, Rider had seen that the man outweighed him by at least thirty pounds. If so, he'd have a hell of a time crawling through that little hole. And with a little luck . . .

Rider patted Kristen's hand, then gently removed it from his arm. When she touched him, she distracted him, and he was going to need all his wits and both arms to take care of their attacker.

Without moving, he turned his head toward the hole. A blue-clad arm pushed through the dirt and underbrush—a blue-clad arm clutching a bright silver blaster.

Relief washed through Rider. The guy was pretty dumb. They'd scraped the bottom of the criminal barrel for him. Rider would have thought they'd have found a better source for their experiments by now.

When the other hand pushed through and Rider was sure the man was relatively defenseless, he reached over and plucked the weapon from his grasp, then grabbed his wrist.

"You should have chosen lethal implantation, bud," he muttered as he gave a sharp twist to the man's wrist, eliciting a choked cry as the bones snapped. Then he stood and kicked the wire fence, pushing the sharp edges into the flesh of the man's back. "That should keep you busy for a while. I'd hate to try to dig out of there with a broken wrist."

"Here, Doc. Stick this in your jeans." He pushed the blaster at Kristen just as a man emerged from the house.

"Hey! What's going on over there? Get out of my yard!"

Rider urged Kristen toward an open gate on the other side of the yard. He waved at the man, then pointed back to the fence that imprisoned their pursuer. "You should get your fence fixed," he called. "Somebody might sue you for injuries."

They ran for blocks, drawing curious glances. Kristen's tee shirt was almost ripped through in the back and floated enticingly on the breeze as she ran. The blaster made a strange bulge in her tight jeans. Her face and arms and clothes were filthy, and she had grass and leaves stuck in her hair.

Rider knew he looked worse. He didn't even have on a shirt, and his back was probably a plowed field of bloody scratches from the fence. He felt them burning, felt the blood trickling down. His sweatpants drooped low on his hips, weighted down by dirt and sweat.

"Where to now, Doc?" he huffed.

She was breathing hard, running beside him, her small strides hardly able to keep up with his. "I... don't... know... " she wheezed.

Suddenly, she stopped, and Rider stumbled to a halt beside her.

"The... hospital," she said between huge gulps of air.

"Are we back to that again?"

"No... I mean... it's probably the safest place... to be."

Rider pulled her into a side street, away from curious glances. "What are you talking about?"

Kristen wiped her face with dirty hands, succeeding in smearing dirt and grass stains over her cheeks. She looked more like an angel than ever, with her wide gold/green eyes shining out of her dirty face. She was beautiful.

Kristen took a couple of huge breaths, holding her side, then spoke breathlessly. "It's Saturday, I think... The hospital will be practically deserted." She looked at him. "We're a mess, but I think I have an idea how we can get inside."

Rider studied her. The hospital. His conditioning caused his brain to rebel at the thought of a hospital.

Don't let them get you into a hospital. Don't let them examine you. They'll know you're not one of them. He shook his head.

"Okay," he said, fighting the qualms his decision brought. "I can't think of anything better. Which way?"

Kristen breathed a sigh of relief. He was going to trust her. She didn't know what she'd have done if he didn't. She was out of ideas.

"It's not far. Back toward downtown," she panted, holding her side where a pain had attached itself and wouldn't let go. She tried to concentrate on getting someplace safe. She needed time to assimilate all that had happened to them.

She'd had buildings blown out from under her. She'd been shot at with a weapon that wouldn't be invented for who knew how many years. She'd crawled through a hole like a soldier in enemy territory, been chased and pursued like a fugitive, found out her brother had been murdered. And she had fallen in love with a man who hadn't been born yet.

It didn't bear thinking on.

She led Rider down side streets and through alleys until they came to the back of the big hospital, where garbage bins sat on either side of monstrous loading docks.

Kristen pulled Rider behind a bin and collapsed. He sat down heavily beside her. When she could breathe without searing pains in her chest, she looked at him. He was shivering with cold and fatigue, and his back was a maze of cuts and scratches.

"Oh, look at you." She touched a raw place on his shoulder, and almost cried when he winced. "You're bleeding. " His back looked like someone had beaten him. It was streaked with blood. Welts and scratches puffed up like insect bites. "You need a tetanus shot. And there's no telling how much blood you've lost."

"I can make more," he breathed.

"Not if you don't get some rest and food." She put her head back against the garbage bin and panted. The fetid stench of rotting food sat on the air like fog. It nauseated her. She peered at Rider who was breathing shallowly and clutching his ribs. Was the nausea her own, or did it come from him? She wiped her face with her forearm and took a deep breath, trying to ignore the smell.

"Rider," she said, swallowing against the sickness, "how do they keep finding us? Are you sure they have no way of tracing you?"

"There's no communication after transfer," he said in a singsong voice, as if he were reciting from rote. "No communication, and no return."

His voice had an uncertain note in it, though, and Kristen searched his face. She knew that tone. It was the tone he used when he recited information that had been fed to him in the conditioning chamber. From what she'd seen, most of that information was false. What else about his mission was false, fed to him like brainwashing, to make him into a zombie for their purposes?

"You're not sure, are you?" she whispered.

He looked at her, pain and doubt filling his eyes. He grimaced, baring his teeth, then took a deep breath. "I'm supposed to be sure. They intended for me to be sure—but no, I'm not." He clutched his middle as pain seared through him. "But if they can be sending people back from farther in the future than me, then anything's possible. Maybe it's even possible that the conditioning's wearing off."

The note of wistful hope in his voice made Kristen want to cry. She laid her hand on his arm, and winced at his pain. "I'm glad. I'm so glad. Just go with it. Don't try to fight it, try to conquer it from the inside."

He nodded. "I've been thinking about how they keep finding us. It can't be luck, and that bastard back there at Skipper's house was no genius. There's got to be something."

"Like a bug."

"A what?"

"A bug. You know, some sort of tracking device. Like in James Bond movies?"

Rider just stared at her.

She sighed in frustration. "Sorry. I guess you don't know about James Bond."

"No wait!" He put his hand out. "Wait a minute. A tracking device..." His eyes glazed and shifted a little to the left of her head and the furrows between his brows grew deeper. "They couldn't have planted it on you, so it must be on me." He stood. "You've got to find it, Doc."

Kristen tugged on his hand, her heart pounding. "Get down. Somebody might see you. What are you talking about?"

"Get up. You've got to help me find it."

She shook her head. "Find what? I don't understand."

Rider glared at her. "It's just like you said, Doc. Something, some kind of device. Look for something tiny, something unusual."

"Rider!" She tugged on his arm again. "Please, get down. Tell me what you're talking about."

He sank down into a crouch. "They have to have planted something on me somewhere. Something foreign."

"Something tiny—something foreign." Kristen thought of the tiny speck in the back of his eye. That had to be it. Whatever it was, a camera, a recorder, just a bug to track them, that was it! The tiny object in his eye.

"Rider, your eye! It's your eye!"

"What? My eye?" He stared blankly at her for a few seconds, then grabbed her shoulders and hugged her. "That's it!

You're a genius! Of course. That's what they were afraid you'd find. Way to go, Doc!" He was still hugging her when it hit him, the conditioned reaction to unwelcome emotion. He choked and coughed.

"God, it's cold," he croaked, and doubled over, arms wrapped around his middle.

Kristen put her arms around him, feeling ridiculously small against his bulk, doing her best to hold him, to shield him. Under her hands, his muscles jerked, and she could feel how sick he was. For the first time, she tried to picture the nameless, faceless beings who were chasing them. The people he said were from the future, like him. The people who wanted to kill her.

Hatred and fury boiled within her, alien emotions. She'd never hated anybody before. But crouched here behind the garbage bins with this man who said he had come to kill her and who had done nothing but protect her since they'd met, she burned with loathing for people who could strip a man of his life, of everything good—who would destroy everything that was important to a human being for their own ends.

"Doc, you said—the hospital is—safe?" Every word he spoke was like a separate agony for him. Kristen wanted to cry at the hopeless pain in his voice. If only there were something she could do to stop these debilitating reactions to his fight against his conditioning.

"Safe as houses," she said, then snorted. "Safer. Come on." She tugged on his arm and prepared to rise.

He had leaned his head back against the bin, and his chest heaved. His hair was plastered wetly to his head, and his face was screwed up in a grimace against the foul odor that permeated the air. "No."

His flat tone frightened her. It was the tone of someone who had made up his mind, someone who would brook no argument. "What do you mean, no?"

"No."

"Talk to me, Rider," she begged. "Don't revert to monosyllabic mulishness on me. They're going to be after us if that's really a camera in your eye."

"Right. Now get out of here."

Suddenly she realized what he was doing. He was trying to be *heroic*, for God's sake! Well, she wasn't having it. "No."

Rider squinted at her. "No?"

"No." Kristen pulled on his arm, trying in vain to force him to move. "I'm not budging without you."

He wrapped his hands around her neck, pulling her face up close to his. "Listen to me, Doc. That damned speck has to be a camera of some sort. They're seeing everything I see. They may even be hearing every word we say. Look at my eye. You're looking right at them. And they're looking at you."

She cringed at the idea that she was staring into some sort of camera lens, and that whoever was behind that lens had seen her naked through Rider's eye. She looked away.

"Look at me! If I go with you, they'll find you." He winced and took a sharp breath.

Kristen felt the pain, too, through his hands, although it wasn't nearly as sharp as the fear of being separated from him. "I'm not leaving you."

"For God's sake, why not?" he growled, his fingers tightening, pulling her sweat-dampened hair.

She absorbed his desperation and fear, and realized that the reason she wouldn't leave was the very reason he was so determined for her to.

This uneasy alliance they had formed, this balance of trust and distrust, was fast turning into something else.

Not wanting to find out if she was wrong, but unable to tear her gaze from his, she answered him, carefully watching his face. "Because I think I would die if I lost you."

Her eyes misted over with tears, but she still saw the shock and fear that clouded his, and she felt the hope that welled in him as if it were her own. Maybe it was.

Now she knew what he had meant when he'd said how frightening hope could be.

"Don't do this, Doc." He dropped his hands, leaving her empty and alone. She wasn't sure she could live without his touch, without those feelings which were now as much a part of her as her own. "If I can't save you, at least I can keep them from you for a while."

"We're wasting time, Rider. It's your decision. Are we staying here, in this lovely little cubbyhole, or are we opting for inside?"

He glared at her, and she glared right back. There was no way she was leaving without him. She lifted her chin, and his mouth quirked in a smile.

"Damn, you're stubborn," he said, moving gingerly to sit upright. "Tell you what, Doc. Let's do a little surgery."

"Surgery?" For a moment, Kristen was disoriented, as if she'd walked into the middle of a movie. "You mean... no!" She couldn't believe what he was suggesting.

"No." She shook her head vehemently. "That's impossible. I've only done the most basic eye surgery as a resident. What if I blind you?"

"Let me see." He held out both hands. "Lose an eye." He looked at his right hand. "Watch you die." He looked at his left hand.

Then he looked at her and shrugged. "No contest, Doc," he grunted as pain darkened his face.

She stared at him, weighing the consequences and realizing he was right. Operate on his eye and take a chance, even if it was a slim one, of escaping with their lives, or refuse to do it and condemn them both to certain death. "No contest," she agreed, and drew a long breath. "Let's go then.

"Fine with me," Rider said through clenched teeth. "I can't say I like the ambiance here."

Kristen rose to a crouch and peered around.

"Wait a minute, Doc."

She half-twisted back toward him.

"If we're right, and this is a camera, we're leading them right to us."

She looked at his eye, imagining the tiny whirring camera imbedded on the back wall of the retina. "So close your eye," she said.

He glared at her, disgusted. "Thank you, Einstein."

She shrugged.

"What next?" he asked.

She wished she knew. He had saved them—how many times? She'd lost count. Now it looked like it was her turn. What could she do? She couldn't go waltzing into the front entrance of the hospital. Well, maybe she could if she was cleaned up, but she'd never get past the security guard looking like a prison escapee.

Her eyes lit on a familiar color and shape. "See those yellow bins over there? That's contaminated waste. Some of it's pretty gross, but sometimes they just throw away scrub suits they use when working with radiation patients, or cancer patients who've been on chemotherapy."

"Yeah?" Rider sounded skeptical. "I don't think I like the idea of radiation."

"Don't worry. It's usually low dose. Besides, doctors and medical technicians work around it all the time. We can use their dirty clothes for a few minutes without any problems."

Rider shrugged, his face pale and sweaty. "Let's just get going."

"I'm going to find us some relatively clean scrubs, so we can get into the hospital without being noticed."

"What about the dirt?"

Kristen looked around. "There's a hose over there they use to wash down the trucks. We'll wash first. Look out!"

She pulled him back behind the bin as a housekeeping aid rolled a stretcher out onto the loading dock, then turned around and went back inside.

"I don't believe it! What luck!"

"What?" Rider said, his teeth chattering against each other. "What luck?"

"I'll show you. First we've got to get washed."

Kristen turned on the water and washed carefully, trying to keep her jeans from getting soaked. She brushed at them, getting the worst of the dirt off. Then she helped Rider wash his face and hands. By the time they finished, he was shaking as if with ague.

Kristen pushed him back behind the garbage bin. "Stay here. I'll get us some clothes."

She pushed open the top to the contaminated waste bin and gingerly moved some yellow trash bags. There! A lab coat. She pulled it out. It was wrinkled and had an orange stain on the front. Probably chemotherapy. It wouldn't be a problem if she took it off as soon as they were inside.

She searched some more until she found a sheet. She shook it out carefully, but couldn't see anything obviously wrong with it. She hurried back to Rider. "Come on. I'm the doctor and you're my patient. Get up on that stretcher."

"I don't think I like the casting of this little drama, Doc. Why can't I be the doctor and you be my patient?"

Kristen caught a faint leer in his tired gaze. She shot him an incredulous look. "Let's see. I know the hospital. I know the staff. I know where we're going. I don't have a camera in my eye."

"Okay, okay," he said grumpily. "I hate it when you're right, Doc."

"Thank you. Now, let's go. That housekeeping person might

be back any minute."

Rider reluctantly climbed up onto the stretcher, and Kristen spread the sheet over him.

"Now, act dead."

"Shit!" He pushed the sheet out of his face and glared at her.

"I'm serious," she said, laughing. If the situation weren't so bizarre and frightening, it would be ludicrous.

Rider fidgeted.

"Rider, dead people don't fidget. Now stop it!" She started to pull the sheet back over his head, but stopped at the expression on his face. "What?"

"You're a knockout when you laugh, Doc. You should do it more often." He grinned at her and winked, reminding her of the camera.

She patted his cheek then pulled the sheet over his head. "Now close your eyes and be a good little corpse," she hissed.

She rolled the stretcher in through the rear doors of the hospital, past the incinerator and down the hall toward the building management offices. She couldn't do anything about the odor of garbage that clung to them, but she checked to be sure her lab coat was buttoned up all the way, covering the filthy, torn tee shirt. Just in time, too, because two young men in the green uniforms of building management employees walked by, gesturing to each other and laughing quietly. They barely gave Rider and her a glance.

Kristen's body trembled in relief. If they hadn't been so busy talking, they might have noticed the decidedly unkempt appearance and wet hair of the doctor wheeling the stretcher. Or the fact that the two of them were coming in through the loading dock instead of the emergency room.

Kristen turned Rider's stretcher toward the freight elevators, checking both ends of the hall. She lifted the sheet off his face and grinned down at him. "Coast is clear so far. How you doing?"

"Dead is hard to play," he grumbled, keeping his right eye shut.

"You're doing great. We're almost to the elevators."

"Where are we going?"

"Shhh!" she hissed, dropping the edge of the sheet back into place as an orderly whisked past them pushing an empty wheelchair in front of him.

"Hey, Doc," the orderly shouted as he scooted past. "Got a live one there?"

Kristen glanced at him, noticing the velvet blackness of his eyes. She smiled nervously. "Well, you know how it is," she commented but he had already careened around the corner.

"I thought you said this place would be deserted," Rider hissed.

"Rider, shut up! It is. During the week this floor is teeming with people." She pushed the "down" button and sighed as the doors opened immediately. She pushed the stretcher in and punched B.

Rider sat up.

"Stop it! You can't do that!" she cried. "Lie down!" She tugged on his shoulders, trying to pull him back down to the stretcher.

"I'm burning up under here, Doc. Where are we going?" He peered at the buttons. "What's—"

She shot out a hand and covered his mouth. She smiled sweetly. "Little pitchers have big ears," she said.

"What the hell does that mean?"

"My nanny said it. I think it means people are listening."

"Oh, yeah," Rider said.

"Oh yeah is right. Now lie down! And close your eye!"

The bell rang, and the doors began to open, so Rider lay back down and let her cover him again. She pushed the stretcher out into the dark corridor, peering around, but it appeared to be deserted.

"So far, so good," she whispered. "Our only problem down here will be the pharmacy and surgical intensive care. Everything else is deserted on Saturday."

"Where are we going?"

"Where do you think? I'm taking your advice." Kristen wheeled the stretcher past the pharmacy window and down the hall. She would have to go in to the surgical suites through the recovery room, since the main doors were right across from the intensive care unit and the family waiting room. She prayed there were no emergency procedures going on.

As she passed the back door to the pharmacy, two pharmacists came out, griping about having to work the weekend. They nodded at Kristen and dropped a passing glance to the sheet-covered form on the stretcher. She nodded back, hoping they wouldn't stop to consider why anyone would be wheeling a dead body *into* the recovery room.

At the automatic doors that opened into Recovery, Kristen paused.

"Rider, are you sure you want to do this?" she whispered. The more she thought about it, the more frightened she got. "I've only handled a laser scalpel one time for a cataract removal." Without waiting for a reply, she wheeled him in through the sliding doors.

"Okay," she said, pulling the sheet off his face. "You can breathe now."

"Thanks," he said wryly. "Where are we?" He sat up gingerly, rubbing his face.

She put her fingers to her lips as she pushed the stretcher through to another set of doors. The rooms beyond the glass doors were dark. She pressed the button on the wall, and they entered the main surgical suite.

There was a noticeable lack of odor in the room, as if the air was conditioned so rapidly and thoroughly nothing was allowed to linger, even cologne or the scent of mouthwash.

Kristen rolled the stretcher up close to an exam table, and Rider slid over, shivering.

"Shit, Doc. These tables are cold."

"I know, I'm sorry. Usually they heat them, but we don't have time for that."

"Yeah, you're right." He sat on the table, enduring the cold of the steel seeping through the thin, wet cotton of his sweat pants. "What now? Where's the equipment?"

"I don't know, okay?"

His angel-doctor was nervous. He reached out and pulled her to him. "Hey, Doc. It's all right. We're going to make it. It'll be fine. Now, can I do something?"

He held her hands, knowing how she depended on her empathic sense to keep her in touch with the world. He drew them to his mouth and kissed the scraped knuckles and the gauze-covered blisters, noticing that the faint discomfort in his gut was a mere echo of his earlier pain.

Kristen leaned over and touched his lips with hers, then shrugged and extricated her hands from his. "Let me see what I can find," she said.

He watched her as she poked around in the huge, sterile room. She stepped into several side rooms and out again, looking more and more discouraged by the minute.

"I don't think they do the eye surgery in a different place," she said uncertainly. "But I can't figure out where the equipment is. Unless . . . "

Flashing a smile at him, she darted off through another set of double doors. Rider sat still for a couple of minutes, but he wasn't about to let himself lose sight of her. So he vaulted up from the table just as she pushed open the doors and rolled in a heavy piece of equipment.

She rolled it over and plugged it into a floor outlet. Immediately a row of lights came on, and something began buzzing insistently.

"Now lie back," she said. "I've got to anesthetize your eye."

He lay down. When Kristen began to pull velcro straps across his arms, he grabbed her wrists. "What the hell do you think you're doing?" She stood there, held in his brutal grip, until he felt foolish and let her go.

"I'm probably going to screw this up anyway, Rider. If you move, I could kill you."

"Shit. And I thought I was having a bad day yesterday." He endured the indignity and panic of having his arms and legs and chest strapped down to the table, but when she pulled a chin and forehead strap across, he growled at her.

"Rider," she pleaded.

"No! I can do it, but you're not going to strap my head down. I'll stay still, I swear." He glared at her until she relented. "They strapped us down. Everywhere—arms, legs, torso, head." He shuddered. "You don't know what it's like. I lay there for hours. I couldn't even move my head, couldn't see—"

His voice gave out, and he had to stop. The memories didn't stop, though. He'd lain there, imprisoned, barely able to swallow, while the leads attached to his temples, his eyelids, his jugular, all his pulse points, fed him information he didn't want, flashed disturbing images across his vision that he couldn't blot out, even with his eyes closed.

They'd made him into someone he wasn't, someone he hadn't wanted to be, and he wasn't sure if he could ever get back to the person he had been before. He wasn't even sure that person was still inside him.

Rider's thoughts slammed up against the wall of that idea. If he had volunteered, why did he hate it so much? Why did he hate the TAINCC if it was helping him avenge his wife?

There were too many questions. Too many mysteries, not the least of which was why he was protecting the very person he'd wanted to kill. His angel doctor. He stared up at her.

She nodded. "Okay," she said softly. "You win. Here goes."

Kristen opened the cabinet on the front of the cart, searching for the anesthetic. There it was, a four percent cocaine solution in a dropper bottle.

"Rider, when I told you I haven't done much of this, I wasn't exaggerating." Kristen knew just how accurate her words were. If anything, she was underplaying the gravity of the situation. On the one hand she understood that if she couldn't do something about the device in his eye, they were doomed. But she had only had that one experience with the laser scalpel, and that was under the supervision of the Chief of Ophthalmology. And she hadn't known that patient. He hadn't been the man she was beginning to love more than life.

"Doc, let's just get on with it. I'm hungry."

Despite her worry, she smiled at him. "You're incorrigible," she said. "Now, I'm going to put something in your eye to anesthetize it. I'd like to put you to sleep, but I don't think we dare chance it." She dropped several drops of cocaine solution into his eye.

His breath hissed between his teeth, and he blinked rapidly. "Shit, Doc. Warn me next time. That stuff stings."

THIRTEEN

The irony of Rider's reaction amazed Kristen. He had endured bruised ribs, blinding nausea, metal digging into the skin of his back, all without complaint. But he griped about a little sting.

She turned to the machine that buzzed behind her and gazed at the electronic display. The laser probe was heavy in her hand. She hefted it, allowing her hand to familiarize itself with its shape and weight. If she held it like a pencil, her forefinger rested on its hair-trigger switch.

Pointing it at the floor she pressed the tiny button. A beam of red light sprang from the tip of the probe, a beam so tiny, so sharp, it was hard to see. She let up on the button and the beam disappeared, but a tiny curl of smoke rose from the floor.

Fear clutched at her diaphragm like the pain of Rider's bruised ribs. She depressed the button several times, getting the feel of the instrument, watching the pattern of laser burns on the floor tiles.

"Doc, what are you doing?" Rider turned his head, straining to see. She heard the edge of panic in his voice—she couldn't delay much longer.

"Practicing," she said, trying to make her voice light.

"Yeah? Well, from the smell of burning plastic, I'd say you're either doing real well or real bad." He relaxed his head and closed his eyes. "Any time, Doc. Any time at all."

Kristen walked around to the head of the stretcher, gazing at Rider's upside down face. "Okay. Is your eye numb?"

He nodded.

"No more head movements, Rider. You say you can keep still. This is it. If you move, I could put your eye out..." Or sear your brain. Her heart lurched at the thought.

For a minute, Kristen stood with her eyes closed. There was a place inside her where she kept the detached professionalism that allowed her to be a good doctor, if she could dredge it up. If she couldn't find it, then they were as good as dead.

Breathing deeply, she willed the tension in her body to flow away, leaving in its place a calm assurance.

She pulled a surgical lamp down close to Rider's head and turned it on. To his credit, he didn't move, although he blinked.

"Stare at the light, Rider. Stare hard, and don't move, please." Relieved, she heard her doctor's voice coming from her throat. Maybe she could do this.

"Doc..."

"What is it?"

"Promise me something."

She sighed. *Don't distract me, Rider,* she begged silently. *Don't say anything that will make me cry.*

"Let's get out of here when we're done. Hospitals make me nervous."

"But it's the safest—" Kristen stopped. Something in his face made her remember his worry about the camera having a microphone. Even if they stayed in the hospital, it wouldn't hurt to make whoever was listening on the other end think they planned to leave. "Let's do. This place is making me very nervous, too. Now shut up and don't move."

The laser probe was cold and hard in her hand as she adjusted the light and positioned it over Rider's pupil. She could just make out the minuscule black speck close to the retinal wall.

She placed a hand on his jaw, marveling at the strength, the tension there. "Okay," she whispered. "Here goes." Carefully, she depressed the button and let go.

It was over in less than a heartbeat.

Rider's breath hissed out like a steam kettle.

"It's done." She hadn't moved and neither had he, but when she uttered those words, his body collapsed like a dropped marionette.

"Rider?" She tightened her grip on his jaw. "Rider!" He was limp. He had passed out.

"I'm so sorry I had to hurt you," she whispered, checking his pulse. It was strong and steady, thank God.

Then she coaxed up the doctor's assurance once more and examined his eye with a narrow magnifying light. The little cube of black that had been attached to the retinal wall was now a misshapen lump. Kristen could see blood welling on the mucous membrane, and she hoped to God she hadn't blinded him, but at least the camera was destroyed.

His eye was turning red, probably from the cocaine as much as from the trauma, so she placed a thin line of antibiotic ointment under the lid and put a bandage over it.

She straightened up and looked at him. His mouth had relaxed, and his jaw was no longer clenched tightly. He looked so helpless and lost, lying there unconscious.

Suddenly, a violent shivering racked her body. Delayed reaction, she diagnosed. She didn't care if she trembled enough to shake the foundations of the hospital now, because now it was over. She had done it! She had melted the tiny square device with its reflective lens into a dull, shapeless lump. Maybe they'd have a chance now. She wrapped her arms around herself and waited for the reaction to pass.

Rider choked and coughed, and Kristen roused herself, quickly and deftly turning him onto his side. He heaved dryly, though, and she realized he didn't have any food in his stomach to lose.

She kissed his pale cheek then spread a sheet over him and rolled the exam table out the door. She prayed no one would see them.

As she pushed the table off the elevator and turned toward the end of the hall where the morgue was located, the orderly who had spoken to them earlier sauntered by. Kristen eyed him, then glanced down the deserted hall, wondering where he had appeared from.

The boy nodded and grinned. "See you've still got that live one. Good thing for you. Where you're headed will be quiet this weekend." He leaned toward her and whispered conspiratorially. "Nobody will die this weekend. Nobody at all."

Kristen stared into the black holes of his eyes, familiarity crawling up her spine like a spider. "Who are you?" she whispered. Up close, she wasn't even sure if it was a boy or a girl.

"Just a bit of a gross prophet," the kid said, and grinned as he saluted her.

She turned and watched as his white uniform disappeared around the corner, then continued on toward the morgue.

"So far so good," she muttered under her breath, then laughed a little hysterically. "You really ought to work on a new line, Doc," she said to herself. "You've used that one quite enough."

Great. Now she was talking to herself. It was probably the idea of being in the subbasement. She hated it down here. It smelled of formaldehyde and dirt. Part of the area under the basement was finished, but part was still just pylons and dirt. The pipe space, Engineering called it. Kristen always felt claustrophobic down here.

Right now though, she was thankful for the deep, dark quiet of this area underneath the basement of the hospital. It was just the place they needed to hide and rest. They'd be safe for a while, if they weren't discovered.

Kristen stopped in front of the double doors to the morgue. She walked around the stretcher and pushed on them. They swung open silently, wafting a stronger smell of formaldehyde and decay toward her.

She heard a moan from Rider. Maybe he was waking up. It worried her that he had been unconscious so long. If he went into a coma...

Quickly, she pulled the stretcher into the room and pushed the doors closed, offering a silent prayer that the odd little orderly was right and no one would die this weekend.

"Okay, Rider. We're here," she whispered and uncovered his face. He was still out, but she thought she could detect a slight evening of his breaths, as if he was asleep instead of unconscious. She looked around. All the exam tables were empty, clean and shiny and waiting for the next guest, who wouldn't mind how cold their steel bed would be.

"No guests today. At least not yet," she muttered as she looked around.

It had been years since she'd done morgue duty, but she thought she remembered a little office somewhere. The red emergency lights were the only illumination, and that coupled with the smell of formaldehyde that permeated everything could easily make her believe they had stumbled into some anteroom of hell.

Leaving Rider on the table, she stepped through a door, finding herself in the office. There was a tiny desk and an old desk chair. A stack of neatly folded scrubs lay on the one side chair, and in the corner was a supply cabinet.

She opened it. Blankets. Blankets and a pillow—for the residents to nap while they did morgue duty. She searched further. She'd never known a resident in her life that didn't keep a stash. Even in the morgue. Sure enough, behind a box of paper clips she found them.

Several little brown vials with typed labels. Aspirin, ibuprofen—she pushed them aside as she read the labels. Ah, there they were. Some hydroxyzine capsules. Not as good as promethazine for nausea, but they would work.

She looked around the room again, squinting in the dim red

light. A narrow white box sat beside an old dilapidated couch.
She stared at the small refrigerator, hardly able to believe her
luck.

Inside there were containers of juice, which had probably
been swiped from the cafeteria, and somebody's leftover lunch.
She sniffed carefully at the paper bag. Nothing obviously spoiled.
Suddenly thirsty, she opened a carton of juice and swigged it
gratefully, then spread two blankets on the couch and carried
two more back to Rider.

She couldn't move him to the couch, so she'd just have to
wait until he woke up. She spread the blankets over him and
touched his forehead. His unbandaged eye was dancing, undulating under the delicate skin of the lid.

"What are you dreaming, Rider?" she whispered as she
stroked his forehead, trying to smooth out the furrows between
his brows. She closed her eyes and tried to glean something
from him, but all she got was a muddle of confused images that
she couldn't sort out. Too tired, probably.

"I hope your dreams are good ones." She wrapped one of
the blankets around herself and sat on an exam table, watching
him. "Please hurry up and come back to me."

                        ***

*Rider Savage gazed out the window of his office, wish-
ing for the hundredth time he could see something besides
a blue haze shining through streaky, scratched glass.*

*He supposed there was some justice in putting the his-
tory department in the oldest building on campus, but they
could have replaced the ancient glass. Still, he loved the
old twentieth century building with its musty smell and the
real wooden beams that creaked.*

*The fading light and his comlink both told him it was
getting late. He frowned as he disconnected from the
school's com, wondering if Marielle would be waiting for
him, or if she'd be gone, like she was so often these days.*

*They had been married five years today. Lately he'd
become more and more convinced Mari had married him
because he was such a good cover for her skipworth underground activities. Who would be more innocuous than a
professor of ancient history?*

*Lately she'd been acting strange, distracted and wor-
ried. He bounded off the last shuttle in the lobby of their
complex and carefully blanked his mind. He'd see if he*

could sneak up on her. Usually she knew every move he made.

He needn't have bothered. When he entered their apartment, Mari was hunched over the ancient radio. She probably wouldn't have heard him if he'd shot his way in.

"What's happened?" he asked, although he was sure he knew without asking. There was only one reason she'd have on the signature uniform of the underground.

When he spoke she jumped, and turned off the radio.

"How'd you get in without me hearing you?" Mari was nervous. He felt the apprehension emanating from her.

"You were concentrating on the radio. What's happened?" Rider reached out for her, but she turned back around toward the radio.

"We've got word there's a raid tonight." She fooled with the dials, causing static to crackle. "We just don't know where."

Rider sighed and leaned over to nuzzle her hair. "Happy anniversary, Commander. When are you going to let someone else take over the field ops?"

She shrugged off his caress. "Rider, stop. Look, why don't you go to the club or something tonight?"

"No. I've told you before, if you're in this, then I am, too. I'd better get geared up." He planted a quick kiss on his wife's forehead. "Promise me something."

She held up a hand. Her brow was creased in concentration. She pulled off the headphones. "We've got to get out of here."

She sprang up and grabbed the blaster that always lay beside the radio. Rider's heart lurched. He sprang to action as quickly as she, throwing the manual lock on the door and turned just as Mari directed a short blast of energy at the radio to destroy it.

He grabbed her arm. "Let's go!"

They headed for the kitchen and the escape hatch they'd cut through a cabinet.

"No, wait!" Mari said.

Rider tensed. "What?"

She turned back toward the living room.

"Mari! What the hell?" He grabbed her arm, but she jerked it away.

"Catwallader!"

"Damn it, Mari." He rushed after her, reaching for her arm again.

She glared at him. *"Stop it."* She shifted the blaster to her other hand and tried to peel his fingers off her hand. *"Cat... Here kitty! Rider, let go!"*

"Mari! Leave the damned cat! We've got to get out of here. They're coming!"

"Cat? Come on, boy. Here, kitty..."

The cat appeared out of nowhere, stretching lazily. Just as Mari reached to pick him up, an explosion shook the apartment.

Before Rider could react, three men in the deep red uniform of the government poured into the apartment, and a ribbon of green light shot toward the cat, leaving a smoking piece of flesh where it had stood.

"You bastards!" Mari screamed.

"Why don't you come with us, Marielle," one of the men said.

Mari leveled her blaster at him. *"Why, so you can wipe me out? I found out what you're planning."*

"We can discuss it later."

"Discuss it? I thought we had discussed it. I thought I was a part of the plan, not just another skipworth to be rubbed out! If you go back to the past and wipe out the original skipworth, I'll dissolve into the ether, just like every other deviant on the planet. And if I don't exist, it will be difficult to give me a cabinet post, don't you think?"

Rider listened, horrified. The things Mari was saying sent shock waves through him, all the way down to his fingertips. He stared in numbed disbelief as his wife, the leader of the skipworth underground, talked about plans and cabinet posts with the enemy.

"How did you find out about that?"

Mari laughed. *"You forget. I've got friends on both sides."*

"Mari, what are you talking about?"

"Shut up, Rider. This doesn't concern you." Mari barely even glanced in his direction. *"I can't let you destroy everything I've worked for, Barkley."*

The man shook his head in what appeared to be genuine regret. *"And I can't let you upset our plans, Mari. You seem to have the idea you're indispensable. Sorry, Mari."*

He leveled his blaster calmly and shot her.

"No!!" Rider dove for her, but it was too late. The room was awash with green light, and Mari gasped as the blast caught her, throwing her body backwards, away from him.

He grabbed her as she collapsed, hugging her to him, trying to hold the life in her by force of will, but it didn't work. The heat from the blaster still burned in her body. He smelled the charred flesh and tissue as death sucked her away from him.

The man named Barkley said something to his two henchmen, but Rider hardly registered his words. Something about the luck of having an intelligent, normal man instead of the criminals they'd been forced to use so far in their experiments with time travel.

Rider didn't even resist when they trussed him with steel bands and threw him into a vehicle. His wife had betrayed her people. She had sold them out for power.

***

Rider's whole body convulsed, and an agonized cry tore from his throat. Kristen jumped up, her head hazy with drowsiness. She grabbed his shoulders, trying to keep him from falling off the table. "Rider! Can you hear me? Relax. You've got to relax."

He fought her, even as the wracking pains streaked through him. She knew she couldn't stand against his strength. The only thing she could do was try to reach him, inside himself, behind the pain and terror that was tearing him apart.

"Rider, please. Wake up. It's okay."

His eyes opened wide, and he stared at her uncomprehendingly. Then his face contorted and he lashed out at her. She ducked just in time.

"God damn you! Bastards!" Then he collapsed back on the table, brutal sobs shaking him.

Kristen held onto him as tightly as she could. His fear and anguish were stunning as they wafted through her, mixed with impotent rage and a devastating bewilderment.

She needed to separate herself from it, from him, so she could think, but she wasn't sure he could stand it all by himself, so she waited, holding onto him, until his ragged breaths began to slow. "It's okay, Rider. It's okay. Here. Swallow these."

He stared at her. "You're the target, aren't you?" he whispered.

Kristen nodded, a thread of fear erupting under her breastbone. What had happened to him while he was unconscious? Was that all he remembered? That she was the target? Would he remember wanting to save her? Or did he only remember his conditioning?

"Come on. Take these," she coaxed. It really didn't matter much, she thought, amazed at her fatalistic turn of thought. If his incredible story was true, she had no doubt if he didn't kill her, someone would. If he wasn't a barking mongrel, as he called it, then they had no chance, because people who could travel through time could probably do just about anything. And if he was a barking mongrel, then so was she, and eventually they'd both be locked up.

His unbandaged eye became clearer, more lucid, as he fought his way back from the nightmare hell he'd been in. "What are those?" he mumbled.

"Anti-nausea pills."

"They're different." He took the two capsules and stared at them, then gazed at her narrowly.

"Give me a break, Rider. Take them or not. I've about decided I don't care." She was so tired. So tired and so confused.

He wanted her to trust him, but he still didn't trust her. She wanted him to trust her, but she was still unsure of him.

He swallowed the capsules without water.

"Now, come on. Let me get you into the office." Kristen led him in and pointed to the couch. "See," she said. "A fairly comfortable bed. At least it won't be ice cold. Now, take off those filthy pants and cover up. You're still shivering."

She doubted he understood much of what she said, because he kept stopping to look at her warily, but he followed her direction and climbed naked in between the blankets. Her gaze followed him. Despite her exhaustion, despite everything that had happened, she was still stirred by the sight of his body.

He let out a huge sigh and closed his eye. "I had—I remembered."

"Yes, I know," she said gently, as her heart pounded with apprehension, and a nameless terror stole her breath. What? What had he remembered? Their lovemaking? His hatred for her? What her descendants had done to his wife? She tucked the blankets up under his chin as if he were a little boy. Sweat beaded on his forehead, and she wiped it away with her hand.

"I don't want to remember this," he said brokenly. "God, I hate being such a slipper! I'm scared."

He allowed her hand on his forehead for a few moments before he pulled away, his gaze focused on something in the far distance—maybe five hundred years away.

"I was a teacher, in a—small college," he started, then stopped, swallowing hard.

Kristen stared at him, fear warring with hope and compassion within her. He was remembering. He was piecing together the broken bits of memory the TAINCC had tried to destroy.

"Rider, don't ever forget, this isn't you. They did this with their conditioning. You're not a—a slipper. You're strong. Very, very strong." She touched his hand, feeling his doubt and fear, wanting to banish it for him, frustrated because she could feel it all, but couldn't stop it.

"You're the strongest man I've ever known. Remember what you told me? They thought their conditioning was permanent. They thought you'd never remember, or they wouldn't have sent you back here." Kristen ached inside with the realization of what she was doing. She was helping him to remember how much he hated her. She was helping him to remember every detail of why he wanted to kill her.

"Got any more of those pills, Doc?" he said, trying to smile.

"You just took two. They'll start working in a minute."

He sighed and wiped his hand over his face, then leaned back against the cushions. His throat worked as he swallowed and took a long breath. "I taught history, if you can believe that. I made all my students learn the keyboard. Probably stupid, since everybody has vidlinks and comlinks nowadays, but I just thought we shouldn't lose the old values, the old talents. It started coming back to me when you were working on your brother's computer." Running his fingers through his hair, he glanced at her, his eyes shadowed with something so dark, so anguished it was hard for Kristen to look into them.

"I had a—wife," he muttered, his hands over his face again. "They killed her. I could smell her burned flesh. God!"

Kristen's heart shattered into tiny pieces at the horror in his voice as he remembered his wife's death. She reached out for him, but he recoiled against the back of the couch. She didn't have to touch him to feel the bitter grief that consumed him. Grief he'd never been given the chance to endure.

"Sorry, Doc," he said, his eyes burning hollowly in his ashen face. "It's all coming back in a flood. I only got disjointed pieces before."

"Sorry for what? You've been tortured, brainwashed. You can't help it." She ached with his new, raw grief. For him, it was as if all the horror had just happened. She understood how he felt.

So why did it create a gulf of loneliness inside her too big for tears? He'd had a wife, and he'd lost her today. Not five hundred years from now, not two years ago, but today. Today, when his brain finally allowed the memory to return, he'd seen his wife murdered. His grief was brand new. His love for her hadn't even had a chance to recede through time.

She hadn't had time to stop and consider how much this man from the future meant to her until now. She hadn't been able to process the feelings that had grown in her. They had grown so fast she'd not had time to recognize them.

When she formed the thought, she didn't even know how long it had been there. She loved him. But as new as her love was for him, his love for his wife was newer. As strong as Kristen's link to him was, he'd been married. Kristen couldn't compete with that.

A searing blast of his anger buffeted her. "God damn them all!" he growled through clenched teeth.

Kristen suddenly couldn't stand it any more. She had to know, had to hear it from his lips. She laid her hand on his arm, needing to feel him, needing to know his reaction when she asked the question that suddenly burned within her. A question she'd give anything to never know the answer to. "It was the Deviants? My—descendants who killed your wife?"

He stared at her for a long time, uncomprehendingly, his mouth a little open, his unbandaged eye wide and vacant.

"Rider?"

He blinked.

"Rider?" The longer he stared at her, the more the certainty built inside her. He had remembered it all. She didn't think she could bear knowing she'd caused the death of his wife.

"What? The Deviants?" He blinked again and focused on her face, his mouth twisting in pain. "Mari was—Mari was a skipworth."

The words came at Kristen like a blow, while his shock and rage shot through her fingertips.

Mari was a skipworth. The words echoed down the corridors of her brain like a gunshot ricocheting off metal. *Mari was a skipworth.*

"How... what?" she stammered, as he grabbed her, his arms jerking as they closed around her.

"She was a skipworth. They killed her. The government killed her. I didn't get home in time. I took the late shuttle, and they killed her." Rider couldn't control the tremors that shook his body as he relived the memories of Mari's death.

"Help me, Doc," he whispered, his lips moving against her neck. "God help me, I was married to a Deviant."

Kristen held him, her palm cradling his skull as if he were a baby. He felt ridiculously like a child as she whispered to him. It didn't even matter what she said. All that mattered was that she was holding him, keeping him safe, loving him.

After a long time the steel coils of his tendons relaxed and he lay back on the couch and pulled her down to lie next to him. He stroked her hair. Her calmness slowly seeped into his bones, although he couldn't control an occasional faint tremor.

He didn't want to talk about it. He needed to assimilate all he'd learned. Needed to try to make some sense out of it. But Kristen was there, holding him, sending a warm comfort through him that made him want to tell her.

"Mari was a skipworth. She was one of the original organizers of the underground movement that formed to combat the government's single-minded efforts to wipe out the Dev— the skipworths."

He'd almost said Deviants. Those twisted quasi-humans who were using their disgusting mind-invading powers to take over the world.

Rider shuddered, and his gut cramped with nausea. The false memories conditioned into him were getting mixed up with his real memories.

"I believed in them. I believed in Mari. Skipworths had as much right to live and be free as anyone." He'd thought his wife believed it, too. He turned his head and buried his face in Kristen's hair.

"Don't, Rider. Don't try to remember. It's making you sick."

He breathed in her warm scent, and a faint tremor rippled through him. He shook his head. "I can't... It's like two different memories at war inside my brain."

Now he had no idea what he believed. According to the

people who'd trained him, his wife had been murdered by skipworths, and he had volunteered to come back to the past to wipe out the Mother of All the Deviants.

According to the memories that were firing like synapses in his brain, his wife had been a skipworth, and had betrayed her people for personal power. According to his newly surfaced memories, she was working with the very people who had forced him to travel back to the past to kill Kristen Skipworth. And they'd killed her when she threatened to expose their plan.

He clenched his jaw against the nausea that threatened as his brain went over the memory of that last night and the horror he'd witnessed.

"Rider, are you all right?"

He swallowed hard and pulled her closer, drawing comfort from her warm, soft body, drawing strength from the place deep inside her that fed him courage and determination and peace through her touch.

"It's just hard, Doc. Remembering."

"Do you want to tell me? I'm here. I'll listen."

He glanced across at her, unable to identify the note in her voice, almost like she was trying to keep from crying, but her face was buried in the hollow of his shoulder and he couldn't see her expression.

He shook his head. "No. I don't want to talk about it now. It's—too new." Kristen tensed in his arms and sat up, her face shuttered.

FOURTEEN

She pulled away from him, needing to withdraw. He was in such pain. *Too new.* Oh, that hurt her. "That's okay. Whatever you need to do."

His memories of his wife were too new, too painful, to be shared. She studied his face. His unbandaged eye was closed, his lips compressed and white at the corners, his face ashen. Tears seeped out from under his closed lid.

She thought she would burst with love for him. She wanted to pull him even closer, to take care of him, to never let him go. Her eyes stung with tears of shared grief and rage, and her heart contracted with love. But he didn't want her help. His pain was too new. He had to live through the death of his wife as if it had just happened.

And the thought of that almost destroyed Kristen.

With grim determination, she gathered her wits. She was a doctor. Whatever her emotions were, whatever had been between them, her responsibility was for his health and well being. He was exhausted, dehydrated, and possibly in danger of becoming hypothermic in the chilly, air-conditioned room. And he was using all his strength in rage and grief and anguished memories. Kristen knew firsthand how draining and debilitating grief could be. She had to keep his memories from sapping what little strength he had. He was her responsibility.

She dredged her professionalism up from within her. Sitting up she touched the bandage on his head. "Let me look at your eye."

Rider raised a hand, touching the gauze pad that covered his eye. "I'd forgotten about it."

"Does it hurt?" She unwrapped the gauze and gently pushed his head back against the cushions. He resisted a bit, watching her warily, but she didn't waver, didn't allow herself to feel anything, and finally her detachment transferred itself to him, and he relaxed.

"I don't know if it hurts or not," he said thoughtfully. "I haven't really thought about it."

"Don't open your eye," she said, lifting the pad. "Let me do it." She carefully lifted the lid. With relief she saw that there wasn't much redness, and hardly any swelling. She pulled the little flashlight out of her pocket and peered through the pupil, holding his eye open as his muscles fought to close it against the bright light. The bleeding had stopped. She sighed.

"It looks fine. Sit up. Now, look at me." She held her hand over his left eye. "Can you see me?"

His right eye opened slowly, the lashes matted with the ointment she'd applied. He blinked several times, but finally his gaze focused on her face.

"Can you?"

He nodded.

A tremor shook her. All her professionalism left her in a rush of breath. "Oh Rider, I'm so glad. I was—so afraid I'd blinded you."

A weak flash of humor lit his face. "I was a little nervous myself, Doc." He leaned back again, closing his eyes.

He was still weak, still too tired.

"Guess what I found while you were out?" She spoke brightly as she retrieved the food from the refrigerator. "Here's some juice and a couple of leftover sandwiches from somebody's lunch. You can eat the bread and lettuce if you can't stomach the meat."

Rider made a face, but Kristen was finally able to make him take a few mouthfuls and wash it down with a creditable amount of apple juice. She was relieved that he could eat without getting sick, although it hurt her that he was so compliant, so helpless.

She knew from within him that he wasn't used to being helpless. He had probably never been sick in his life, until he had been hurled back through time. He'd probably never known a day when he wasn't in control of his life, until the day his wife was murdered.

"Now," she said in her doctor voice. "Mister Rider, I want you to go to sleep."

He looked at her. "It's Savage. Rider Savage." A grimace crossed his face. "At least it was."

She bit her lip against the tears that threatened. "Okay, Mister Savage. Get some sleep. That's doctor's orders, and if you don't, I'll give you a sedative." She pushed the blankets up under his chin and pressed gently against his chest until he relaxed back against the couch cushions. She watched his eyelids droop as he fought sleep.

"How long have we been here?" he asked drowsily. "That one mongrel they sent was an idiot, but they can't all be. They figured out how to get metal through time."

"Don't worry about that," Kristen said. "We've got plenty of time. They won't find us this weekend."

"How do you know?" His words were becoming slurred as he began to drift off to sleep.

How did she know? The orderly's words echoed in her brain. "I'm the doctor, remember? Besides, it doesn't matter anyway. You're not going anywhere until you get some sleep."

"I hate it when you're right, Doc," he whispered.

Kristen watched him for a while, trying to absorb all he'd told her. It should be easier to think of him as crazy than to accept the things he had said. But it was getting easier and easier to believe him.

Five hundred years from now, people with her name were being persecuted—for what? For having an innate ability to know what other people were feeling, even what they were thinking? A small resentment began to build inside her.

People were people. Why did someone always have to think that one person was better than another? It didn't matter if it was skin color, religion, race or telepathy. Bigotry had no place in the world. It was sad that even five hundred years from now people were still being caught in the same traps.

At least then, as now, there were people willing to fight for human rights. She touched Rider's cheek. Like him. Like his wife.

A stabbing pain shot through her heart. His wife. Stubborn and tough. Yes, his wife would have been stubborn and tough. She smiled. She'd have had to be.

Kristen sighed and stood. She was tired, too. She looked at the clock. Four a.m. She didn't even remember when she'd last slept. It must be Sunday morning. Well, the strange little orderly had said no one would die this weekend.

"I hope you're right," she muttered as she opened the door to the bathroom. She turned on the water in the shower, un-buckled Skip's computer pack from around her waist, dropped her filthy clothes and stepped in. The stinging spray felt good on her stiff neck and shoulders. She raised her face to the stream of water and let it beat on her forehead and temples where a headache was lingering, then she turned around and let the hot water massage her neck.

His wife. His wife who had died two years ago and five hundred years from now. What had Rider said? Time travel was a one-way trip? You could never go back?

He'd also said when he'd left the future they couldn't transport weapons, but Kristen had seen a blaster, had felt it burn her skin. She peeled off the sodden bandage and stared at the line of blisters across the back of her hand. Several of them had burst. She gritted her teeth and let the water run on the burns, washing the open wounds.

Finally turning off the water, she wrapped herself in one of the soft cotton blankets, letting it absorb the wetness from her skin. She stepped out of the bathroom and sat down in a chair, still bundled in the blanket, to wait until Rider woke up.

She loved to watch him sleep, and she knew how much he needed it, with all the trauma his body had endured in the past hours. He looked so young and untroubled when he was asleep. Kristen's heart filled with love and compassion. She loved him so much. How would she ever live without him?

A ripping fear tore through her. Without him. What if he was wrong? What if he could go back?

She tried to remember everything she'd ever heard about time travel. Everything she'd ever read. H.G. Wells. Robert Heinlein. Dozens of B movies as well as some fairly good ones, both serious and funny.

What if he could go back to the future? What if he could go back and do things differently? Take an earlier shuttle home that night? Could he save his wife? Would he?

A deep shivering racked Kristen's body as she sat wrapped in the warm cotton blanket. Of course he would. She gazed at his face, hard-planed and beautiful, with its determined chin and its strong jaw.

He would go. There would be no question. She wrapped her arms around herself, trying to stop the shivering, trying to stop the thoughts, but they kept coming.

She couldn't blame him. He'd been married. He'd had a life. Why would he want to stay here, five hundred years away from everything he'd held dear? Five hundred years away from home.

Leaning back in the chair she closed her eyes, trying to stop the tears of loss and regret that forced their way through her closed lids. Could she do it? Could she give up her whole life for him?

Now? No question.

But what if the choice was different. What if it was two

years ago and the choice was between Rider and Skipper? Would it be as easy?

She knew it wouldn't. For her, loving them both, it would be impossible. She was almost glad the choice wasn't hers to make.

She loosened one cramping hand from its grip on her shoulder and wiped tears from her eyes. Rider's problem wasn't the same.

Mari had been his wife. Kristen was just the target.

His voice echoed in her head. *Lose an eye, watch you die. No contest, Doc.* She smiled for a second, remembering.

But this was between her and his wife. They'd been married for five years. There would be no contest. He would go back. Anyone would.

Kristen quashed the unbidden prayer that he was right about there being no return, and closed her eyes. Maybe she would doze for a few minutes.

***

Rider opened his eyes, panicked for an instant until he remembered where he was. It took a moment to orient himself to the room, to the couch on which he was lying naked, covered only by a cotton blanket, to the fact that he had remembered.

A rage burned inside him, at first as hot as a blaster burn, but slowly turning to a smolder. Flameless heat, all the more dangerous because it could burn for hours, days, even years, before it flared.

Mari hadn't been killed by skipworths. She had been a skipworth—the leader of the Underground. And she had betrayed them. Her own people.

It was too new, this acid disgust for the woman he'd thought he'd loved. He'd never even known her. Never known what she was really doing.

She had always tried to keep him out of her underground activities. He'd thought it was to protect him. What a fool he'd been.

She'd been working for *them* all along. Mari was the one who'd destroyed his life. She and the bastards in the TAINCC. They had turned him into that most hated of beings, a tank. They'd taken his memories from him and put false ones in their place.

And they'd sent him back in time to kill Kristen Skipworth. His angel-doctor. The only good thing in his life. If he got the chance, he'd slaughter them.

A movement across the room brought him back from his deadly thoughts.

The Doc. She was sitting in the chair, slumped a little, her arms wrapped around herself, her hair damp and curling around her face. He still thought she looked like an angel, although now his angel's eyes had faint blue shadows beneath them, her hair was damp and messy, and her face was shiny clean, more like a cherub's face than an angel's.

She was brave, his angel. His mouth curved into a smile as he recalled the valiant lift of her chin, the defiant stare, her intense concentration as she'd prepared to destroy the camera in his eye. Then his gaze wandered lower, to where the blanket had slipped and was draped over her arms, leaving the tops of her breasts bare.

His body stiffened, and an aching desire suffused him. He wanted her. Through all the pain, despite the tortures they'd used to ensure that he would feel nothing, he actually ached with need for her.

Even when he'd thought she was the instrument of Mari's destruction he'd still wanted her. He squeezed his eyes shut and leaned back against the couch cushions, the memories flooding over him, twisting his gut with the nausea that accompanied what he now knew was the breaking of his conditioning.

He remembered the torture, all the pain. He remembered that, far from volunteering, he'd been conscripted, forced to endure it.

And he remembered that all through it he'd sworn, even when he'd been strapped down with leads and tubes and helpless against the onslaught of lies and false memories, that he would use their training, their conditioning, against them.

He hadn't fought the conditioning. He'd known that was useless. He'd used it, turned it for his own purposes. Reveled in their torture, knowing if it didn't kill him, it would make him stronger. Even after they'd conditioned out his real memories and replaced them with false ones, the determination had remained, draped like a blanket over every moment he'd spent in their torture chamber.

Even after the brainwashing was complete, when he hadn't been able to remember anything else, the resolve lay inside him like his soul. When he hadn't even known why, he'd still known how important it was for him to become the strongest, the best.

A grim satisfaction rippled through his breast that he'd managed to do it. Kristen was right. The bastards had thought their conditioning couldn't be broken.

Rider felt the vague nausea tickling at the back of his throat. He savored it, holding on to it as a reminder of what he owed them.

It looked like they were getting better, smarter, more technologically advanced. They were pretty good. But they weren't good enough. Not good enough to beat him.

With his eyes still closed, he assessed his physical condition. He was a lot better. His ribs didn't hurt quite as much as they had, the wracking pain and nausea associated with anything that went counter to the TAINCC's conditioning was fading. He was no longer starving, thanks to his angel doctor, and he didn't think he'd suffered any permanent damage to his eye. Yes, he thought he could do pretty well, considering.

Which was good, because to protect his angel doctor, he would have to be the best.

He opened his eyes to find Kristen watching him. As their gazes met, she smiled, and Rider's heart contracted as he gazed on the beauty of her face. For an instant he wished Australia were a free state for skipworths in this era like it was in his. He'd like to take her there and keep her safe for the rest of his life.

Keep her safe. It was a need as strong as the other, baser need. Stronger. Yes, he desired her, but the determination that had kept him going in the TAINCC now had a purpose. His revenge now had a name. If it meant his life, he would protect Kristen Skipworth.

How ironic that they'd sent him down the centuries to destroy her and now he was prepared to die to save her. What was it, this need that was deeper than sexual desire? Was it love?

His heart went cold at the thought.

He'd loved Mari, and she'd betrayed him. Mari had never loved him. She'd used him, that was all. He studied Kristen, her wide, amber-shot eyes, her vulnerable lips, her small, lithe body.

Did he love her? The thought sent fear swirling around his brain and desire swirling through his loins. He didn't know. He just knew, as surely as he knew Mari had betrayed him and her people, that his angel doctor needed him. And he knew one other thing. He couldn't imagine a future without Kristen Skipworth.

"Rider? Are you okay?"

He focused on her amber-shot, trusting eyes. "Yeah, Doc. Just drifting I guess."

"Well, you need to take a shower. It'll warm you up and help to get you rehydrated. I've already had one. It was great. Come on." Kristen stood before she remembered she was wrapped only in a blanket. She hiked the sliding material up on her shoulders, shivering in the air-conditioned emptiness of the morgue, and grabbed a set of scrubs from the side chair.

"When you get out, I'm sure some of these will fit you."

When she looked up, Rider was standing silhouetted by the red lights. Kristen thought she'd never seen anyone so beautiful. He looked alien, primal in the blood red light, the planes of his body harshly shadowed, like a boldly rendered oil painting.

His eyes were no longer glazed with sleep. They were on her—blue, intense. He walked over to her and took the scrubs, tossing them on the floor. He spread his fingers around her arms, pulling her up close to him. As he did, the blanket fell. Kristen, her pulse beating like a drum in her throat, reached for it, but his hold on her was relentless, so she let it drop.

In the red glowing light, his features looked cut from granite, his eyes deep-shadowed. He was frowning, his dark brows furrowed. She couldn't take her eyes off his face as he bent his head.

"Rider, what are you doing?" she whispered breathlessly as his lips touched hers.

"Shhh," he breathed against her lips, then trailed his kisses from her mouth to her neck, where he nuzzled against her skin. "I don't think I can make it to the shower without help."

Kristen's body tightened with something she could only identify as pure lust as his mouth moved on her skin. She steeled herself against the pleasure that flamed within her.

"Don't do it, Rider. It's just not—" she almost broke down as his sadness and pain came to her through his fingers. She wanted more than anything to respond to him. She wanted his love more than life. But she was a doctor, and doctors were practical and realistic, and her training told her a man couldn't lose his wife whom he obviously loved and be in love with someone else on the same day.

"I'm the doctor, and I say you need to guard against the

effects of your conditioning. You need sleep. You need some time to come to terms with your newly found memories. You're too weak. Too debilitated." Too vulnerable, too strong, too tempting, with his hot breath on her neck, his scent in her nostrils. She gritted her teeth against the sensations he was stirring in her.

"No," he growled. "I've lived too long with death. You smell like life, Doc. I need you. I'd die without you." He said the last so softly that Kristen wasn't sure she'd heard right. But she couldn't mistake what his hands on her body were telling her, what his mouth against her skin was silently whispering to her.

Whatever he felt for his dead wife, he cared for *her*. He desired her so badly, he would withstand any pain, live through any torture, just to have her. She could feel that within him, and she thought she could settle for that.

Desire. Sometimes it was enough, wasn't it?

Then she felt the faint waves of nausea wafting through him. "No!" She tried to break his hold. "I can't let you. God, Rider, how can you stand it?"

"Just shut up, okay? Just shut up." He put his thumbs against her lips, silencing her.

Then he ran his hands down her back, his fingers trailing heat where they touched, burning fire on her air-cooled skin. He cupped her buttocks and pulled her against him until she felt his unrestrained hardness against her, and her belly contracted with desire. She whimpered, moving her lips against his neck, where a pulse beat steady and fast. "You're shivering. You need to shower."

"I love it when you're right, Doc," he whispered against her hair as he pulled her toward the door. "Come on."

"But I've already had a shower," she protested weakly.

"I know."

The bathroom was still foggy, the steel-lined shower hadn't even cooled off yet.

"Turn the water on, Doc," he murmured, his lips near her ear. "I haven't quite mastered the technique."

She manipulated the handles until a warm, stinging spray beat down on them. Rider shuddered and lifted his face to the steamy spray. Kristen could feel his body relaxing against her. She shivered, too, at the contrast between his cool skin and the hot water.

"God," he breathed. "You have no idea how good real water feels, after the chlorine spray they used on us."

Kristen sighed with the inevitability of it. Yes, she had to admit, sometimes desire was enough. She had learned a lot about herself under his gentle tutelage, and one very important lesson she'd learned was that she couldn't live without the feelings he bred in her. For a while, at least, she didn't even care what was driving him. Perhaps it was just that he'd lived too long with death—that all he wanted was the reaffirmation of life, after having relived the death of his wife.

If that was all he wanted, she didn't even mind, so strong was her own need. She could do it, not only for him, but for herself as well.

FIFTEEN

She ran her hands over his muscular shoulders, tracing their shape as the water flowed over them in rivulets, washing away the dirt and blood. His biceps were like river-worn rocks— smooth, hard, worn by time but still unyielding.

Water streamed down his face and body as he turned to her, his skin glistening vermilion in the low lights. He smiled and pushed wet strands of hair out of her face.

If she lived a thousand years, or ten thousand, she'd still be knocked out by his smile. When he smiled, she could believe in the future, in him, in forever.

He pulled her close, wrapping his wet slick body around her, giving her everything he had to give. She knew it was everything, because she felt the faint nausea lingering at the back of his throat, she tasted fear and pain in the flavor of his skin.

Hugging him as tightly as he was hugging her, she gave him back everything she had to offer, hoping he understood how hard she was trying to believe in him.

He pulled away and grinned. "Soap?"

"What?" She blinked, still lost in the warm wetness of his skin. "Oh." She brushed water out of her eyes, then peeked out of the shower stall. She hadn't bothered with soap before. She'd just let the water wash the sweat and dirt off her skin.

"Naturally," she muttered, and stepped out onto the cold bathroom floor.

"Where're you going?"

He'd tried to make his voice light, but she heard the worried note. She sighed as she pressed on the soap dispenser on the wall.

He still didn't trust her completely. She couldn't blame him, because she couldn't totally open herself to him, either. It was sad, because they both needed that trust badly.

If they were different people, it would be so easy. They were attracted to each other like magnet and steel. But they were five hundred years apart, and someone was trying to kill them.

Filling her palm with pink, gooey soap, she stepped back into the shower stall. "It's what always happens when hospitals are designed by bureaucrats instead of the people who work in them. They put the soap out of reach of the shower."

The viscous liquid was luxuriously thick and smooth in her hands. She spread it over him, her fingers delighting in the sleekness of his body, the hard, sculpted beauty of his form. She caressed him with the slick suds. He took some from her hands and began the same erotic ritual on her body.

They rubbed each other all over, caressing nipples that stood erect, sliding their hands down to each others' bellies, pressing, shaping them. Then, incredibly, they moved lower.

Kristen moaned as Rider's hands slipped between her thighs to slide seductively over and into her. She touched him, too, hesitantly, unsure of what his response would be.

When her fingers closed shyly over him, he threw his head back and uttered a short, sharp cry. He'd already been hard, but he leaped in her hands. Coupled with the feelings he was drawing from her, his desire flashing through her almost made her knees buckle.

"Doc!" he cried, and pulled her to him. "Doc." The second one was a whisper. "Don't touch me. You don't know—"

She caught his face with her hands, alarmed, peering through the streaming water, trying to assess his appearance in the dim red lights. "What? What did I do? Are you sick?"

He slapped the handles that controlled the water to the off position. "Yes," he growled, pulling her from the shower stall. "Sick with desire. Sick with wanting you. Sick with—" He stopped, his face twisting, then took a deep breath and dragged his gaze from hers to look around. "Where are the towels?"

"No towels," she said. "We have to use the blankets."

He wrapped her in one and hugged her to him, using the soft cotton to blot away the water, then he pulled it down, his gaze riveted on her body.

Kristen's head was swimming. Nothing she had ever read, no anatomy class or medical text had prepared her for the reality of making love. She'd thought she had reached the pinnacle when his hands had moved on her, but she was wrong. He was drawing a response from her now that couldn't be described in words.

It was pure sensation, pure desire. She thought she must have reached light speed. Every molecule of mass in her body transformed into pure, erotic energy.

Rider pushed her onto the couch, lowering her gently onto the blankets. Then he knelt on the floor and laid his head on her breast. The tickle of his damp hair on her nipples brought a gasp of arousal. Her breasts tightened, her nipples hardened just from the brush of his hair.

She stroked his head as he moved his hands over her body, driving her senseless.

He ran his hands over her skin until every nerve ending was on fire. She squirmed against the sweet torture, but he growled and held her still until she was forced to relax.

Then he sat up and began again. He explored each breast, touching the underside, the swell, tracing blue veins from the apex to the soft outer curve, touching her nipple, coaxing it into full erection.

"Rider?" Kristen's body was wound so tight she was going to scream if he didn't give her some release soon. Her breasts were aching, her body was quivering with her need. "Please," she gasped.

He paid no attention to her as he left her breasts and moved his exploration to her belly, spreading his hands over her, measuring her with his fingers. Then he moved lower, over the little thatch of hair, then even lower, until she arched, senseless with desire, against his hand.

Through it all, she watched his face. It was set, his mouth grim, his brow wrinkling a bit when a pain would tear through him, but his eyes were on her, triumphant, shining damply.

Then suddenly he was above her and in her, his face buried in the juncture of her neck and shoulder. He muttered under his breath, "This time, Doc. This time I promise it won't hurt. This time it'll be good, I swear."

"It already is," she murmured, prepared to forget the five hundred years that separated them, prepared just to feel.

She ran her hands down his body, over his corded muscles, his lean flanks, his hard, long thighs. As he moved inside her, swelling and throbbing against her flesh, an answering desire built inside her. Her breasts ached with it, her belly quivered, her loins burned.

Rider lifted his head and gazed down at her, his brilliant blue eyes on her mouth, then he kissed her, and as he did, his movements quickened, and Kristen found his rhythm.

Just as before, when he kissed her, she could feel it all. She felt him swelling, ready to burst, at the same time as she opened to receive him. They reached the peak together, and Kristen thought they must have exploded, the searing, ecstatic shock was so great.

He collapsed beside her, his chest heaving, his breaths fast and uneven.

"You okay?" Kristen was tucked into the hollow of his shoulder, weak with expended passion.

He nodded. "Easier, this time," he croaked as he stroked her hair. He coughed, and his belly spasmed, but he didn't double over in pain, and he didn't jump up and run.

"Good," she said, snuggling tighter into his embrace. "It tends to make a girl insecure to have a guy puke after he makes love to her."

"Very funny."

"Thank you," she said, but he didn't hear her.

His breaths had evened out, grown softer, and his belly had quit its wrenching contractions. He was asleep.

She nuzzled into the hollow of his shoulder and tried to be content with what he had given her. But the sweet beast inside her had other plans.

It had awakened, and while she may have thought it could be satisfied with mere physical pleasure, she was wrong.

Kristen dozed and drowsily vowed that, no matter what the cost, she would fight for this man who had coaxed from her the love she'd thought she'd never dare to share. A faint apprehension grew as she wondered how she could compete against a woman five hundred years away. If there was a way for Rider to save his wife, Kristen couldn't even try.

She turned her nose toward the sleepy redolence of his skin and slept.

When she woke, she felt like she'd been asleep for hours. She stretched and snuggled against Rider's hard, warm body.

"Hello," she said, turning her face up to gaze at the underside of his chin.

He peered down at her and smiled. "Hello to you."

His smile took her breath. "Did you sleep? How do you feel?"

He closed his eyes for an instant. "Surprisingly good for having slept in a morgue and made love to someone who usually makes me puke."

"Very funny."

"Thank you." He chuckled quietly. Kristen could feel the rumble deep in his belly. It stoked the fire inside her, and she moved restlessly against him.

He turned her mouth up to his and kissed her. "Doc," he breathed against her mouth, then moved to lift himself over her, but Kristen had had enough of his exquisite torture.

She shook her head and pushed him away.

His eyes narrowed, but before he could speak, she twisted her body so that she was poised over him. "My turn," she said, grinning wickedly, and proceeded to seduce him.

She nuzzled his neck. "You tell me if you're getting sick," she whispered, running her tongue around the shell-like cartilage of his ear.

His eyes were closed, his jaw tense, but he only grunted in agreement. She laid kisses along each centimeter of strained tendon in his neck and licked the scratches on his shoulders until his muscles trembled under her mouth.

He grabbed her arms, tugging her up so he could cover her mouth with his. "No fair!" she mumbled against his lips. "It's my turn. Let go!"

With a glare and a moan, he obeyed her. She turned her attention back to his body.

The little juncture where his muscular shoulders met his chest fascinated her, the hollow where she had snuggled comfortably several times in the past few days. She kissed it lovingly, then moved downward over his pectorals where his nipples were hard and taut, and apparently sensitive, because he sucked in a hissing breath when she lowered her mouth onto one.

She chuckled, delighted by the reaction her unschooled lovemaking was eliciting from Rider, who had come into her life so hurt, so rigid, so terribly, brutally sad.

His fists were clenched at his sides, she hoped in an effort not to grab her and ravish her. The alternative would be a return of his wrenching pain and the sickness caused by his conditioning. A glance at his face reassured her of what she already felt inside him. His face was twisted, but not in pain, in almost unbearable ecstasy.

Good. She wanted to torture him just like he had done to her.

His steel-banded belly took a lot of her attention. After she had run her tongue and her fingers over every ridge, every taut muscle, she laid her head there and gazed at the display below her.

He was hard and ready for her, but she dragged her attention away from his aching flesh. Instead, she reached out and ran her thumb over the colorful, stylized dagger tattooed on his left thigh, near the juncture.

He hissed again, and through his skin, she felt the blistering pain, the burning nausea, and he withdrew.

Suddenly, she was cold and alone. All the warmth, all the

passion had dissipated from his body. She might as well have been resting her cheek on a stainless steel exam table.

She raised her head and looked at him. "Tell me about it," she whispered, taking his face in her hands and turning it so he had to strain not to look at her. "Tell me."

He closed his eyes and withdrew physically, as he had withdrawn emotionally seconds before. He sat up, pulling the blanket over him. Kristen crawled under the cover with him, but she didn't think he even noticed.

"The mark of the TAINCC." The singsong quality was back in his voice, signaling to Kristen that he was reciting something he'd been told.

She grabbed him, her hands on either side of his face, and shook him. "No!" she grated. "I don't want to know what they told you. Tell me what *you* know."

His eyes widened for a second, then he turned his face away, shaking off her hands as easily as drops of water. His arms cradled his midsection, as if he expected the worst.

"I thought I was over it," he muttered between clenched teeth. "I thought the worst of the remembering was over. Goddamn them and their TAINCC!"

He hugged himself, his face contorted with pain. "They took me—Mari's burned flesh still in my nostrils—to a place, a room. I don't know where. And they started in on me."

Kristen put out her hand to stop him, afraid the memories might shatter him, but he wasn't with her. He didn't even know she was there.

"They wanted to know how much I knew. They wanted to know if I knew what Mari was doing, if I knew who else was involved." He shuddered. "They stripped me. They probed and tortured—they had methods you can't imagine..."

He stopped, sweat dripping down his face, his eyes haunted. "The mark. It's not just a mark. It's part of the conditioning. A mark of shame. Nothing is supposed to distract a tank. It's part of their torture. Sexual desire makes it burn like fire."

He stared at her. "I can't—I *won't* tell you what they did when they imbedded it, but you're right. They thought their conditioning could never be broken."

Kristen couldn't stand listening any longer to the horrors he'd endured, the pain he'd gone through to make love to her. She didn't think he could stand it, either.

She put her fingers against his lips. "Please don't tell me any more. I don't have to know what they did, because I know what you did. You broke their conditioning. You are so brave and so strong you make me ashamed. Don't talk about it any more."

"I'm not a martyr, Doc. I did what I had to. I wasn't brave. Sometimes I think I've been scared shitless my whole life."

"It's the people who are scared who are brave, Rider. The ones who aren't scared are fools."

He began to relax. He unclenched his fists and stretched out on the couch. He was like a marble sculpture, muscles honed, more beautiful than Michelangelo's finest work.

Rider shivered, the sweat cold on his skin, Kristen's body warm where it touched him. He'd been wrong days before. Bad memories were not better than no memories. If he'd never remembered Mari's betrayal, never relived the tortures they had put him through, he would have been happy.

Still, it gave him even more incentive to thwart their plans, to use their careful tooling of his body and mind to his advantage, to exact revenge on the bastards who had tried to dehumanize him.

Kristen shifted, her soft, warm body pressing closer into his side. He felt the renewed stirring of desire that had fled when she'd touched the tattoo on his thigh. This time the burning and the pain were like an echo.

He tightened his arm around her and she raised her head. Her eyes glistened with tears as she laid her palm against his cheek.

"They hurt you so badly. I'd like to kill them for what they did to you."

With a kind of horror, he experienced her empathy. It reached inside him and extracted the pain, transferring it from him to her. He closed his eyes, selfishly allowing her to ease his suffering with her touch.

Then she was gone.

His eyes flew open in time to see her kneel between his legs.

"Doc, what...?"

"Sh-h-h." she whispered, glancing up at him with an impish gleam in her damp eyes.

"Come here," he pleaded, reaching for her, but she ignored him, growling when he touched her arms, so he gave up.

He lay back against the couch cushions and watched her, as helpless as he'd ever been in the TAINCC, although she had him trussed with nothing but sensation.

As cautiously as she had handled the laser probe, she touched the mark imbedded in the skin of his thigh with her thumb. Rider drew a deep, sharp breath and steeled himself against the pain.

Her thumb caressed his tattooed skin, traced each brightly colored line, inspected each separate segment of the stylized dagger. The sensation was powerful. Erotic impulses like electric charges ran from that super-sensitive point through each nerve in his body.

He moaned, unable to think, hardly aware of where pain ended and desire began. Just when he thought he couldn't bear another second of her gentle exploration, she moved. Her attention shifted from the mark on his thigh, to another, even more sensitive place.

When she touched him, he couldn't control himself. His body arched. His erection leaped against her hand, and he cried out.

He couldn't stand one more second of her exquisite torture, as maddening in its way as the TAINCC's, but suffused with pleasure instead of pain.

He reached for her, pulling her up over him, her legs spread, her eyes shining. He touched her, and her gasp told him she was ready. So he positioned her above him, his hands about her waist, and let her have control.

She held on to his arms and lowered herself onto him, her head thrown back, her breath puffing through parted lips. The joining was electrifying, from the first touch to the moment when their bodies pressed together in complete fusion.

Then, when she began to move, leading the dance, he could do nothing but follow, each movement sending shock waves of desire through him until he lost control and arched, his hands at her waist holding her fast against him as he spilled his seed and his soul into her.

As he did she cried out, her nails digging into his flesh, and he felt her contract around him, drawing from him the last of his strength.

She crumpled on top of him, her head against his chest, her hair tickling his nose. Rider felt more vulnerable than he could ever remember feeling. Not only was he completely drained, he had a disgusting urge to cry.

What had his angel-doctor done to him? He cradled her head and thrilled at her soft murmur of contentment.

He was afraid she'd given him back his humanity. Afraid

that the urge to protect her was something much more than just honor.

He was afraid, deathly afraid, that he loved her.

His heart contracted, and he winced as a faint wave of nausea tickled the back of his throat. The conditioned aversion to emotions was almost gone. He'd rediscovered his humanity, his life, in the arms of his angel doctor.

And he was terrified. With the conditioning, he could be the killing machine the TAINCC had tried to make him. Without it, he wasn't sure he could beat them.

He buried his face in her curly black hair and breathed deeply of her scent one last time. With a sense of profound regret, he knew it was time to go.

"What time is it?" he asked.

She turned to look at the clock on the desk. "Eight o'clock."

"What day?"

"Sunday. Sunday night."

Rider frowned. "How long have we been here?"

Kristen shrugged. "Since sometime early this morning."

He sat up. "We've got to get out of here. We've been here too long. They'll find us."

"But how can they? We destroyed the camera. Even if they'd had sound, we said we were leaving the hospital."

He was up, pulling on the scrubs, looking around for his shoes. "Come on, Doc. Think. They can come back from the future. We don't know what they may have developed beyond my time. They could be watching us right now. I mean, that one guy was pretty stupid, but that doesn't mean they all are."

Kristen looked at him thoughtfully. "He was pretty stupid. How'd he get sent back? You're not that stupid."

Rider gave her a disgusted glance. "Thank you."

She laughed, and he watched her mouth, thinking how much he wished he could give her laughter for the rest of her life.

"You know what I mean," she said.

"I told you, Doc," he said. "Most of these guys were criminals. I was a volunteer... No!" He shook his head. Sometimes his brain was still fuzzy. "No. I wasn't a volunteer. I was forced into it. I had something those other poor guys didn't have. I had my hatred for them to sustain me. Even when I couldn't remember it, it was still there to motivate me. Now, get dressed. We've got to get out of here."

His words hurt Kristen. He hated them because they'd killed his wife. But she knew he was right. Even with the assurance of the strange little orderly that no one would die over the weekend, now it was Sunday night, and the hospital would be getting busy. They always admitted a lot of patients on Sunday night for surgical procedures on Monday.

The corridors would be teeming with people before many more hours.

"You're right. We've got to go," she said.

She got up and got dressed quickly, running her fingers through her hair.

"I guess we'll just walk out," she said as she dressed. "We'll both have on scrubs, and we'll look terrible. They'll probably think we're residents on call. If anybody says anything, just let me talk."

"No problem," he said, pushing her through the office door ahead of him. "Lead the way."

Kristen stepped out into the dark corridor as she buckled Skipper's belt pack around her waist. She looked both ways. "Looks like the coast is clear. The elevator is this way." Rider was right behind her, the blaster in his hand.

"Put that away," she whispered. "You can't walk around with a blaster! Maybe if you were twelve years old, they'd think it was a toy."

"You could tell them I'm an escaped mongrel," he muttered.

"That would certainly work," she retorted as they rounded the corner to the elevator lobby and heard the bell ring.

Rider stopped her with a hand on her arm. They pulled back against the wall.

"We can't sneak around here like spies. We look suspicious," Kristen whispered urgently. "We need to just walk right by whoever it is."

"Just wait."

They stood pressed against the wall and watched the elevator doors through the wide-angle mirror that was mounted at the turn of the corridor. As Kristen watched, a very big man got off the elevator. He was dressed in white, but there was something strange about the uniform. The distorted image made it difficult to study details, but it looked too white, too pressed, too perfect. He was carrying something in his hand.

"I know that guy," Rider whispered in her ear.

"You know...?" Kristen stopped. "But you don't know anybody... oh."

"Yeah, oh," he said, then almost jerked her shoulder out of

its socket. They ran silently back down the hallway.

They were both in sneakers, so Kristen could clearly hear the click of the man's boots as he walked down the hall.

"Who is he?" she whispered, certain she already knew the answer.

"He trained with me."

She nodded and slowed down as they approached the morgue.

"No!" Rider hissed at her. "There's only one way out of there. Where can we go?"

She looked at him blankly. "We're in the subbasement, two stories underground. There's no way out anywhere. The elevators are the only exit."

"There's got to be something. Come on!"

"Wait!" She stopped, but Rider grabbed her and pulled her along. As he did, she glanced behind her at the other end of the hall. She could still hear the man's boots, clicking, clicking, coming inevitably closer. "Why isn't he running?

Rider jerked on her arm. "Maybe he knows there's no hurry. What the hell?"

Rider pulled up short and Kristen bumped into him. The corridor dead-ended into a piece of plywood.

"What's behind there?"

"I don't know. The pipe space, maybe. There's unfinished space down here, but I thought it was on the other side of the elevator lobby." She looked at the plywood barrier. "On this side..." What was on this end of the building? Something was tickling the edge of her brain.

"Oh! I know. A long time ago they were thinking about building a tunnel to the Medical Arts Building across the street. But I think they abandoned it when they couldn't guarantee the structural integrity. There's some kind of clay around here that shifts and slides, and they decided the tunnel wouldn't be safe." The click-click of their pursuer's boots echoed relentlessly in her ears.

Rider pulled on a corner of the plywood. "It's probably safer than what's behind us."

Kristen's heart contracted with fear. "No, we can't go in there! I don't know how far they got. It could still be a dead end."

"Want to fight him?" Rider jerked his head backwards, then pushed her out of the way. "Stand back." He stepped away from the barrier, stood for a few precious seconds with his head bowed and his arms raised in what looked to her like a placating gesture, then with a yell and a movement so quick she couldn't follow it, he kicked a hole in the plywood.

Dust and stale air buffeted them. Kristen coughed and fanned dust away from her as Rider pulled her through the hole.

On the other side was a dirt tunnel bolstered with thick boards, like an abandoned mine in an old movie. It was barely high enough for Kristen to walk upright. Rider had to crouch. He pushed her in front of him. "Lay on, Macduff," he said.

She turned around to look at him, surprised by the reference. "That's Shakespeare."

"Yeah? I know a little Chaucer, too."

"Well, I guess it's good to know humans haven't lost their taste for good literature."

"Actually, they're considered quite racy. They aren't allowed in the schools."

"You're kidding."

Rider pushed on her bottom. "Get a move on, Doc. We can discuss how tastes in literature have changed in the past five hundred years—or the next five hundred years—later. What do you think's up there?"

She pushed through cobwebs and dust, trying not to recoil, trying not to think of what might be living down here in the dark. "I don't know, okay?"

She tripped on a fallen board. "It's dark. Did I tell you I'm really afraid of the dark?" She heard her voice trembling. *Get a grip, Doctor Skipworth. Don't be such a slipper.*

Rider must have heard the note in her voice, too, because he spoke gently to her. "Hey, Doc. It's going to be all right. You're doing great."

"No, I'm not," she said shakily as the pallid light became dimmer and dimmer. She looked back over her shoulder, her eyes starving for the last glimmer of light back down the corridor. "I'm scared. I get really claustrophobic in the dark." She could hear the edge of panic in her voice. She gritted her teeth against the temptation to break and run back toward the light.

Rider put his hand on her neck, caressing her nape. "You're brave and tough. You're a hell of a partner, Doc."

Behind him he heard the unmistakable sound of blaster fire. It was faint, and he hoped his angel-doctor hadn't heard it. If she had, she might panic. The bastard had probably been too lazy to kick his way through the barrier, so he'd blasted it.

He remembered the guy. He'd barely started his training when Rider had been hurtled back into the past. Rider almost hadn't recognized him. He looked older. It made Rider's head hurt to think about the reasons a man younger than he was would look older after a few days.

He picked up his speed a bit, crouching enough so he wouldn't hit his head, and urging Kristen forward when she faltered. "Come on, Doc. It won't be much further, I'm sure."

"I guess if it's too dark for us to see him, he can't see us, right?"

"Right." Rider didn't tell her his fears, that if they could send metal back into the past, there was no telling what kind of weapons his TAINCC buddy back there had. He could have night vision goggles. Suddenly, he remembered what he had been in prison for. Torture and mutilation.

"Rider?"

"Yeah, Doc. What is it?" The edge of panic was still in her voice. She'd done so well so far. He couldn't afford to have her bark out on him now.

"Do you see that?"

"What? All I see is black."

Then he saw it. A tiny pinpoint of light ahead. After so much darkness, it was hard to believe his eyes.

"Well, well," he said lightly. "Egress."

Kristen sped up slightly, which was okay with Rider. He was ready to get out of this hellhole, too.

Slowly, agonizingly slowly, the pinpoint of light got larger. By its size, Rider figured if it was an exit, it was about twenty miles ahead.

He laughed to himself bitterly. He'd never tell Kristen, but a light that tiny couldn't be anything more than a flashlight or a single bulb. She'd find out soon enough.

Still, the question was, what was it? Or who? Was it a beacon to safety, or a lure to destruction? Grimly, he continued.

As they got closer, Rider saw that the pinpoint of light was exactly what he'd thought it was. A single light bulb. Where it had come from, how it was powered, he had no idea, but as they approached it, he tensed, ready for anything.

"Hi, there. Going my way?"

Except that.

He whirled and pointed the blaster in the direction of the calm, slightly amused voice right behind him.

Kristen jumped and whirled at the same time. He could

hear her rapid breathing.

In the semi-darkness, it was hard to make out the speaker until she stepped into the pallid circle of light cast by the bulb. "You..." Kristen muttered.

He turned to look at Kristen, then back at the small figure confronting him. "You two know each other?" he asked wryly. They ignored him. The little girl was grinning at Kristen. "So you finally recognized me?" she asked.

"What's going on here, Doc? You recognize her?" Rider studied Kristen out of the corner of his eye while he kept a watch on the other, smaller figure. His angel doctor was no longer terrified. In fact, she seemed relieved, lured into calmness by the strange little person confronting them.

Kristen stepped up beside him. "No, not until just now. Why have you been following me?" she asked the girl. "It was you, wasn't it? Every time?"

"Could someone tell me what's going on here? We don't exactly have all day to chat." Rider was getting fed up. They didn't have time for Old Home Week here. "We're being chased by a psychotic murderer."

Kristen stared at him. "He's psychotic?"

He glared at the girl. "You know how to get out of here?"

"Just keep on the straight and narrow, and don't waver," she said, then disappeared into the shadows.

Rider stepped toward the spot where she'd vanished, but there was nothing there. He ran his hands along the dirt wall, bent over and examined the floor. "What the hell was that?"

Kristen put her hand on his shoulder. "I don't know, but I swear, Rider, she's been everywhere."

He stood, dusting his hands on the scrub pants, peering through the dimness at Kristen. "What do you mean?"

"She was a runaway in the alley, then she was the homeless old woman who told me about houses being safe, and the electric company." She shrugged fatalistically, as if she knew he didn't believe her, didn't even understand her. "And the orderly, too," she finished. "She said no one would die this weekend. I know, it doesn't make any sense to me, either."

Rider stared at her in the semi-dark, trying to absorb what she was saying. "You're saying she's some kind of guide or something?" He thought about it. A guide—sent by who knew who—from who knew where—to taunt them with cryptic remarks that didn't make sense? "I guess it's no more unbelievable than what I've told you. But where did she come from.

Where did she go?"

And why didn't she take them with her?

Kristen grabbed his arm. "Listen," she said.

He did, and heard the crunch of heavy boots echoing down the dirt corridors. "Let's go."

He pushed Kristen ahead of him on through the corridor. It got blacker and blacker, darker than he'd known anything could be. Was this what death was like? An unending void? A black hole in life? He shuddered.

The trip back to this time had been like being born in reverse. He'd left a light, sterile room in the TAINCC and hurtled through darkness so deep it had shrouded him like fabric, clinging to him, suffocating him. Then he'd been slung into a solid wall of brick like a piece of rotten fruit tossed by an angry kid.

Had that darkness been any darker than this? With his heart pounding against his chest wall, with the smell of wet dirt and mold in his nostrils, with the memory of that tiny light teasing his retinae, he wasn't sure.

Kristen's breaths were becoming more rapid and shallow. He knew how she felt—he was terrified and exhausted, too. He reached out in the darkness and touched her arm.

She gasped, a tiny choking breath, then put her hand over his. He understood what she was seeking with that touch—she needed to feel his assurance, glean courage from his calm.

It was what he needed, too. So he gritted his teeth and tried to give her what she wanted, knowing what he tried to broadcast was a lie. But he did it anyway. If she found out he was terrified, she might break, and if she broke, he didn't have a chance.

Her quiet bravery kept him going, so he did his best to send her messages of strength and courage, and in doing so, realized that it helped him. She was the reason, the instrument of his determination.

He had to keep her safe. Her safety was worth more than his life. He had to be brave to protect her.

Behind them walked certain death. Ahead of them—Rider swallowed the dregs of bitter panic that suffused his mouth—ahead of them was the unknown.

The bizarre little person had told them to keep on the straight and narrow, and Rider couldn't see any more logical reason for not believing her than for believing her.

He was going to have to think about where she had come from at some point. There was only one way he knew of for someone to appear out of the blue. The same way he had. Through time. But when he'd left the future, the trip had been one way. Had they perfected the return?

"Oof!"

Kristen stopped abruptly, and he ran into her.

"Ouch," she said. "I—think this is it." Her voice quavered just a bit.

Rider's heart filled with admiration for her. Admiration and something else. Something so wonderful and so awful he wasn't sure he could bear it.

Somewhere along the way, Kristen Skipworth had become the most important thing in the world to him. Important in a way that had nothing to do with Mari's betrayal, with the TAINCC, or even with the need to protect the skipworths through time.

His hands shook, and he swallowed hard. He wanted to see her amber-green eyes. He cursed the darkness for depriving him of the pleasure of her face. He wanted to hold her, tell her everything would be all right, even if he didn't believe it.

She deserved everything he could give her, and he was so damned afraid of what was going to happen. He'd lost what objectivity he'd had. And without it, he wasn't sure he could keep her safe.

Her bravery made him ashamed. She had believed in him, had struck out into the darkness with him. He wrapped his fingers around her neck and massaged the knotted muscles there. "You think this is what?" he asked.

"The end," she said flatly.

SIXTEEN

Rider's fingers tightened on her neck as her hand touched his. Her fingers pulled at his, urging him to let go, urging his hand forward until his palm flattened against cold damp dirt.

"See. The end of the road."

He could tell she tried to laugh, but it came out sounding like a sob.

His stomach knotted in panic. The end of the road. Was it? Did it end here, with him and his angel-doctor flattened against the cold wall of dirt while the tank picked them off like little dots in a vidgame?

"Just a minute," he muttered, listening. There was a soft whoosh of air coming from below them. Kneeling down, he ran his hands along the wall. At about knee height, he encountered a void. "There's still a tunnel here," he said, pulling her down to kneel beside him. Her limbs quivered.

He touched her cheek. It was cold as ice, and wet with tears. "It's awfully narrow, but it's a tunnel."

"Straight and narrow," Kristen murmured.

"What?"

"That's what she said this time. Everything she's told me has been true. Oh, Rider, I don't know if I can do it." Her voice cracked, and she crumpled to the ground.

He reached for her and found her turned in on herself, arms wrapped around her knees, face buried in her arms. "Sure you can, Doc."

He wrapped her whole body in his arms, holding on to her as tightly as he could until he heard her muffled voice.

"What if it's a dead end?"

He almost shuddered, hearing his thoughts echoed in her broken little voice. But he checked himself and took a long breath. "Didn't you say that little girl was right every time?"

She nodded against his chest.

"Well, then. Shouldn't we trust her?" He couldn't believe what he was saying. Despite his confident words, Rider's whole body tensed with fear.

He, too, was afraid of being caught like a rat in a trap in that small space. It was too much like the chambers in which he'd been locked while being conditioned—dark, inescapable. He didn't want to die that way, didn't want to die at all.

It was strange, this new urge to live. For a long time after he'd learned of Mari's betrayal, it hadn't mattered to him. He'd begged for death, cursed God for cheating him out of it. But that was before he'd learned to use his hatred to keep him strong, before he'd sworn vengeance on them, before their conditioning had made him forget that it was them he hated, not the skipworths.

And now his angel-doctor needed him, and that was more than enough to live for.

Wrenching his thoughts back to the matter at hand, he put his palm against her cold cheek. "It's your call, Doc. I'll do whatever. We can fight him from right here if you want to."

"Which way do you think is a better chance?" she asked quaveringly.

Don't make me tell you, Doc. Don't make me say we've got a cometsicle's chance in hell either way. Don't make me tell you you're going to die here with me, and I can't do a damned thing about it.

He wiped his brain of the cowardly thoughts, still not quite convinced she couldn't read his mind as well as his feelings. "Maybe we should believe your little prophet."

She shivered, sending ripples through him. "Prophet. She called herself a gross prophet."

"Well, then, that settles it." He unwrapped himself from around her and let his lips replace his fingers on her cheek, which was still damp, still cool with tears. Then he urged her up and pushed her toward the hole. "After you."

Suddenly, he heard the unmistakable whir of blaster fire, and at the same instant the tunnel lit with green and a searing pain ripped through his shoulder. He cried out involuntarily.

"Rider! What?" Kristen cried as he whirled, grabbing his blaster and returning fire.

The silhouette of their pursuer shadowed the pale light of the bulb they had left behind. Rider fired again, his jaw clenched against the burning agony in his shoulder, and pushed Kristen toward the hole as the green ribbon of light burned all too close to her.

"Get going, Doc. I'm fine."

"You're hurt! I can smell—"

"Damn it, Doc! Go!"

"You're coming?"

"Yeah, now go!"

The tunnel was still lit with fading green light as he saw her sneakers disappear into the hole. The blaster jerked in his hand as he fired again at the dark figure and hit him. The bastard didn't even flinch. Metal reinforced body armor, he thought grimly. Damn!

He set off a long blast, watching to see how much damage it did, trying to aim for the guy's hand. He heard a gutteral cry as the tank stumbled backward from the force of the blast.

Whirling, Rider ducked into the hole, the hairs on the back of his neck tingling. He half expected to feel a green, burning blast rip him in two, but nothing happened. His shoulder was a wall of fire, fuzzing his brain as he doggedly crawled after Kristen.

She was crying softly, but she never faltered. "Rider, you okay?" Her voice was nearly absorbed by the dirt all around them, and weak with fear and pain. "Your shoulder." She slowed down, turning back toward him. "Let me—"

"Move!" He slapped her on the bottom. "It's nothing, Doc. A flesh wound. Go! Fast as you can!"

She sobbed once, but she kept going.

They could have crawled for days. Rider was oblivious to time, and apparently so was Kristen. They didn't talk, they just doggedly continued.

Sometimes the passage got so narrow he wasn't sure he was going to make it. Despite what he'd told her, the pain in his shoulder stole his breath. His flesh continued to burn long after the green light had faded.

He clenched his jaw and tried to ignore it, but it just kept on, searing deeper and deeper, until finally, aeons later, it let up.

He did his best to keep from scraping the sides of the narrow tunnel, but when he couldn't avoid it, the cold wet wall of dirt set off the searing pain again. Even in the chill that existed thirty feet below the surface, his face and body poured sweat.

Kristen whimpered and stopped. He ran into her.

"What is it, Doc?" His jaw was still clenched against pain, and he sounded grim and bleak to his own ears.

"Can't..." she whispered, her breath catching on a sob.

"Come on." He deliberately lightened his voice as he groped in the darkness for her. He touched the small of her back. "Just a little farther. You can do it!"

Her body was shaking with silent sobs. "No, no, no..."

"Don't give up on me, Doc," he begged, patting her back.

"Talk to me. What is it?"

"Too—narrow. Can't..."

She was almost incoherent. If he was cold, with his layers of muscle and thicker, tougher skin, she must be freezing. In the cramped space, there was nothing he could do but urge her forward.

Horror laid its icy fingers on his spine. What if the passage was too narrow. If she couldn't get through, he knew he couldn't. They'd be stuck. Doomed.

No! Rider stiffened, allowing the resolve that had kept him going all this time to override his compassion for Kristen, his fear, even his good sense. He would not be stuck here like a cartoon character in a hole too small. He shoved her, hoping he wasn't pushing her over the edge into a complete breakdown.

"Get going, Doc! Get your damned ass in gear! I'm the one back here with my butt stuck up like a damned bullseye. Get a move on!"

He shoved her as hard as he could, allowing the anger to suffuse his brain. If he touched her, would his anger, his resolve, transfer to her? Could she use it?

He felt resistance, and it almost panicked him. The passage was getting narrower, ominously narrower. Still he kept a constant pressure on her shapely bottom, and he kept up a constant barrage of crude remarks designed to infuriate her.

"I can't believe I got myself stuck in a damned tunnel with a debutante! Move it! Get that fat little bottom out of my way so I can get out of here!"

If they hadn't been in such dire danger, if they hadn't been buried thirty feet underground, in the darkest darkness he'd ever known, he'd have thoroughly enjoyed the experience. He'd love to see her face.

"Shit, woman. My hair grows faster than you move!" He punched her bottom lightly, prodding her gently onward. "Hard to drag all this bulk around, I guess?"

"Rider, if we don't die, I'm going to kill you!"

He almost laughed aloud at the quavery, defiant voice. A sense of triumph inundated him. They were going to be fine. He leaned forward and kissed her behind with a huge smack.

"Way to go, Doc!" he said, then groaned when his shoulder brushed the wall. The passage was narrowing again. "Keep it moving!" he gritted out through jaws clenched against the fire in his shoulder.

He'd said his shoulder was just a flesh wound. As badly as it hurt, he was pretty sure that was true. Just a graze. A deep one, probably a half inch of flesh and muscle had been plowed, but a graze nonetheless. It just burned like hell.

Somehow, the passage didn't seem so narrow all of a sudden. Rider breathed a wary sigh of relief and continued crawling, no longer able to feel his knees, hardly noticing the searing pain in his shoulder.

Kristen stopped short in front of him. He hadn't even realized his head was down, his eyes were closed, but when he looked up he saw light. "What is it?" he asked, trying to peer around her.

She crawled a little farther, and suddenly disappeared.

"Doc!" he shouted, lunging toward the pale glow that blinded his dark-adapted eyes. He put out his hand to pull himself another foot forward, and encountered nothing.

He overbalanced, his breath gone and his heart slamming against his chest, and tumbled down a slimy, curving wall on top of her.

He rolled and struggled to stand, but his arms and legs cramped so much he couldn't move for a moment, could only writhe there on the floor until the muscles gave up and relaxed. Kristen was already upright, stretching her legs and back and crying softly.

"It stinks in here," she whispered, looking at him through her tears.

Rider laughed. He laughed until his gut hurt. It felt so good to laugh, so good to stand up straight, so good to be with her. "Of course it stinks, Doc. It's a sewer."

He pulled her close and kissed her, scratching his lips on the grit on her face, filling his mouth with the taste of dust and grime mingled with her flavor. "You did it, Doc," he muttered against her mouth.

"No," she whispered. "You did." Her eyes flashed brilliant gold in her dirty face. "And if you ever say anything else about my butt, I'll kill you."

He hugged her, molding her to him, dirt and all. He didn't want to ever let her out of his sight. Ever.

"So, you made it."

Pushing Kristen away, Rider whirled, raising his blaster. It was the girl from the tunnel.

"Just who the hell are you?" he demanded breathlessly,

shocked by her sudden appearance.

"Name's Darwin," she said, grinning.

He took a good look at her. She was tiny, probably no more than five feet tall. He'd thought she was a child the first time he'd seen her lit only by the pallid bulb, but now he saw that she was definitely a woman.

Her compact, perfect body was encased entirely in a black, shiny substance that looked molded to her. Her hair was black and pulled into a topknot from which a straight black braid hung down her back. Her face was gamine, the kind that was ageless, with a child's translucent skin and naturally red lips.

Her eyes, though, were deep black holes, old as the universe.

"Darwin? What kind of name is that? It's a joke, right?"

"Not at all," she responded, and danced toward them.

Rider stared. There was literally no other word for it. Her step was so light, so bouncy, it could be called nothing else.

Kristen stared, too. "Why are you following us?" she said suspiciously.

Rider hadn't lowered the blaster, and his finger tightened on the activator button as he waited for Darwin's response.

"Somebody had to."

"Who are you?" he said again. For some reason, every word she uttered irritated the hell out of him.

"I told you. Darwin."

He took a step forward, pressing the blaster into the soft top of Darwin's breast. "Tell me more, and stop talking in riddles, damn it. We don't have time for games."

An exaggerated sigh escaped her lips and she pouted like a child who's been told to come inside. "My name is Darwin. I'm from the future. I'm here to help you."

"Great," Kristen muttered. "Like the government."

"What?" Rider said, not wanting to be distracted from his careful observation of Darwin, but not wanting to miss what Kristen was saying, either.

"Never mind," she said. "Why are you here to help us? And why were you following me?"

"Where in the future?" Rider asked, fear and hope suddenly battling within him. *Had* she come from the future? And if so, how far? The questions raged within him, especially the one, most important one. Could they go back?

"Much, much farther forward than you, Rider."

He assessed her through narrowed eyes. "You know me?"
She nodded.

"Then you know why I was sent back here."

"Yep."

"Do you also know why I didn't accomplish my mission?"

"Yep."

"Well, what about our friend back there? Do you know what's keeping him?"

"Yep."

"Look, Darwin. I'm beginning to get real tired of your monosyllabic answers." Rider ignored a snort of amusement from Kristen and pressed the nose of the blaster just a bit more firmly into Darwin's breast.

"Okay, sorry." Darwin pushed the blaster aside with a finger, and Rider let her. "You kind of messed up his shooting hand with your blaster, although I see he didn't do badly with your shoulder, either."

Kristen looked at Rider's shoulder when Darwin gestured. "Oh, Rider. Look at you."

"Don't worry, Doc. You haven't had the pleasure of the full effect of a blaster wound, but when you do, they're sort of self-cauterizing." He shrugged, wincing at the pull of burned flesh against fabric.

He hadn't looked at it yet, didn't particularly want to see a half-inch furrow plowed in the flesh of his shoulder, or check to see if bone had been burned. No tendons had been severed since he could still move his arm. "Not that it usually matters to the wounded party whether a blaster wound is cauterized or not. Anyhow, this one's okay for now. So what happened to our friend?" He turned back to Darwin.

"He stopped to patch up his arm with plasmanique, then he'll probably go outside and try to find a way in here from up there." She jerked a thumb toward the top of the huge pipe they were standing in.

Rider studied her, his brain whirling too fast for coherence. "Probably? Why don't you know? Don't you know what's going to happen to us?"

As he spoke, he thought he saw a shadow cross her face, but it was gone so quickly he thought—he hoped, he might have been mistaken.

"No. It can get pretty complicated," she said, spreading her hands.

Rider thought complicated was a mild term for what it could get.

"See," Darwin went on, looking at her hands.

Rider couldn't help thinking she was avoiding their eyes.

"We can't know more than we know. In other words, I'm from the future, and I'm here right now, so right now is all I can know about your time. Tomorrow, I or someone else from the future, can know what happened up until then."

Kristen pushed her hands through her hair. "But what if you went back to three weeks from now yesterday. I mean..."

Rider turned to look at her. "What the hell are you talking about?"

Darwin threw Kristen a sharp glance, then laughed. "I know. See what I mean? All I can say is I can't know what's happening here until it happens. And if something were to happen that changed the future, then I wouldn't know it because it would have changed the future, which would have changed what I had done, et cetera, et cetera, ad nauseam."

"I don't understand," Kristen said.

Rider agreed with her, sort of. He didn't understand a lot of things, either, but he'd seen the glance Darwin had thrown her. He was certain at least part of what the tiny girl said was a lie.

One thing was perfectly clear to him, though. These people could travel to the past and back again. They apparently could control where they went pretty accurately. His brain was having trouble with the implications of that.

If he'd thought he was confused before when he'd tried to analyze his feelings for his angel doctor, it was nothing to the turmoil in his brain now. If he could go anywhere, forward or backward in time... with an effort, he forced himself to concentrate on Darwin's words.

"What are you two going to do now?" she asked.

Kristen assessed Darwin, not quite sure of the sensations she was receiving from the other girl. There was something peculiar, something not quite true about Darwin.

It wasn't that Kristen didn't trust her. That was just it. Kristen had an overwhelming urge to trust Darwin. But she couldn't figure out where the urge was coming from, because she couldn't *feel* a damned thing from Darwin. And she had the very definite notion Darwin was holding her feelings back deliberately.

She dismissed the thought, turning to Rider. "We've got to get out of here before Darth Vader figures out where we are."

He frowned. "Who?"

She nodded back toward the hole through which they'd crawled. "Him. Your psychotic buddy." Kristen didn't think she was getting through to him. He was distracted. She put her hand on his arm and gleaned bewilderment within him. Bewilderment, fear, and a devastating hope that ripped at her heart.

"I know," she said. "It's confusing. But Darwin is here to help us."

He stared at her, the frown still creasing his brow. "That's just it," he said, glancing at Darwin. "The stuff you told the Doc, how'd you know what to tell her if you can't know what's going to happen in the future? She said you told her to watch out for the electric company."

Her heart pounding as she realized the truth of his words, Kristen looked at Darwin. "And that the morgue would be safe this weekend," she said quickly. "That's right. How did you know those things?"

Darwin looked decidedly uncomfortable. She shifted her gaze to her hands, then back to Kristen. "I can't tell you. Like I said, it's really complicated. Look, I've got to go..."

Rider's face darkened ominously. He grabbed Darwin. As Kristen watched in astonishment he twisted her arm brutally, eliciting a cry from her.

"No! You're going to stay right here until you explain something to me."

There was an edge to Rider's voice that had never been there when he talked to Kristen. Even when he'd threatened her.

He sounded ruthless, virulent. She could see the cold-hearted resolve the TAINCC had conditioned into him, and she was afraid for Darwin. Looking at his face, she could almost believe Rider would kill the girl if it served his purpose.

Darwin laughed nervously. "You haven't quite gotten it yet, have you, Rider? You can't keep me here if I want to leave. You'll be left holding a fistful of air."

He yanked her arm up behind her while Kristen watched. "Rider," she said, her empathic sense mirroring the pain in Darwin's arm, even though she still wasn't receiving anything from the other girl. "You're hurting her."

"Damn right, I'm hurting her," he growled. "And I'm going

to hurt her more if she doesn't tell me the truth."

"About what?" Darwin's voice was strained.

"About time travel. Can we go back?"

Kristen's heart lurched, and sudden hot tears stung her eyes. Here it was, the thing she had been afraid of. She had known it was coming. She had no reason to be upset. She'd thought she was prepared, ever since the moment when she'd realized what the possibility of returning to the future would mean to him.

"Back where?"

Don't, Darwin, she wanted to shout. *Don't play with him! You don't know what he's been through.*

But didn't she? She caught Darwin's eye and saw a shadow there, a shadow of sadness, or regret? It was decidedly uncomfortable when someone from the future looked at you like that.

Rider tweaked Darwin's arm, and Kristen winced. She knew how those little tweaks could hurt.

"Back into the future."

Kristen had thought her heart was already sore, but his words wrenched it until she expected her chest to bleed. *Back into the future.* She knew what he meant. *Back home.*

His words were so wistful, so full of desperate hope. Home, where he wanted to be. Back with his wife.

It was what she'd known would happen. *No contest, Doc.* She could almost hear him say it. No contest. His wife would win. It was the way it had to be.

Darwin gave Kristen an unfathomable look, then twisted her head toward Rider. "There's a possibility," she said, her voice still strained by pain. "For you."

He let her go, as if he couldn't stand to touch her any more. He gazed at Kristen for a long moment, and she could almost read the thoughts behind those blue eyes. "Are you saying Kristen couldn't go?"

Darwin had her eyes closed and was carefully manipulating her arm, her face blank. "That's what I'm saying," she said. "Look. You can't stay here much longer. And I sure can't. I've got to go."

"Darwin, wait!" Kristen rushed to her and caught her hand. Darwin gave her a shocked look and recoiled immediately, snatching her hand away as if she'd been burned, but not before Kristen felt it. She was buffeted with sensation. As much as from Skipper. Almost as much as when she touched Rider.

The echo of Darwin's touch reverberated down Kristen's spine. Love, pain, regret, heartache, a profound pity, and something else, something familiar but elusive, which nagged at her memory like a whiff of a forgotten scent.

Kristen tried to shake off the shock of that touch, tried to lighten her voice. "You can't go yet. Don't you have any more gross prophecies for me?"

Darwin smiled sadly, and Kristen's heart turned over again. What else could there be? How much more could she take if Rider left her, too?

"Actually, I do. Although it's going to get me in even bigger trouble than I'm in already," she muttered, as if to herself. Then she pointed a finger at Kristen. "Don't forget what Skipper told you when your parents died. Every word."

She turned to Rider. "You have to make your own decision, Rider Savage. I pray it's the right one." She disappeared before their eyes.

"No, wait! Darwin! How did you know what— " Kristen stopped. She was talking to air. Darwin's words echoed in her ears. How did Darwin know what Skipper had told her?

Kristen's heart contracted, and tears burned her eyes as she recalled what her brother had said that awful day when they'd buried their parents.

Rider stared at the spot where Darwin was standing, until Kristen laid her hand on his arm. When he looked at her, his eyes were opaque and as dull as unpolished turquoise.

Through his arm she felt the regret, the doubt. "I know what you're thinking," she whispered.

"No," he said flatly, shrugging off her hand. "You don't. Let's get out of here before our friend catches up with us."

He grabbed her arm and pulled her with him toward the faint light that indicated an opening to the outside. "Is there one more place in this fair city where we can hide? Or have we used them all up?"

Kristen didn't like his hard-bitten tone. It was as if he had changed in the few minutes while they had been talking to Darwin. Changed into the killing machine they'd tried to make him. His hand gripping her wrist didn't give her anything. No emotion at all. It was the first time she hadn't been able to glean his emotions from him through his touch. She was bereft.

"Doc? Got any ideas?"

She tried to think, to pull her thoughts away from the void she sensed within him. Where could they go? The clinic had been blown up. Her apartment had been blown up. For all she knew, Skipper's house had been blown up by now.

Skipper.

"We could go to Skipper's boat," she said.

"Boat? Your brother had a boat, too?"

She nodded. "Oh yes, he had a boat. Skipper always had a boat." And it had cost a lot to keep the house and the boat these two years, but she had. She had never wanted to confront the reality of his death enough to get rid of his things. Now, it seemed, it was a good thing she'd kept them.

"What kind?"

"A sailboat. A thirty-foot sloop, I think is what he called it. It's at the city marina."

Kristen squinted as bright sunlight assaulted her eyes. Had they really crawled through that tunnel all night long? When she'd looked at the clock in the morgue office, it had been eight in the evening. Now, it was broad daylight. Monday morning. Her arms and legs quivered with exhaustion. How much longer could they last?

They were in one of the big viaducts that ran under the city. Above them were the hospital and the Medical Arts Building. She could hear the rush of traffic on the streets.

"The marina's about fifteen miles from here. We need money."

Rider laughed harshly. "Ever done any begging, Doc?"

She put her hands on her hips and encountered the belt pack that held Skipper's little computer. "This is a real long shot," she muttered, "but Skip was always stuffing his change wherever he could find a place. He was so careless."

Suddenly, she was inundated by thoughts of her brother. Frowning at her when she'd admonished him to take better care with his money. Irritated when she wouldn't join him and his buddies on the boat. Intense as he concentrated on his project, bent over the computer. Sad and strong as he took her arm the day their parents were buried. Her throat closed up, tears clogging the back of it.

She missed her brother almost more than she ever had before. So much reminded her of him. His house, his boat, the little computer case.

"Doc?"

She blinked hard, angrily dashing away the couple of tears that fell, and unzipped the pocket on the front of the case, groping around inside. She found two pens, a notepad, and a small vial of dark red liquid labeled *K SKIPWORTH*.

"Yuk, Skipper," she muttered.

"What?"

Kristen held up the vial. "He's got a vial of my blood in here." She kept digging. "Bless you," she whispered as she came up with two dollars and thirteen cents in change.

She grinned through her tears at Rider, who was surveying the vast concrete riverbed in which they stood. "We can ride the bus," she announced triumphantly, holding out her hand.

"Great," he said without conviction. "Where's the bus?"

"There's a bus stop right in front of the Medical Arts building, if we could just get up there."

Rider looked around. "Down that way."

Just as they were about to climb up the metal spikes that served as steps in the concrete wall, Darwin materialized in front of them, brandishing a handful of twenty dollar bills.

"Don't take the bus. You won't make it. Here. Live high. Take a cab." She stuffed the bills into Rider's hand and disappeared again.

Rider scowled at the shimmering air where she'd been standing just a split second before. "I don't like her," he muttered.

"Rider," Kristen admonished. "She saved our lives."

"Yeah, well. I don't trust her." He frowned at the bills in his hand. "These are probably fake. We don't use money in the twenty-fifth century. Why would they, even farther in the future?"

Kristen laughed and tugged on his arm. "Come on, they're not fake. And even if they are, they're probably good enough to fool a cab driver. Let's climb up to the street and hail a cab."

As they climbed out of the viaduct, a mottled gray cat ran across the street in front of them.

Kristen's heart turned over. "Sam! I forgot Sam! How could I do that!" The big yellow tomcat who'd shared her apartment ever since Skipper died had given her something to focus on, someone to care for, to talk to. How could she have just left him there to fend for himself after her apartment exploded?

She grabbed Rider's arm. "We've got to go get Sam!" Poor thing, he was probably starving.

Rider stared at her as if she'd lost her mind. "Sam? You mean that damned cat?" He shuddered, and Kristen felt the ripple all the way through him. She still didn't understand his aversion to cats.

"No way! Come on." He twisted his arm out of her grasp and took firm hold of her elbow.

"Rider, please. He's been out there, lost and alone, ever since the apartment blew up. I can't leave him!" Suddenly, her cat was the most important thing she could think of. He was her responsibility. She was supposed to protect him.

"Listen to me, Doc." He jerked her around and grabbed her shoulders, his hands transmitting cold bleakness to her. She shivered, hating his new control that kept her from knowing his feelings through his touch. It was almost as if he were already gone.

"We are *not* risking our lives for a goddamned cat—" His breath caught and he coughed dryly, his fingers digging into her arms.

Unable to stand the desolation, she wrenched away. "I've got to," she said, beseeching him with her gaze. "Please. It won't take more than a few minutes."

"No!" he thundered, his face inches from hers, his eyes black with rage. "He's a *cat*. He's not worth your life. Now shut up and come on. We've got to get out of here!" He grabbed her arm again and pushed her toward the curb. "Call the cab."

"No. You're so determined to leave Sam to starve in the street, you figure it out."

Rider stared at his stubborn, maddening angel-doctor, fury churning in his gut. He wanted to grab her up and shake sense into her. He wanted to hold her so close she'd think she was him. He wanted to forget cats and blasters and the stink of death, just for a few minutes.

"I said no. The goddamned cat is not worth your life," he gritted between clenched teeth, swallowing against the bile that choked him. He glanced around, trying to figure out which of the hundreds of smelly gas-burning cars were cabs.

His eye caught a bright white figure down past the hospital, walking deliberately, stiffly. He held his right arm against his side, and his left hand was in a pocket of the jacket.

"Shit! There he is, Doc! Come on!"

Kristen shot him a terrified glance, then pointed toward a garishly painted car.

A ribbon of green light whirred past Rider's head as she opened the car door. He pushed her in and dove in behind her.

"What the f—" the sleepy driver exclaimed as Rider righted himself and pulled the door closed. A blast shattered the back window of the cab and burned a neat hole in the front window.

"Go!" Rider shouted, pulling Kristen's head down below the level of the window, unsure of why he thought being out of sight would protect her against blaster fire. It could go through plastic. "Get the hell out of here!"

"Hey, mister—" the driver started, but Rider grabbed his neck with one hand.

"Let's go for a nice drive, what do you say? Or I'll snap your spinal cord..." he said conversationally.

"Shit! Damn! Shit!" The driver's neck immediately slicked with sweat, but he pulled on a lever and they shot forward just as another green ribbon of light flashed through the window, putting a smoking hole next to the first one.

Rider looked back and saw their pursuer hailing another cab.

"Wh-where?" the driver stuttered in between curses.

"Just drive very fast," he said, then turned to Kristen. "Doc? Where to?"

She lifted her head from his lap and peered out the back window. "Is he following us?"

"Yeah. Now quick. Where to?"

She shot him a sharp glance then looked back behind them. "Gable," she said to the driver. "Forty-four hundred block."

The traffic was closing in behind them, and Rider couldn't see whether the tank had gotten a cab yet. "Turn here!" he shouted at the driver. "Take the side streets. We've got to lose somebody."

"Look man, who's gonna pay for my cab?" the driver whined. "I got all my savings tied up in this car, and I just had it washed."

Rider touched the driver's neck again. "You just drive, mister, and hope you're insured against blaster damage."

"B-blaster damage...?" The driver's wide eyes caught Rider's in the mirror.

Rider knew what he was thinking. One for the dog catchers. He turned back to look behind them. Lots of traffic, several other yellow cars, but he didn't think he saw the one the tank had been waving at.

Kristen had been tucked up against his side, shivering, but now she sat up and moved away, tension gripping her. When he touched her arm she cringed. Not much. Barely enough for him to notice.

"Doc? You okay?" He glanced at her quickly, but she was watching the road ahead. He looked around. "Is this the way to the marina?"

The driver's gaze caught his again in the mirror. "Heck, no," he said. "Gable's downtown."

Rider grabbed Kristen and shook her. "What the hell are you doing?" he growled. "You're going to get us killed."

She wouldn't look at him, kept her gaze averted, even when he pulled her up close. "Damn you, Doc!"

He thrust her away, disgusted with her deceit. He swallowed hard against the nausea that crept into the back of his throat. She was still trying to go get that damned cat! How could she be so stupid? How could she throw their lives away for a dumb animal?

Just like Mari! He shivered. She'd gone back for the cat, and they'd killed her. With a great effort, he clenched his jaw and relaxed, pushing thoughts of Mari and the cat out of his mind, concentrating on saving Kristen, despite her determination to get them killed.

He touched the driver's neck and was rewarded with a moan and a terrified glance in the rear view mirror. "The marina," he whispered. The driver nodded.

"Marina. You got it."

Kristen took a quick breath like a sob, but Rider didn't care. He'd be damned if he'd let her get herself killed for a cat. He'd kill her himself first.

He saw the water long before they reached it. It stretched out all the way to the horizon, blue and endless, meeting the sky in the hazy distance, far beyond his imaginings. He'd never seen the ocean, although he'd heard about it.

But what he'd heard in his time, what he'd seen on vidlink, couldn't compare with the beauty stretched out in front of him. He could smell it, too. A fresh, salty smell, like nothing that had ever been in his nostrils before.

Maybe, maybe on that endless stretch of water he could keep her safe.

If only they could escape into time. What had Darwin said? He could go, but Kristen couldn't. He could be safe, but his angel doctor never could. As long as she lived, her life was in danger. Her life and the life of all the skipworths down through time.

The car rolled to a stop, startling Rider out of his reverie. He blinked, and discovered that the cab driver and Kristen were both watching him, the driver with wide-eyed terror, his angel-doctor with a expression that was at once pensive and sad.

He hoped to hell she couldn't read his mind. If she could, she'd know how damned scared he was, how cowardly he felt. She'd know he didn't think he had a chance in hell of keeping her safe. He averted his gaze from hers, wiping his brain of terrifying thoughts, not only because he was afraid she could glean them from him, but also because too much thinking brought on the emotions, and emotions kept him from acting logically.

He thrust two of the bills at the driver. "Is that enough?" he asked him.

The other man barely glanced at them. "Yeah, yeah! Just get out of my cab," he pleaded.

Rider grabbed Kristen's wrist and pulled her out with him. "Where's the boat?" he asked.

She lifted her chin and stared defiantly at him. He twisted her arm up behind her. "Have we got to go through this again, Doc?"

"I'll scream," she gasped.

"Go ahead. Then we can both be locked up by the dog catchers and wait for him to knock us off like targets in a vidgame." He shrugged and let go of her arm, thinking how tired he was of the game. Of life in general.

It was complicated, as Darwin had said. He thought, for a brief instant, he might actually be better off if he'd not hesitated back in the clinic when he could have killed Kristen Skipworth with a flick of his wrist. His life would have been much easier. Empty, damned, but easier.

The familiar nausea flickered in his throat. He had hesitated. He'd given his brain a split-second, and that had been enough to change his life forever.

SEVENTEEN

Rider looked at Kristen and saw the sadness in her face again. It hurt him deep inside for her to be sad. If he gave his brain a split-second now, he'd know why she was sad. He'd know he hadn't been fair to her, hadn't told her everything. If he thought about it, he'd know she had the wrong idea. But they didn't have time right now, and he had to keep himself rational so he could do the things he needed to do to protect her.

"Come on, Doc! What's it going to be?" He grabbed her again, deriving a grim satisfaction when she yielded. "Where is the boat?"

She pointed vaguely with her free hand. "Down there," she said. "It's the *Whale Song.*"

"Let's go." He gave her a little shove and let go of her arm. Standing behind her, he watched to see what she would do.

Her shoulders slumped a little under the grimy cotton of the scrubs. The curve of her neck disappearing under the tangled black hair drew his gaze. He longed to touch it, not threateningly, as he'd done so many times, but lovingly. He wanted to put his mouth there, right where her hair curled. He wanted to bury his nose there and breathe in her scent. The scent of life.

His gaze traveled down her back to the seat of her pants, filthy where she'd sat on the cold earth inside the tunnel. Down her long legs to her feet, then back up. Her hands were clenched into small fists at her sides, but she walked resolutely down the pier, and he followed her.

She stopped at a sleek blue boat with blue canvas covers and the name *Whale Song* stenciled on its side, with a stylized, curving shape Rider recognized as one of the ancient creatures he'd studied in some mythology class he'd once taken.

She'd promised him she'd show him whales one day. He wondered if they'd have the chance.

"Well, here it is," she said, a falsely bright ring in her voice. Grief shone from her eyes, grief tinged with fear.

"You can do it, Doc," he murmured and touched her shoulder. With a little wince, she pulled away. He knew her so well. He was trying to shield his thoughts, his emotions from her, and that wince told him he'd succeeded. Well, it was for her own good, her own safety.

Kristen didn't want Rider touching her. She was confused, tired, sad. And Rider was holding himself apart, somehow shielding his feelings from her.

Feeling more alone than she'd ever felt, she climbed onto the boat, her heart aching as she surveyed Skipper's pride and joy.

It was so neglected. Skipper would kill her if he knew she'd let the *Whale Song* go like this. Just like his house, she'd avoided the boat since his death—pretended it didn't exist, in fact.

Now, as she stepped aboard, a faint echo of her brother roiled deep inside her. Was it real, or just her battered emotions commingled with the memory of him laughing, tossing his head in the wind as he shouted at her to cast off? Kristen shivered at the vividness of the image.

She stopped and Rider bumped into her from behind, grabbing her and a halyard at the same time to keep them from tumbling off the deck.

"Hey Doc, come on. What is it?" He urged her forward, but she resisted. "Are you all right?"

She shook her head at his dumb question. "No," she said in a small voice. "I'm not all right. I don't want to be here. I never came to Skipper's boat for a very good reason—so I wouldn't be bombarded by the essence he left behind. Oh God, I miss him so much." She wanted to cry, to turn around and jump off the boat. "I can't believe they murdered him, but I have to believe it, don't I?" She lifted her chin and looked Rider straight in the eye. He looked away.

"Who am I, who was Skipper, that people would hunt us down like animals and kill us? I don't want to be here. I don't want to know this." Her voice cracked, and she pushed her fingers through her hair.

Rider turned her around. "Doc? You okay?"

She stared at him uncomprehendingly for a moment, still caught in her nightmare memories and bewildering questions. Then the intensity of his blue eyes burned past her thoughts, and she focused on him. "I'm tired, Rider," she whispered, hating herself for her weakness.

She understood the gravity of their situation. How could she not? She had blisters on her hand, scrapes and scratches all over her. Rider had a seared shoulder, bruised ribs. They both were exhausted. And they both were still in danger.

She knew it. She just couldn't handle it any more. "I'm so tired. I don't know if I can stay here, where he was. I can feel him already, just standing here on deck. I could almost believe he was still alive. No! I can't do it!"

She pushed against Rider, desperate to get away from the feelings, desperate to jump off the boat and just run anywhere. Anywhere to get away from the whale songs.

Rider held onto her, though, and pulled her with him as he made his careful way down the deck into the cockpit. He held her around the waist, and Kristen couldn't even fight him, because with him touching her, she was under a double assault from the two of them.

Skipper, his life snuffed out but his essence lingering, eating away at the wall she'd built around her grief in the past two years. And Rider's essence, open to her again, stronger than her brother's, because Rider was right here, touching her, transmitting his anger, his fear, his sorrow to her in waves. And with it, the other feelings, those overwhelming yearnings he'd built in her, the longing she knew she'd never again be able to live without now that he'd kindled them.

So she yielded, letting him drag her into the cabin and deposit her on the forward bunk. She was barely aware of his words as he pulled a blanket over her.

"Maybe your little detour threw our buddy off, Doc. I hope so, because I don't think either one of us is able to do any more fighting today. With him or with each other. I'll go up on deck and keep an eye out. You rest. I think you need it more than I do right now." He pushed a strand of hair back from her forehead, his fingers lingering, then he disappeared.

She heard him go up on deck and sighed in relief as the distance dulled his emotions inside her a little bit.

As she pumped water into the tiny sink in the head and sponged off her sweaty body, she fought the sense of Skipper that was so strong here. Why here so much more than at his house?

Even as she asked herself the question she knew the answer. Skipper had loved the boat, ever since the first time their dad had let him take the wheel. Skip had been fascinated with boats all his life. He always said the sea itself was the ultimate whale song, calling to those who would listen, ready to nurture, to keep safe anyone who trusted her.

The sea was his first love. And that love, as much as the

coincidence of his surname, was what had earned him his nick-name.

She grabbed a towel from the cabinet and dried her hair and face and body, turning her nose up at the faintly mildewed smell of the cotton. Then she walked naked into the front berth, looking in the drawers for something she could wear.

She found a pair of white shorts that would do for Rider—they were much too big for her. She held them for a moment, savoring a snapshot memory of her brother, tanned and sleek, scrubbing the bilges and cursing boats.

"They're just a hole in the water into which all your money pours," he'd said more than once, but Kristen wasn't fooled. He loved the boat and the sea.

Her eyes hazed with tears as she searched deeper in the drawer and pulled out an old, faded tee shirt that said "Save The Whale Songs." She'd given it to him the same day he'd gotten the name painted on his boat. She slipped the soft shirt over her head.

"No matter what happens, Krissy. I swear, I'll take care of you.".

With a cry, she sank to the bunk, hugging the tee shirt around herself. He could have been right in the room with her, as real as the voice had been. She squeezed her head between her hands.

"Get out of my head, Skipper," she muttered, pressing harder on her temples with the heels of her hands. "I can't stand it!"

"No matter what...to the end of time."

Oh, God!

"Stop!" She bit her lip, her own cry startling her. She hoped Rider hadn't heard her. Stopping the pressure of her hands, she sat motionless for a few moments, listening. No. He hadn't heard her, or he didn't care enough to check on her. Either way, it was fine with her.

She had to think about what had just happened. It was what Darwin had told her to remember. She could see Skipper, thin and gangly, pathetically grown-up looking in his somber suit. And herself. She'd had on a navy blue dress with white piping, and black patent leather shoes with little heels and her first pantyhose.

They'd been twelve when their parents died. Twelve years old, not even in puberty, and left totally alone when their father's private jet had crashed in the South Pacific. Wealthy, but alone.

Kristen had just been entering puberty, and their deaths had left her devastated. For days she couldn't speak, and Skipper had hovered around her like a mother hen, protecting her from the friends and acquaintances and business associates.

As they had walked back to the limousine from the gravesite, he'd put his arm around her shoulders, even though she was two inches taller than he then, and said the words that echoed now in her ears.

"To the end of time, Kris. Don't worry! I'm starting a stash, as soon as I get the trust fund. It will always be there, always. In Daddy's Bible, okay? We'll never touch it, unless our lives are in danger."

She nodded, just like she had back then, and a poignant amusement rippled through her breast. That had been the beginning of Skipper's conviction that people were out to get them. He was positive enemy agents had killed their parents.

With the knowledge of the last few days, Kristen wondered if he'd been closer to the truth than either of them could have ever imagined. She shivered. Until Darwin mentioned it, she had forgotten their conversation, but now she realized Skipper had kept his promise... for as long as he could.

She stuffed her knuckles between her teeth to keep from crying aloud. Wrapped in his tee shirt, curled up in his boat, she sobbed quietly. He'd kept her, protected her, through all the bad times, through the good times, until his song had died.

Now she had no one. Everyone who'd loved her had died, except Sam.

Brushing tears off her face, she sat up. Sam. He was probably starving and scared to death. She pictured him going back to her apartment—where her apartment had been. She wondered what his little cat brain had thought when there was no apartment there. She had to get Sam and get back before Rider woke up.

She jumped up, running her fingers through her hair and dashing away the last of the tears. Closing her eyes, she searched for Rider with her senses. Not much. Maybe he was asleep. He had to sleep sometime. Or he'd withdrawn again, out of her reach.

She dug a pair of swim trunks out of a drawer and pulled them on, drawing the drawstring tight around her waist and pulling the tail of the tee shirt over them. Pretty baggy, but not awful. At least she was covered.

Daddy's Bible. Where would Skipper have put it? She glanced around the forward berth. "Please let it be here," she whispered. "Come on, Skipper. Where?"

In the main saloon, she searched the shelves over the berths where his collection of sailing books and science fiction were. Then she knelt down to look in the drawer under the centerline table.

There it was, the big family Bible that had always sat on their parents' coffee table. She opened it. There, nestled in the hollowed-out pages, was more cash than she'd ever seen in her life. A huge roll of thousand dollar bills. Rolls of hundreds. And a stack of twenties.

Not stopping to count it, she just grabbed a handful of twenties and stuffed them into the pocket of the tee shirt before putting the Bible back in its drawer.

Nor did she stop to wonder how Darwin had known about it, either. Those thoughts were too bewildering, too distracting, and Kristen had to go get Sam.

She tiptoed up the companionway ladder and stepped into the cockpit, her sneakers making no noise on the boat's slick surface. She'd seen some canned food in the galley, and her plan, if Rider was awake, was to pretend she'd come up to ask if he was hungry.

But he was leaning back against the mast, sound asleep. For a moment, she was stopped by his vulnerable beauty. He'd washed, too. She wondered when, then she saw that the scrubs were damp. He'd probably dunked himself in the bay, clothes and all.

Carefully, trying not to rock the boat at all, but knowing her weight was enough to set it undulating on its lines, she stepped off the side onto the pier.

Rider didn't move. From within him she felt the exhaustion, sensed the disturbing thoughts that were trying to sort themselves out in his battered brain. She silently wished him a good sleep and crept up the pier toward the marina offices to call a cab.

***

Rider jerked and bumped the back of his head on something extremely hard. He jumped up, trying to expel the last of the sleepiness, and quickly glanced around. He was on a boat—Skipper's boat.

Damn, he'd been exhausted. He never should have slept.

It could have been fatal to sleep that deeply. He was going to have to arrange watch with Kristen until they decided what to do.

A twinge of fear deep in his gut reminded him that they didn't have much time. He shook his head to dispel the last dregs of drowsiness. He had to figure out what to do. What the best way was to keep his angel doctor safe.

Whose bloody brilliant idea had it been anyway to wipe out the skipworths?

"Damn the bastards and their TAINCC," he whispered.

And damn Kristen for starting it all? No. How could he blame her? Even when he'd thought she was the enemy, he'd never really been able to blame her, or hate her. In fact, if he were completely honest with himself...

"Shit!" he said aloud, running his fingers through his hair. He couldn't love her. His damned emotions were getting in the way too much. He had to stop them.

They came, though, so hard and fast they doubled him over. He was sickeningly afraid of those thoughts. He pressed his palms against his temples, trying to squeeze them out. If he loved Kristen, how would he protect her?

He'd thought they could escape to the future or the past, but according to Darwin, that was impossible. And if they stayed here, they'd never be safe. They'd both be scared to death all the time, and Rider knew how fear and love played hell with logic and cold resolve.

Deliberately pushing away his disturbing thoughts, he stood and stretched, his skin tight and hot where the sun had dried the salt water. He flexed the awful, blackened burn on his shoulder. It even felt better, although he didn't think he'd dunk it in salt water again, not now when he knew what salt did to a blaster burn.

He shuddered. Still, it was good to be clean, even salty clean. He'd take a real shower later.

Right now he needed to check on her. His stomach rumbled. And get some food.

Even before he got down the stairs into the cabin, he knew there was something wrong. Something was missing. Something that had been with him ever since he'd wrapped his fingers around her ankle in the alley. His heart slammed against his chest wall. She was gone!

He refused to believe it. Tearing through the whole boat

looking for her, he tried to tell himself she'd walked to the marina store to buy juice or something. But he knew.

As much as it scared him to admit it, he knew if she was close he'd feel her. It was something else he hadn't acknowledged until now. He knew, as surely as he knew she sensed his emotions, that he could sense her as well. Not as strongly, but it was there. A link between them, like a silver thread binding them together. His pulse pounded as his brain acknowledged what his heart already knew.

He couldn't stand the idea of something happening to her. The realization that she was gone scared him more than the TAINCC, more than the killer that they'd sent after them, more than anything had ever scared him in his life.

What had she done? Nothing could have happened to her. The tank would never have left him alive. No, if he could just get his brain to working, shake off the exhaustion that was fuzzing his mind, he could figure it out. He looked around the cabin, searching for a clue to tell him what she'd done. Had she just run away?

He didn't think so. As Rider had told her often enough, he was her only chance—her only protection. And he was sure she believed that as much as he did.

Also, this was her brother's boat. It was the last safe haven she'd had. Everything else had been destroyed. The clinic, her apartment...

Her apartment!

"The stupid, fucking cat!" He grabbed gratefully onto the anger to tamp down the paralyzing fear. She'd defied him and gone after the cat.

The fear that rocked him was worse than anything he'd ever experienced. He was sure his heart would burst inside his chest. *Be safe, Doc,* he begged. *Please don't get yourself killed over a stupid cat.*

If he found her alive, he'd kill her. He slammed his fist down on the first available surface.

When he hit the table, a drawer rattled and gaped open. Rider slid the drawer wider and saw a Bible. A Bible with several green bills sticking out of it.

He opened the cover and gaped at the sight that greeted him. Judging by the numbers on the bills, there was a considerable fortune rolled up and stuffed inside the hollow book.

"You never give up, do you Doc?" he muttered as he stuffed

several of the smaller denomination bills into the pocket of the scrubs. He pushed the drawer shut with his foot and took off to find a cab to take him back to Lombard Street.

By the time the cab pulled up in front of her apartment building, Rider was fuming, and terrified. If the tank had followed them and missed their detour, he would have ended up right here. They knew where her apartment was. After all, they'd blown it up.

He leaned in the window and waved some bills at the driver. "Another twenty if you wait," he said, then took off to find Kristen.

As he rounded the corner of the building, he saw her sitting on the ground, her head in her hands. Seeing her unhurt almost undid him.

Love, aching awful wonderful love, rushed through him, leaving his eyes wet and his limbs shaky. Oh, God, he loved her.

He clamped his jaw until his neck hurt. They were doomed if he couldn't get control of his emotions. Blinking away the foolish stinging in his eyes, he ran up to her and grabbed her shoulders, jerking her to her feet, furious and weak with relief.

He shook her. "Doc! What the hell do you think you're doing? Don't you have any damned sense?"

She lolled limply in his hands, not even resisting him, so he stopped and pulled her to him.

"God, you gave me a scare." His hands were trembling, so he pulled her tighter to stop them. Her head rested under his chin, and her tears were damp against his neck.

"Listen to me," he whispered to her. "You can't go running around like this. You can't ever take anything for granted again. One of *them* could be anywhere. Understand?"

He cradled her skull and turned his face into her hair, burying his nose in the clean, dark strands, breathing deeply. He clenched his jaw against the emotions that churned inside him. "God, Doc. I was so afraid I'd lost you..."

"I can't find him, Rider."

"I know," he said absently, glancing around the street, the hairs on the back of his neck prickling. "Come on, we've got to get out of here. I've got a cab waiting."

"No!" She pushed away from him. He held her fast, though, so all she could do was strain her neck back to look at him. "I'm not leaving without Sam."

"Doc, it's a *cat*! You're being an idiot. Leave it alone." He shuddered inwardly at the thought of the animal. Cats! He'd like to kill them all! He wiped his brain of the image of the smoking pile of flesh that had been Mari's cat, and the limp body he'd held in his arms that had been his traitorous wife as he urged Kristen toward the cab.

"No!" she shouted and hit at him, her eyes glowing amber. "I'm not leaving without him!" She twisted and writhed, trying to escape his grip, so he grabbed her shoulders again and shook her.

Her chin raised defiantly, and if the golden lights in her eyes had been lasers, he'd be dead, cut in two by their beam.

"I'll carry you bodily."

"I'll scream."

"What the hell is it about that damned cat?" he grated, his fingers tightening on her arms. He started to shake her again, wanting to shake the notion of saving the stupid cat out of her, wanting to shake into her the understanding of how dangerous it was for them to be standing there, unprotected, in the alley, wanting to pick her up and carry her over his shoulder, kicking and screaming, back to the boat.

But when he met her gaze he saw the anguish there, and he hesitated, waiting to hear what she said, knowing it was going to rip another layer of skin away from him.

He was so vulnerable now to her every mood that it scared him to his toes. He tried to find the detachment inside him, but it was gone. And in its place was enough love and fear to drown him, enough to get them both killed.

"I couldn't save Skipper," she said brokenly, tears running unchecked down her face.

"Damn it, Doc." Her grief suffused him. He let her go. He couldn't stand to feel her emotions as if they were his own. When he did, he saw the red marks on her arms where his fingers had pressed.

"I didn't get the chance to try. I can't let it happen again. I can't leave Sam without even trying." Her eyes pleaded with him to understand.

He turned away. He did understand. He understood too well. He still harbored a deep regret inside him that he hadn't been able to save Mari. Traitor or not, she'd still been his wife, and he hadn't saved her. Maybe that was part of his obsession with Kristen. That he was trying to do it right this time.

But no. Kristen was much, much more important to him than Mari had ever been. He loved his angel doctor more than his own life. He'd realized it when he'd seen her sitting unhurt and safe on the curb.

But even if he weren't in love with her, she was still the Mother of All the Deviants, and he still had an obligation to save her.

"Doc, I swear I'll come back after the cat. Right now, we've got to get you to someplace safe."

He grabbed her, just as he heard something. "What was that?" he whispered.

Kristen stiffened in his grasp. "Sam!" she shouted. Her face transformed so suddenly, so totally, it almost knocked him backwards.

He thought about the first time he'd seen her, when he'd thought she was an angel. Then later, when he'd decided she was older than he'd first thought. Right now, with her face tear streaked, with her hair tangled where she'd run her fingers through it, with red fingerprints slowly turning blue on her arms, he thought his first assessment must have been right.

She was an angel, and she'd definitely rescued him from hell.

As he watched, she strained her eyes upward, shading them with one hand. "Sam? Is that you? Oh, look, Rider. He's sitting in the window—well, what used to be the window of my apartment." She clicked her fingers. "Come on, big guy. Look at you."

Rider watched in incredulous horror as the yellow cat climbed down the fire escape and jumped straight into Kristen's arms. It tucked its head under her chin and purred so loudly Rider could hear it from his vantage point several—quite a few—feet away.

Kristen murmured to the cat and scratched its neck, her face glowing like a madonna's.

"Doc. Come on." He kept his distance as they walked back toward the cab.

Kristen had just gotten into the back seat with the cat when the tank stepped out of the shadows of another alley several yards away and fired at them.

Rider ducked behind the car as a green ribbon of light angled through the front windshield, burning a hole in the cab driver's head.

Kristen screamed and the cat yowled.

"Stay down, Doc," Rider shouted.

The tank fired again, low, the blast bursting the right front tire.

"Doc!" he yelled. "When I'm away from the car, push the driver out and drive like hell."

He didn't listen for her answer, just dove from behind the car toward a garbage bin, praying the tank would follow him rather than going for the car. If he didn't...

Rider cringed at the heat of a blast too close to the back. As he'd feared, their pursuer aimed one more blast at him then turned back to the car.

Had Kristen heard him? The interior of the cab was dark. But he hadn't heard the door open, and he didn't see the driver's body on the street.

"Come on, Doc. Get out of here," he muttered, praying to whatever might be up there to pray to that she'd do what he said.

He heard a crackle of heat, like blaster fire on metal. Damn! The cars here were made of metal, not plastic. One or two regular blasts wouldn't penetrate metal! She was safe, if she stayed down. Safe at least until he reached the car. His hands shook with relief, and he cursed his reaction.

Where was the detachment? Where was the cold resolve?

All he could find was a gut-wrenching fear that he'd let her down. A fear that his uncontrollable emotions would keep him from acting swiftly and logically to save her. *Get a grip,* he told himself. The best thing he could do for her was forget how important she was to him and concentrate on how important she was to the future.

Drive, Doc! Get out of here!

As the tank walked resolutely toward the car, Rider crept up behind him. He rushed him, counting on surprise and the momentum of his body to knock him down, but not entirely hopeful. He remembered fighting the guy once or twice in training. He never remembered winning.

"Oof!" Surprise was on his side though, and when he rammed the tank in the small of his back, the big man crumpled, and the blaster fell from his hand.

Rider intertwined his fingers and slammed his knotted fists into the bigger man's neck, the reverberations echoing all the way up his arms. He did it again and again, trying to smash his spinal cord, until the tank shrugged him off like a nuisance fly. The man must have steel for nerves, he must not know what pain was. And the guy was half again Rider's size. All Rider had going for him was surprise, and the surprise was over.

Maybe he had one other thing going for him. His agility. The tank was bulky with muscle. Rider, though sore and exhausted, with bruised ribs and a shoulder that didn't want to work just right, just might be more agile and quick.

It was one thing he'd learned in basic. The only way to keep from being hurt badly by the bigger guys or the clumsy robots was to keep moving until the round was over.

As Rider dove for the dropped blaster, a twinge of fatalistic humor curled his lips. Who'd ring the bell for this round to end?

He grabbed the blaster a split second before the tank's kick landed right in the middle of his rib cage. Indescribable agony seared through his diaphragm. If his ribs weren't broken before, they crunched ominously now.

His breath whooshed out, and he couldn't get it back. He gasped, trying to steal enough breath not to pass out. Had he punctured a lung?

With an effort born of panic, he rolled underneath the car and fired the blaster at the foot that had kicked him. He smelled burning flesh and saw a satisfyingly large hole erupt in leather and flesh.

The tank hesitated, just for an instant, but that was enough time for Rider to aim a blast at his other foot. That stopped him longer.

Rider scooted farther away, backing toward the other side of the car. His ribs hurt so badly he could barely breathe, but he tamped down the pain, covering it with a fierce determination.

Nothing but death would make him stop. He would not allow Kristen to die! She needed him, and he would not fail her.

As he slid out from under the car, the dead cab driver tumbled out on top of him.

"Good, Doc. Now get out of here!" he gasped as he kicked the dead man out of his way and crouched behind the car, breathing shallowly to minimize the searing pain in his ribs.

The tank reached for the passenger door, and Rider heard the rip of metal as he tore the handle off and threw it aside, then slammed his fist through the passenger window.

"Doc! Drive!"

"Get in," she cried.

"No! Drive! I'll be fine. Go!" He leveled the blaster at the tank's eyes and watched as the green ribbon of heat missed its target and plowed a part through the man's hair. A sizzling sound and a nauseating smell gave Rider a bit of hope as the car behind which he crouched took off.

"All right, Doc," he whispered. "I knew you were lying about not being able to drive." His limbs were weak with relief that she'd finally listened to him. He ignored the faint regret that he might never see her again. At least she'd gotten her damned cat.

Unbelievably, the tank still stood. He lumbered toward Rider. Rider backed away, aiming a blast at the other eye. He pressed the activator button, but nothing happened.

His mouth went dry. Out of energy.

The tank kept coming. Faintly, in the back of his mind, Rider heard something familiar, but it didn't quite register as he frantically considered his options.

He crouched on the balls of his feet, ready to move quickly, hoping with all of his being that the man was more injured than he appeared. He darted sideways.

Suddenly, the noise that had tickled at the edge of his brain coalesced into an identifiable sound—a car engine.

EIGHTEEN

Rider whirled just in time to see the cab bearing down on them. He dove onto the sidewalk and rolled, gasping for breath over the crunching pain of his ribs. He looked up just in time to see the cab slam into the tank.

The big man crumpled, no match for the bulk and force of the moving car. Rider lay on the sidewalk and watched in amazement.

Kristen backed the car up at least a hundred feet, then ran over the body again. She backed away, turned the car around with a scream of wheels, and shouted to Rider through the open driver's window.

"Come on! Let's go!"

Rider glanced back at the body of the tank who'd been sent to kill them and wondered how soon they'd send another.

He limped over to the car, holding his side, and flung himself into the back, almost passing out when his body bounced on the seat.

Kristen didn't speak, just took off. Rider lay as still as possible, breathing in short, unsatisfying puffs, wanting to take a deep breath but unwilling to find out just how badly his ribs were messed up.

He didn't move until the car stopped.

"Come on, we're here," his angel doctor said impatiently, holding the door open. He peered at her through narrowed eyes.

She was holding the damned cat in one arm and had her other hand on the car door. Her face was a mixture of fear, pity, and irritation. He searched her gaze, but he couldn't read anything more. Certainly not the love and trust he'd hoped he would find.

He blinked, trying to believe that the stinging in his eyes was from the pain in his ribs, not the ache in his heart. Carefully, wearily, he pulled himself out of the car.

Kristen reached for him, but he shrugged off her grip. "Keep that damned cat away from me," he whispered, shuddering and wincing at the grinding in his midsection.

She winced, too. He didn't miss that. He moved resolutely away from her. He didn't want her pity. Didn't want her to feel his pain. He was hurting, confused, and closer to breaking down than he'd ever been in his life. All he wanted was to be left alone.

He climbed onto the boat by himself and took his position against the mast.

"Come below," she said," and I'll clean you up and wrap your ribs." She put her hand on his arm. He didn't even have the strength to shrug it off this time, so he let it stay there, but he bent every last bit of will he had left to shielding his feelings from her. He had to. He didn't have the strength to deal with her empathy, her pity, her need right now. It was all he could do to keep from crying.

He didn't acknowledge her at all, and after a few seconds she took her hand away and went below.

Rider had never felt so totally alone in his life. It was a horrible feeling, the worst thing he'd ever experienced. The worst in what seemed now to be a lifetime of worsts.

He sat, warily relaxed, breathing carefully. He should feel great, triumphant. He and Kristen had won. His angel-doctor had acted brilliantly. He should be proud of both of them.

And he should be planning their escape. But he was so damned tired, and so confused. Hot tears squeezed out from beneath his closed eyelids. What had happened to him? He was a trained killer, for God's sake!

All emotions should have been sucked out of him in the TAINCC. He longed for that distance, that wall of protection that the conditioning had given him. Or had it?

He'd never been fully conditioned, he thought resignedly. The whole time, even after they'd successfully wiped his memory of his wife's real identity, he'd rebelled against them. And it had worked. He'd kept his humanity—well, most of it— kept his resolve to wreak vengeance through all the torture, all the brainwashing. And he'd kept his emotions.

He clenched his fists and took a deep breath, almost like a sob. He didn't want them. He didn't want the feelings. Feelings were too hard. Physical pain was nothing compared to the pain of loving and losing someone who meant more than his own life.

Damn Kristen Skipworth! Damn her for making him care again. Damn her for making him love her. Loving her took too much out of him. Loving her was too dangerous for her. She needed a protector, not a lover.

Maybe Darwin could find her a protector who could keep his head. Someone who wouldn't be paralyzed by fear every time he thought of losing her.

His eyes spilled over with tears, and he cursed himself for his weakness. Cursed his angel-doctor. Cursed the stupid cat. The cat. He shuddered. Still, the creature had helped trigger the return of his memories. Rider supposed he should be grateful to it for helping unlock the secrets buried in his unconscious mind.

Because if he'd never remembered, he might have succeeded in killing Kristen. If he'd never broken the conditioning, he'd be just another tank lost in time. Maybe he'd even be a hero back in the future. The tank who'd successfully wiped out the Deviants. That was a whole dilemma. Darwin certainly had a gift for understatement. Complicated hardly covered it. She said she was from much farther in the future than he, which seemed to indicate that the skipworths weren't wiped out.

He brushed angrily at the tears with his arm, blotting them on the sleeve of the scrub shirt. It was all so damned confusing.

He'd hoped he and Kristen could hide in the corridors of time. Have a life together. But Darwin had said Kristen couldn't go.

He wiped his face again. Tanks didn't cry. Humans cried. Vulnerable, expendable humans.

He felt a warm weight on his lap. Drowsily, he glanced down and caught his breath when he saw what it was. The damned cat.

He wanted to spring up, to scream and throw the disgusting animal as far as he could, to wring its neck. But he didn't move. It was as if he was paralyzed, pinned down by the warm weight.

Sam raised his big yellow head and stared at Rider with round, wide eyes, making a peculiar chirruping sound.

His hand trembling, Rider touched the cat's ear. Sam flicked it as if Rider's touch tickled, and Rider's breath caught in a sob. Kristen had managed to save the cat, and Rider had managed to save Kristen, so far.

Now what?

"Now what, Sam?" he whispered, running his finger along the cat's chin. When he did, Sam lifted his head and began purring loudly. Rider's fingers still shook, but he scratched Sam's chin and watched the cat's eyes close and his nostrils dilate in ecstasy.

Kristen. His angel doctor, whose stubbornness and courage had torn down the wall of pain and hatred he'd lived behind, whose empathy had made him human. Too damned human.

She needed someone who could protect her—someone who wasn't in love with her. She'd be better off without him. He was such a slipper, he couldn't even keep from crying. Rider leaned his head back against the mast and let the tears fall unchecked.

Kristen lay in the forward berth, her brain in turmoil. She couldn't rest. Rider had been so remote. No, not just remote. Hostile. As if he were furious at her.

She'd been terrified when the cab driver had been killed. In all her years as a physician, she'd never seen anyone murdered before her eyes.

And with the blaster there wasn't even any blood, which somehow made it even more shocking. She was a doctor. Blood she could handle.

But this thing—this ribbon of bright green heat that could burn through flesh, was ghastly, alien. She shivered, remembering how close it had come to her, how close it had come to Rider.

She had been so afraid for him. She'd wanted to jump out of the car and help him, but thank God she'd had enough sense to know that the car was the best weapon they had.

It was a bit horrifying, the satisfaction she'd experienced when she'd rammed into that inhuman monster with the car. The crunch of metal against flesh had thrilled her. She wondered if she'd killed him.

A whisper of pain and grief rippled through her from Rider, bringing her thoughts back to the present. She glanced upward involuntarily. She'd been gleaning those whispers from him all afternoon.

It dismayed her to know he could almost shield his feelings from her. He was apparently making a huge effort to do so. He was getting better at it, too. These tiny waves were all she'd gotten in the past several hours.

At first she'd thought he was asleep, but when Sam had jumped down off her berth and scrambled up the ladder to the deck, she'd followed the yellow cat, to make sure he didn't jump off the boat.

When she'd come up on deck, she'd seen a sight that had at once thrilled her and broken her heart. Rider sat, his back against the mast, holding Sam on his lap.

Holding her cat.

Rider, who was terrified by cats because they reminded him of the day his wife died, was holding Sam on his lap and stroking him.

She'd retreated into the cabin where she lay now, Rider's presence like a rain cloud above her, hurt by his distance, his careful guarding of his emotions.

This was what it would be like when he left. Worse, much worse than after Skipper died, because although she and Skipper had been closer than siblings, they were brother and sister. And although before the last few days Kristen wouldn't have agreed with anyone who said there was a connection closer than family, she now knew there was.

The void Skipper left in her life would never be completely healed, but Rider's presence had filled an empty place within her she'd never even known was there. Now, when he held himself apart from her, the void was deeper, wider, a wound which would gape in her life forever.

She shifted restlessly. The cabin was hot with the hatch closed, but she'd been reluctant to open it. She didn't want to interrupt Rider. She didn't want to do anything that might push him closer to the decision she was sure he would make.

He would go back. He'd have to. The thought that he might be able to go back there and save his wife obsessed Kristen. She knew it must be obsessing him.

With a sorrow too deep for tears, Kristen lay on the bunk, staring at the sky through the plexiglass hatch, and worked on getting used to Rider being gone.

She didn't even dare think about what would happen to her without him. She shuddered, thinking about the monster that had come after them. The people who were intent on killing her wouldn't stop. They would send more.

They probably had millions of them and could drop them back into the past like summer rain on asphalt, so that no matter where she went, one would be there, or two or a dozen. And it would only be a matter of time.

She would have to live her life being suspicious of everyone. She would never be able to trust anyone. Even on the open sea, she'd be vulnerable. She had thought she was alone when Skipper died. Now she would be totally alone. Totally.

She closed her eyes against the tears that kept threatening. Tears would accomplish nothing, she told herself for the thousandth time. In fact, breaking down could probably get her killed. She had no time for tears anymore.

She had to learn a harder lesson now. She had to learn to steel herself, not only against the emotions of others, but against her own traitorous heart. She couldn't let feelings get in the way, not if she was going to survive.

She heard a noise above her. When she opened her eyes, she saw Rider opening the hatch. He slipped through, and she scooted out of the way so he wouldn't step on her.

He lowered himself gingerly to the berth, leaving the hatch open, groaning and holding his ribs as he relaxed beside her.

"Damn, it's hot down here, Doc. You taking a steam bath?"

Kristen eyed him suspiciously. He sounded almost cheerful. She touched his arm and when she did, his mouth turned up in the quirky, heartbreaking smile that always thrilled her. She bathed in the glow from that smile, knowing the time was near when she would never see it again.

Through her fingers on his arm she could sense the deep sadness that had overlaid his soul from the beginning, but beneath it was a center, a calmness that hadn't been there before. And that calmness ripped her heart into shreds, because she knew what it signified.

He'd made his decision.

Her shredded heart lurched so painfully she had to cover the place with her hand. Her eyes filled with tears in spite of herself. She blinked furiously.

When she could see again, she looked at him. He was still staring at her with that smile on his face, and when her gaze met his, the smile faded into a frown.

"Why so sad, Doc? We're safe. At least for the moment."

He was reclining on the bed, leaning on one arm. He'd taken the scrub shirt off, and Kristen saw the scars of his battles.

His shoulder was charred, his chest covered with scratches and scrapes. His diaphragm and belly were a watercolor in blues and yellows and greens, the old bruises bleeding into the new ones. She touched his ridged belly and felt his muscles contract.

"You're so hurt," she whispered, longing, despite her sadness, to stretch herself against his whole length, longing to feel his naked chest against her breasts, feel his hardness against her softness, his skin against hers. She shivered a little.

When she brought her gaze back to his face, he was still frowning. He touched her cheek with one callused finger. When he did, her head moved toward his touch, and he made a rumbling sound deep in his throat, then wrapped his fingers around her neck and pulled her to him.

His hand caressed her nape as his mouth touched hers. The touch was electrifying, sending waves of desire through her—not just her desire, but his, too.

He did still desire her. He still wanted her with a fierceness that frightened her. A fierceness that overlay the pain, the sadness, even the grief. She was awed by the strength of his desire for her.

His mouth opened, and she opened hers beneath it. As his kiss deepened and her senses swirled faster, he began to move his hand from her neck down to trace her collarbone, then lower, to caress her breast beneath the soft cotton of the tee shirt.

He pushed her onto her back and slid his hands under the shirt. Kristen's stomach contracted as his fingers trailed across her skin. She raised her arms and let him strip the shirt off her, just like he was stripping her emotions raw with his kisses.

He found and loosened the string that held Skipper's swim trunks on and pushed them down, cupping her buttocks in his hands and pulling her close to him, until his erection throbbed against her.

She couldn't stand not seeing him, so she pushed on the elastic of the shorts he wore, hooking her thumbs in them and pushing the pants down. He kicked them off with a grunt, leaving nothing between them.

Nothing at all, except five hundred years.

That almost stopped her, but coincident with it, he slipped his finger into her, knocking every last coherent thought out of her head. She writhed against him.

"Please," she begged. "Rider..."

"What?" he whispered. "Tell me what, Doc. Kristen. Tell me what you want."

"You," she hissed. "Just you. Now."

Then he was over and in her, filling her, taunting her with his teasing thrusts, until she grasped his buttocks and pulled him closer, closer. If she could, she would have melded with him, forming one complete being, so he could never separate himself again.

"Kiss me, Rider," she begged, knowing when he did she would feel it all, even if it were for the last time.

He kissed her and she felt it. Felt his overwhelming desire. Felt the ribs grinding painfully in his chest. Felt her own need growing until her throbbing body sent its signals to his and he quickened his thrusts.

His climax grew inside her just like her own until they both shattered.

Afterwards, they lay together, still joined, for a long time. Finally Rider moved, and Kristen let him go, unable to keep him inside her any longer. As he withdrew physically, leaving her cold and empty, he withdrew emotionally at the same time.

The shields went back up around him. He'd needed the release, needed her, one more time, but that was all. The link that bound them wasn't strong enough to override his love for his wife.

She knew this. She could deal with it. She'd just have to collect the tattered strips of her heart and go on without him.

Sitting up, he put his head in his hands. Kristen trailed her fingers down his back, not willing to lose him just yet.

"Doc," he said, and it sounded like an admonishment. She drew her hand back and pulled the sheet up to cover herself.

That was it. She needed it to be over. She didn't think she could take him being here and holding himself away from her. She needed him gone now, if he was going, so she could start trying to get used to it.

Oh, God, why couldn't he just be a psycho?

"Rider," she rushed in to fill the silence before he spoke. "I know. It's all right."

He turned and stared at her, his eyes dark as midnight. "What do you know?"

She squeezed her eyes shut and twisted the sheet in her hands. "I know you've got to go back to try to save your wife. I understand. I'd do the same thing for Skipper if I could."

When she opened her eyes, his back was to her again, and his hands were clasped together, his elbows on his knees. "You don't know a damned thing."

She saw his body trembling, and she longed to pull him close, to comfort him, but she could feel the sadness in him, too innate to be helped by comfort, too deep for him to shield from her. She just sat there and waited for him to continue.

"I need to tell you about Mari, Doc. I need to explain to you just what she was. See, she..." He stopped, his voice cracking. The pain in his voice cut into Kristen's heart like a scalpel, until she wanted to tear it out just to get rid of the pain.

"Mari was a skipworth, Doc. But she was something else, too." He looked at her, his eyes dark and bright as cobalt glass. "She was a traitor."

Kristen stared at him, her heart in her throat. What was he saying?

"She sold out the skipworths for power. Then, when she found out the government was experimenting with time travel to destroy you and therefore destroy all the skipworths, including her, she sold the government out. They killed her for that."

His beautiful shoulders undulated in a shrug, and he made a small noise when his broken ribs stabbed him. He turned around to look at her, an unreadable expression on his face, undecipherable emotions crowding his heart.

Kristen could hardly speak, her heart was pounding so painfully in her chest. "What—what are you saying?" she breathed.

"I'm saying I don't want to go back and save her, Doc. What I want to do is stay here and keep you safe, but I can't do that."

Kristen stared at him, trying to make sense of his words, trying to sort out the various messages she was getting from his closeness, but he dropped his gaze, and the sensations stopped.

"What do you mean?"

He didn't look up. "I was hoping we could travel in time. When Darwin said I could go back, I thought that would be the answer, I thought we could just hide in time. But you can't go. And I can't protect you." He picked up the scrub pants off the floor and left. She heard him go out on deck.

For a long time she just sat there, hugging her knees, staring at nothing, bewildered by his words, by the turmoil of his emotions. He said he couldn't protect her.

If he couldn't, then there was no one in the world who could.

Maybe she should be worried about all her descendants. Maybe she should be thinking of the people five hundred years in the future who were there because she was alive now.

But she just couldn't think that broadly. She was here, now, and she was in danger of losing the man she loved more than

life. More than her own life, more even than the lives of unnamed generations in the future.

But he said he couldn't stay with her.

She jerked on the tee shirt and went up on deck. He stood,
his back straight and rigid, holding on to a halyard and gazing at
the sunset. Sam was draped over one arm with his head tucked
under Rider's chin.

Looking at them, her heart broke.

"You know," she said, interrupting her intolerable thoughts,
lifting her chin as he turned to look at her. "I can take care of
myself. Darwin told me to remember what Skipper said when
our parents died. He said no matter what..." Her heart was
pounding so hard she was having trouble getting enough air to
talk, but she took a deep, shaky breath and continued.

"No matter what, he'd protect me. To the end of time. He
has, you know. He left me a stash. He taught me a little about
sailing, too. So I'll be just fine here. I'd suggest you find Darwin and go back where you came from."

His mouth quirked up.

"Don't laugh at me! I'm serious. You can go back and—
and do whatever it is you think you need to do. I know you're
only trying to spare my feelings. I promise I won't get killed for
a few years yet."

"Doc, you're priceless. Now, get below before the wind
catches that tee shirt again and you make a spectacle of yourself."

Kristen put her hand on the hem of the shirt, holding it
down.

"Here," he said as she turned. "Take the damned cat with
you."

He followed her, chuckling irritatingly.

In the cockpit, she let the struggling cat down and whirled
on Rider, the tears she hadn't been able to blink away rolling
down her cheeks, tickling her skin. She clenched her fists, refusing to wipe them away. "You have no right to laugh at me,
damn you. You don't think I want to be tied to a man who gets
nauseated around me, do you?" To her dismay, she burst into
tears.

Rider tried to gather her into his arms, but she resisted,
pushing at him. "Leave me alone, you bastard. I just... hate
good-byes, that's all. I don't need you."

He pulled her to him, pinning her arms like he had aeons

ago in the street. His breath was hot on her cheek as he whispered to her. "Oh, God, Doc. I hate good-byes, too." He sighed raggedly. "What am I going to do with you? I can't leave you."

Kristen stopped struggling, but she couldn't stop crying. "What—what do you mean? I'll be fine."

"Doc, shut up, okay?" He shook her gently. "I'm probably the worst protector you could have. I've got all these damned emotions churning around inside me, keeping me from thinking straight." He held her at arm's length and gazed into her eyes. "I don't know if you should trust me to keep you safe. I love you too much."

Kristen stared at him, dumbfounded. "You—love me too much?"

He nodded, not taking his eyes off her. "Too damned much to be logical. Too damned much to be safe for you. But Doc, I can't leave you. I can't just walk away from the most important person in my life." He shrugged. "I know how stupid it is. I'm so scared. So afraid of losing you. So afraid of leading you into danger."

He shook his head slowly. "You need somebody brave, somebody who's not eaten up with love and fear."

His words floated around her like dandelion fluff in midsummer, too wonderful and lovely to be believed. She stared at him, trying to absorb their meaning. She laid her fingers on his forearms and felt his sadness. "You are the bravest man I have ever known," she said softly. "I told you before, the people who aren't afraid are fools."

"So, Doc," he said. "Looks like you're stuck with me." He frowned, and she could have sworn there was a glimmer of doubt, maybe even fear, in his intense gaze. "That is, if you want me."

Her eyes were hazy with tears, and she was baffled by what she was hearing. "Are you sure? Are you really, really sure?"

"Listen to me." He sat down and pulled her down beside him, holding her hands in his. He held her fingers to his lips as he talked. "You are more important to me than anyone, anywhere, any time. I don't think I can face a future that doesn't have you in it."

Kristen's heart was doing battle in her chest. Fear and hope, pain and love, grief and overwhelming joy were fighting inside her. "I don't want you here if this is some kind of badge

of honor, Rider." She pulled her hands away from his distracting lips. "I told you. I can take care of myself."

"Look inside me, Doc. Find your answer there." His eyes
blazed cobalt under his furrowed brows. He gazed at her
unblinkingly, and she accepted his challenge. She placed her
palms on either side of his neck and closed her eyes. He leaned
forward until his forehead was touching hers.

From within him she felt a growing warmth, a warmth that
flickered, then blazed. His skin burned under her hands. She
was suffused with love, saturated with hot desire. She nodded,
rocking her forehead against his, and felt a swift jolt of relief
from him.

"I love you, Rider," she whispered as his arms encircled
her and his head angled, his mouth seeking hers.

"Well, it sure took you two long enough."

Rider tensed and let go of Kristen. He stood with a grunt.
"Darwin, I presume," he said sarcastically.

"Hi!" Darwin stood on the deck, her black fatigues and
heavy boots ludicrously out of place on the light, airy sailboat.

Kristen wanted to giggle at the disgusted look Rider gave
the girl, but she thought it might be better not to.

"What the hell are you doing here?" he asked her. "Got
some more platitudes for us?"

"Only one," Darwin said, grinning from ear to ear as they
climbed up on deck. "I want to offer you two my congratulations."

Kristen stared at her. "Congratulations? For what? Are we
safe?"

A shadow crossed Darwin's expressive face. "No, Kristen.
You're probably never going to be totally safe, although you do
have a good idea about sailing around. It will be awfully hard
for anyone to find you that way, especially if you keep contact
with others to a minimum. But no, my congratulations are for a
very different upcoming event."

Rider still looked disgusted and bewildered, but Kristen
suddenly knew what Darwin was talking about. She wasn't
sure if Darwin's glance at her was telepathic, but she had no
doubt about the message, however the other girl had managed
to send it.

Kristen placed her hand protectively across her stomach,
and as she did, another thought occurred to her. "Oh my God,
Darwin."

Darwin nodded gleefully. "Isn't it wonderful? And deliciously ironic?"

Rider growled. "Would someone mind telling me what is going on here?"

"I'll leave that to your wife," Darwin said and started to disappear.

That is, she disappeared for a split second, but then she popped back. "Here I go again," she muttered. "I'll probably be in probation for the rest of my life for this one."

She shrugged and took Kristen's hand. "I need to ask you a very big favor, Krissy."

Kristen was surprised to hear Darwin use the nickname Skipper had given her.

"May I please have Skipper's computer?" Her expressive face was dark with apprehension. "You won't need it any more, and I know someone who wants it very badly."

Kristen stared at Darwin. She thought about all of Skipper's things, his house, his boat, his computer, and how they had saved Rider's and her lives in the past few days. The computer was something of Skipper's, something that held a tiny bit of his echoes still, but somehow she didn't mind Darwin having it. After all, Kristen had his boat and her memories.

She shrugged. "Sure, Darwin. I don't mind."

Darwin's little face lit up like a Christmas tree as she darted below deck and popped back with the nylon belt pack. She kissed Kristen on the cheek. "Go sailing, Krissy, and watch for the whales." Then she was gone.

Kristen was almost knocked down by the gentle love and the faint echo of her brother that blasted her when Darwin touched her. She gaped at the spot where Darwin had been standing—all that was left was a shimmer.

Blinking and frowning, she tried her best to make sense out of Darwin's words and the sensations she'd left with her, but the only thing that made sense was impossible.

"What the hell did she mean by that?"

Kristen allowed Rider to interrupt her crazy thoughts. She shrugged and laughed a little. "Another gross prophecy, no doubt."

Rider glared at her. "You're awfully smug all of a sudden. Did I miss something?"

"Oh, Rider, of course you did." Kristen kissed him. "Doc..."

"Okay." She took his hand and placed it on her flat stomach. "You'd better enjoy my girlish figure while you can," she said. "Because it won't be girlish much longer."

Rider turned ashen. "You mean you're—"

She nodded, smiling. "I'm pregnant."

"But how—I mean how do you know?"

"Trust me," she said. "Women know these things." She patted his hand where it rested on her belly.

"But, Rider, there's something else about this particular baby," she said.

He stared at her uncomprehendingly for a long moment, then his face became even more pale as the realization dawned on him. He sat down abruptly.

Kristen knelt in front of him, holding his hands, feeling his disbelief, his fear, his joy through them as he finally relaxed and the color came back into his face.

"You and—me?" he said incredulously.

She nodded, her heart filled to bursting. "You and me," she repeated. "I may be the Mother of all the Deviants, but sir, you are their father!"

He jumped up so fast, he almost knocked her over. Then he realized what he'd done, and he turned back to take her arm as carefully as if she were ninety years old.

"Doc, I'm sorry. Are you all right? How long have you been pregnant? When I think you were out there, chasing that damned cat..."

Kristen looked at him. How long had she been pregnant? She thought about it. "Probably only an hour or so," she said quietly.

Rider smiled at her, the heartbreaking smile she'd loved since the first time she'd seen it. She would love that smile forever.

"I've got to get to work," he said, patting her arm.

"Oh, stop it." She shrugged off his hand. "I'm not an invalid. Where are you going?"

"I've got to get you out of here. We're the hope of the future, the parents of all the Deviants, and the first one is on its way. We've got some sailing to do."

She reached up to kiss him, but something far out on the horizon caught her eye. "Rider, look," she whispered.

"What?" He frowned and squinted in the bright sunlight.

"Out there. See?" She pointed toward a shiny black shimmer in the water beyond the docked boats, out where the water was almost as blue as the sky.

"What is it?"

She took his hand again and laid it on her belly, holding it there while the happiness she'd thought she would never again feel suffused her. "It's a whale."

"A whale," he said wonderingly, pulling her close and wrapping his arms around her.

She nodded. "And I promise you, Rider, some day we'll hear them singing."

He didn't stop smiling, even when she kissed him.

EPILOGUE

Several days later, Darwin sat on the pier out of sight, dangling her feet in the water, and watched Rider and Kristen prepare to set sail. She smiled to herself, satisfied that she'd done all she could without *really* interfering.

Even her last remark, and the sensations she'd allowed Kristen to glean from her, as heavy with meaning as they had been, hadn't really *revealed* anything. The important thing was she'd kept the promise she'd made.

Her supersensitive ears heard a familiar sound behind her. The faint, almost silent whir of a blaster recharging.

She whirled, just in time to see the tank raise his blaster and point it at the couple embracing on the *Whale Song*. From the angle of his aim, he'd burn a hole right through both of them—no, through all three of them, Darwin corrected herself.

She sighed. "They'll send me back to pre-history for this one," she muttered, drawing a minuscule sizzler from her pocket. She aimed and fired.

He disappeared in a puff of acrid brown smoke.

She was just about to pop back home when she felt it . . . the unmistakable pull. She was being snatched.

"Oh, no, you wouldn't dare!" she hissed, knowing the camera imbedded in her right eye would pick up her whisper. "Don't!" She knew firsthand how dangerous snatching was. She'd done it herself.

She had finally gone too far. Not even her father could get her out of this one—if he'd even want to. She was supposed to be a watcher. Their motto was "hands off."

She had pulled major interferences twice now, and what did they say—three strikes and you're out?

Prehistory would be way too easy a sentence after she'd interfered this time. She was probably on her way to observe the oozing of the primordial ooze.

Damn. And she'd been looking forward to planning her honeymoon.

Don't Miss
Rickey Mallory's

HEART OF THE HERO
ISBN: 1-893896-33-1

SHADOW OF THE CAT
ISBN: 1-933417-97-8
(Coming in 2006)

Visit our web site at http:// www.imajinnbooks.com for
great prices on all our books!

Printed in the United States
47438LVS00003B/322